THE ROUGH SIDE
OF PARADISE

THE ROUGH SIDE OF PARADISE

NIKOLA HARVEY AND KIRAN CHALRES

Kiran Charles

Contents

I

"It's only one night." Vince let the words float around in his head as he gazed at his reflection in the mirror. His hair hung almost below his eyes and he ran a hand through it, pushing it back before placing his Stetson on his head. He brought his hand back up to his face and ran it over his chin. He'd made the mistake of letting his mother convince him to trim his beard before the wedding. With his long hair hidden and the beard much shorter, it struck him that he looked like a different person. That he looked so much closer to the Vince from "before." Before the pain, before the death, before the running. Movement in the mirror caught his eye and his line of sight focused on Jaskian, as it tended to do more often than not. He smiled a little to himself as he realized he also looked like the Vince before Jask, and that person wasn't someone he wanted to be ever again. He'd take on all the pain in the world and beyond if it meant getting to keep Jask with him. Which was why the words "only one night" were so hard for him to wrap his head around. They'd had enough of being apart and yet here Jaskian stood, packing a bag to spend the night with Astarte instead of in their bed.

Vince knew he was being unreasonable but he and Jask had already spent so much time apart, just the thought of one night without him was making him uneasy. The past two months of moving and searching for Johnny's body had been hard on them both. Making the decision to move forward with the wedding had been something they'd decided together. A day to look forward to, something to celebrate their love and its endurance. Vince felt excitement anytime he thought about finally being able to marry Jask. Jaskian Veris was the best thing to ever happen to him because Jask meant home to him. This stupid night before the wedding tradition could be ignored. He decided to tell his fiancé exactly that.

"Jask, neither one of us is even a bride. This is ridiculous. Stay home. Stay naked." He turned to face him, flashing what he hoped was a charming grin.

Ice blue eyes stared back at him. "Believe me, I wish I could, but our story has enough tragedy in it... why risk it? I don't want to screw this up."

"Nothing could screw this up. We're meant to be, remember?" Vince stepped closer and put his hand over Jask's, effectively stopping him from packing.

"I remember. But Vin, it's just a night. As much as I wanna stay, this tradition is important to my mom. It's more for her than anything, it's the last night I'm *just* her son and not someone else's husband."

The word husband caused a happy flip in his stomach. After tonight, he'd have the honor of calling Jask his husband. He could deal with a night of discomfort if that reward waited for him. "Alright, but let's not make this a habit."

"Wouldn't dream of it," Jask said with a smile. His hands

cupped Vince's face and he leaned in, kissing him gently. "It won't be easy for me, either. I might freeze to death."

"You can take my blanket." Vince stepped away to grab it and packed it in the bag.

Jask kissed him a lot deeper after that, like he was trying to take all the heat from Vince's body. They'd have kept going and Vince might've been able to convince him to change his mind, but Edis knocked on the door to kill the fun. "Times up, gotta take him."

"If we stay very quiet, maybe he'll go away," Vince whispered, dropping his head to Jask's shoulder and wrapping his arms around his waist.

With a soft chuckle, Jask planted his lips to Vince's head. "He won't, but you're adorable. Ed, give me a minute."

"You've got two, but that's it," Ed said. The door closed a moment later.

"Vin, here." Jask carefully tried to extricate himself, but Vince wouldn't budge. "I want to give you something, but I can't until you let me go."

Vince hesitated for a second before loosening his grip, "Fine, but I'm not going far." He stepped back half an inch to give Jask some breathing room.

With a shudder, Jask let out his jet-black wings. Every trace of the white they used to be was long gone. "You gave me a ring, but I realized I never really gave you anything. So... before it was too late, I wanted to..." Jask trailed off, then made an adorably constipated face as he plucked one of his own feathers and let out an exaggerated whine. "Give me your wrist."

Vince frowned and made sure Jask's wing was okay before

doing as requested. "Is this some weird angel ceremony I should know about?"

"No," Jask said as he tied the feather around his wrist. "This is just me saying I love you. And now you can have a literal piece of me with you wherever you go... unless you don't want it."

"I do! I absolutely do. Thank you," Vince pulled him close again, kissing him gently. "I love you, too."

Jask smiled against his lips and broke away only when Edis knocked again. "Times up," Jask said sadly. "I'll see you tomorrow."

"I won't sleep without you," he sighed, "but if I can handle growing up with Leota, I can handle this." He kissed Jask one more time before reluctantly letting him go with his brother. Vince stood in the same spot for a few moments as he processed the silence of his now empty house. Jask was going to Astarte's and Amaranth's home for the evening and Edis would go back to Lee and Arro. Only Vince would be without company.

He felt a sudden pang of grief, overwhelmed with a need to talk to Johnny. Johnny would've been able to distract him, help him forget about his worry that he could fuck something up. Because Vince was an expert at fuckups. He ran a hand over his face and walked into their kitchen. A flash of light from the window caught his attention and he checked to see if it was Jask and Edis. It was unlikely, as they had most certainly teleported. Vince didn't see the point since they all lived in the same cul-de-sac, but to each his own.

He directed his gaze to the buildings lighting up the night sky to his left. Settling on the outskirts of the city had been a unanimous decision, but Vince would be lying if he said he didn't miss seeing the stars.

He shook himself out of that thought and pulled open a cabinet, frowning when he saw their liquor seemed to be missing. He was sure his mother had something to do with that. She'd given him multiple lectures about being late to his own wedding, her main concern being a drunken stupor. He couldn't seem to convince her that nothing would make him late to marrying Jask. Seemed like she'd taken matters into her own hands. He slammed it closed and grabbed his keys. If he couldn't drink here, he'd go to the bar. No way was he getting any sleep without some type of alcohol in his system.

It'd taken some trial and error to find a bar when they'd first moved but eventually, they'd found a place that accepted demons, angels, and even the occasional human. No one batted an eye when Jask and Vince walked in together that first time. He started up his old truck and drove into town, whistling along with the radio as he sped down the road.

Already, being apart from Jask was making him antsy. They'd spent so long fighting the bond, so long separated. Now that it was safe for them to be together, they were hardly ever divided. They weren't joined at the hip every moment of every day; their new jobs wouldn't allow it. However, every other spare moment Jask was by his side. Until tonight. He knew it was temporary, a fleeting moment in the years they'd have, but his chest was still tight with anxiety.

They still didn't know who'd taken Johnny and that meant there was an unknown potential enemy out there. If he wasn't with Jask, he couldn't protect him. Vince huffed out a small laugh as he pulled into the bar. If anyone in their odd little family didn't need protection, it was Jaskian. Yet, the worry stayed in Vince's mind, sitting like an unwanted guest.

He wasted no time in entering the bar, waving to a few regulars. Herchel was behind the bar, glaring at a group of loud demons in one corner. Vince took his favorite stool and looked over at the crowd before turning back, hanging his hat on his knee. "Trouble?"

Herchel shook his head and dropped a glass in front of Vince, pouring him his usual. "Nothing old Bess can't handle," Herchel tapped the bar above the spot he kept the shotgun Vince knew was there. He'd seen it enough times, luckily never pointed at him. It suddenly struck him as odd that he hadn't been in a bar fight in so long. It had almost been a weekly occurrence before Jask. He shook his head as he picked up his glass. He was proud of himself for kicking that habit and he wasn't about to pick it back up now... no matter how much the men in the corner were asking for it. No matter how much he missed it. He was getting married tomorrow. Jask would murder him if he showed up with healing bruises. The idiots were getting louder, and Vince tossed back the whiskey, motioning for Herchel to keep them coming.

He could ignore them. He was not getting into a fight tonight. He took a sip of the second drink, savoring it. A few blissful moments passed as he envisioned what Jask would look like tomorrow, how he would smile when they stepped into the venue at the same time. The daydream got even better as he began to mentally plan out the honeymoon. They weren't going very far, but they'd both taken a week off work. Vince was determined to keep Jask in bed for *at least* five of those days.

He was rudely knocked out of his reverie when a small voice called out in pain. Vince couldn't stop himself from looking, turning his head to glance over his shoulder. A young angel kid, probably barely old enough to drink, had caught the attention of the ruffians in the bar. They'd shoved him to the floor and were circling him. He saw the look of terror on the boy's face and his brain flashed him back to that day with Damian. To the glassy eyes that had stared up into nothing as the blood seeped into the cold cement floor. One kid was dead because of him, he'd be damned if something happened to this one while he could stop it. Vince slowly sat the glass back on the bar before pushing his hair back and settling the cowboy hat back on his head. He watched Herchel reach for the gun and shook his head as he stood. "I got it, Herch. Leave Bess sleeping for now." Looked like he was getting into a fight tonight, after all.

He pushed a couple of the instigators out of the way and held a hand out to the victim. After a brief hesitation, the kid took it and allowed Vince to pull him up. Vince confirmed with him that he wasn't hurt badly before dusting him off and sending him away. He felt a shove from behind him. He turned, clenching his teeth and facing what he assumed was the ringleader.

"Hey," the drunk slurred. "We was just having fun."

"Oh, were you? *He* didn't seem to be." Vince took a second to roll up his sleeves.

"Angel bastards. Better to teach them early how rough the world is."

Vince shook his head. "It's only rough because of assholes

like you. Herchel's is a safe space. If you can't abide by his rules, you need to go."

"Make u—."

When Vince told this story later, he would tell anyone that would listen that he hesitated. That he thought out the pros and cons of a fight the night before his wedding to the love of his life. That is *not* what happened. Vince's fist connected with the jaw of the speaker before the words had finished leaving his mouth. Almost in slow motion, Vince watched him hit the ground, out cold. A pool stick broke across his back and he turned his head with a raised eyebrow. The man looked at the broken stick and then back to Vince, who hadn't budged even an inch. With no other options, he tried to punch Vince in the stomach. Vince easily sidestepped the hit.

"Really?" he demanded before grabbing the guy by his shirt and tossing him hard into the wall. The rest of the mob jumped him at that point and Vince almost regretted getting involved. Not because he was worried he wouldn't win, but because he'd done so well in staying out of fights. He brought his elbow up and into the chin of an assailant, the vibrations traveling up his arm as he felt the man's teeth break. He ducked the next swing and gripped the man by his throat, lifting him into the air before body-slamming him into the floor.

He stood and looked back to the bartender. "Herch! Jask does *not* need to know about this!" Herch's hands went up, palms facing Vince in agreement as he shrugged. Vince could only hope he wouldn't rat him out. He was tackled from behind, stumbling forward a few steps. He reached back and grabbed the guy, swinging him forward over his shoulder and onto the pool table. After a few more moments, he had them all running out the door. He kicked the last one in the ass as he watched them flee.

"Hot *damn* that felt good!" He came back to the bar and took the bottle of water Herchel handed him. He downed the entire thing before catching his reflection in the bar. He'd managed to get a nice cut on his cheek, he lifted his fingers to it and winced. It should be healed by morning, or at the very least hidden well if he cleaned it up. He sat back down on his stool and laid his hat on the bar, picking up the glass Herch had waiting on him. A throat clearing to his left had him looking over to find the boy he'd just saved sitting next to him.

"Thought you'd left." He took a drink of the whiskey, loving the burn as it traveled down his throat.

"No, I... Well, I-I'd like to buy you a drink. For what you did." The blush on his cheeks and the stutter were adorable. Two years ago, Vince would've taken him home. Now all he wanted was to get past tonight and get back to Jask.

"That isn't necessary but thank you for the gesture." Vince thought that would've been the end of the conversation, but the kid didn't move.

"I should be the one thanking you. Please, there has to be something I can do."

Vince finished his drink and turned to face him. "There is. Take care of yourself. Don't let assholes like that get you down." He patted the kid on the shoulder, paid his tab, and waved to Herch as he left the bar. He was just buzzed enough that his nerves were mostly settled, but not bad enough that he couldn't make it home. Once he pulled into the drive, he had a moment of weakness and started walking towards As-tarte's. He just wanted to check on Jask... but something made him stop in the middle of the cul-de-sac. Jask wanted this and Vince needed to respect that. He took a breath of the cool night air and spun around, letting himself into his silent, empty home. He stripped off the clothes he'd worn, tossing them in the washer to try and stop the blood stains from set-ting in. After a quick shower and a cold beer, he finally sank into the bed. He rolled until his face was buried in Jask's pil-low and drifted off into an uneasy sleep. It felt like seconds after he closed his eyes that he was opening them again. He stretched a little and wrapped his arms around the pillow, fully intending to go back to sleep.

~

"You did well tonight. That kid definitely has a crush," an *achingly familiar voice said, hitting him like a train.*

Vince was up and on his feet before he'd even made the decision to move. "Johnny?"

"Heya, Vinnie. Miss me?" Johnny smiled at him and Vince took three long strides, pulling Johnny into his arms. He knew he was probably crushing him, but he didn't care. Johnny was here and Vince was just so relieved to see his best friend again.

"I'll take that as a yes." He felt a hand pat his back and he stepped back. It was then that he actually noticed his surroundings. There were no walls, no doors, no windows. Nothing but an ongoing white around them and his bed behind him. He turned in a slow cir-cle before looking back at Johnny. Poor, innocent, loyal Johnny who

was smiling at him still, even if it was tinged with a bit of sadness now.

"This is a dream. It's not... you're not real. Fuck..." The grief hit again, fresh and raw. Vince stumbled back until he hit the bed. He sank down into the mattress and rubbed his eyes.

Johnny nodded and took a seat next to him. "You're right, this is just a dream. But does it matter? I'm still here... in one way or another." He flashed that boyish grin Vince missed so much and nudged him with his elbow. "Miss me yet?"

"You have no idea, Johnny." Vince looked his friend over. "I'm sorry. You didn't deserve it."

He shrugged, seemingly unbothered. "I know. None of us deserved what happened that day... or the days after. You figure out who took my body yet?"

"Well, no, not exactly." Vince pushed down the guilt that was threatening to overwhelm him. "We're going to! I promise. It's just... Jask and I... we're getting married tomorrow."

Johnny beamed and wrapped an arm around him. "It's about time. I'm happy for you. But... don't think so hard about who took my body."

"No, Johnny. I can't let this slide. Like I said, you didn't deserve it, so we'll find the bastard." Vince paused, weighing his next words in his head before asking, "Johnny, are you happy? Wherever you are."

His friend shrugged, shifting his glossy eyes to his own hands. "Just confused, mostly. And tired... I can't rest until my body is at rest." Johnny shifted suddenly, turning to face Vince fully. "Why didn't you burn my body? Why'd you bury me when you burned everyone else?"

"Draz started digging the grave..." Vince started but stopped *with a sigh. He looked over at Johnny. "Truth? I should've stopped him. Should've put you on a pyre like everyone else. But doing that made it so much more real. It meant you were actually gone, and I wasn't coping well with that."*

For the first time, Johnny looked truly uncomfortable. "Actually, about Drazan..."

Vince frowned and waited for Johnny to continue. What could he possibly have to tell Vince about Draz? Johnny's mouth opened, but instead of words, a loud blaring alarm replaced Johnny's voice.

~

Vince shot up in bed as his alarm clock rang on the bedside table. His breathing was coming quick as he searched the room for the threat, tossing the blankets off of his legs. His eyes landed on his alarm clock and he sank back onto the bed. Vince reached over and turned it off, running his other hand over his face. A dream, that's all Johnny was now. He allowed himself a moment to grieve again for his fallen friend.

The phone buzzing on his bedside table had him rolling out of bed and answering his mother. A brief conversation and one hot shower later, Vince smiled at himself in the mirror. Today was the day Vincenzo Riskel got married.

JASKIAN

Leaving Vince even for a single night was painful. He knew it was necessary, but still... after everything they've lost, everything they've suffered... it just seemed wrong to purposefully separate. He went through the motions with Astarte before she finally turned in for the night, and that alone was enough to make him wish he'd thrown tradition out the window. For two solid hours, all he heard from her was how grown up he was and how much she wished his father could've been there to see it.

Part of him was really starting to believe she'd gone mad. It had taken a great deal of effort not to remind her that Athar wasn't around for a very simple, extremely terrible reason. *I killed him,* he reminded himself silently. *Because he thought this very union was unholy enough that he tried to kill us.*

But that path was dangerous. All it ever did was cause him to think about the other things they'd lost in recent years. Athar, Cidos, Johnny... Drazan. Knowing his best friend was out there somewhere and hurting was almost too much for Jask. Drazan had given him *everything...* and how did Jask repay him? He'd gotten his boyfriend killed, and nearly got *him* killed, too.

Nothing was the same anymore. Happiness felt like something cheap, something stolen — not something to be grateful for. He wasn't sure if he'd ever be able to move past that, ever be able to look at Vince or his brother Edis and not think of all the things they'd suffered together. Sure, on some level, that brought them all closer. They'd die for each other. Kill for each other. But it didn't stop the memories from trying to swallow Jask whole.

A knock on his window caught his attention, and Jask sat up slowly from the bed. Grinning, he made his way over to peek through the glass and expected to see Vince — maybe he'd had enough of tradition, too. But when familiar, bright, hazel eyes stared back at him through the dark, he knew exactly who it was... and it wasn't his soon-to-be husband.

He opened the window so quickly that the glass actually vanished. "Drazan?!" he whispered, waving him in. "What the *fuck*, Draz! Where have you been?"

Draz climbed in through the window, straightening his clothes as he turned to face Jask. "You almost sound unhappy to see me, Jask."

Too many emotions flooded Jask's system at the sight of his best friend. He didn't answer right away. He couldn't. Instead, he surged forward and pulled Drazan into a tight hug. "Of course I'm happy to see you, you idiot."

After a moment's hesitation, Draz hugged him back, hand awkwardly patting between Jask's shoulder blades. They stayed in the silent embrace until Draz stepped back, clearing his throat. "So. Tomorrow's the big day?"

"Yeah," Jask said quietly. He ran a hand through his hair and sat on the edge of the bed, realizing pretty quickly that whatever warmth they used to share was gone. "Vince figures we've put it off long enough."

"Well, what are you doing here? Shouldn't you be out at a strip club? A bar?" Draz gave him a small smile and Jask could see a hint of the old Draz behind it. He almost missed what

Draz was saying as he continued. "It's barely eleven o'clock. You're getting old, Jaskian."

It was true, but he still felt a little defensive. "Edis has a kid now, and it's not exactly like my best friend was around to plan a bachelor party for me. I don't... I don't have anyone else. Not really."

"Well," Draz said as he shrugged, pulling Jask up off the bed. "I'm here now. Let's go celebrate."

"Yeah?" Jask stepped in close, trying to take in the familiar lines of his friend's face. "Might get my ass kicked by the future missus, but I can't say no if you're offering."

"You know I'll take any chance I get to annoy Vince. Let's see if this shit still works." Draz put a hand on Jask's shoulder and Jask could feel him pull on his power. A blink later and they were outside a bar. Draz put his hands on his knees and took a few deep breaths. "Fucking hell, that's always so exhausting. I think I'll stick to mirrors."

Jask chuckled. "Aww, poor baby. Come on." He clapped Drazan on the back and lifted him upright by his shoulder. "What are the rules for these kinds of things, anyway? Am I supposed to still be a good little angel?"

"Why are you asking? Looking to get into some trouble?" Draz opened the door, revealing scantily clad dancers on poles. "Because this is where we'll find it."

The last thing Jask needed was trouble. But old habits died hard — and some died much harder than others. He stepped through and smirked over at Drazan. "Trouble seems to find us, D. Let's see what happens."

"That's what I like to hear. Go find us a table and I'll get the drinks." Draz winked and headed to the bar, eyeing one of the dancers as he passed.

Jask wasn't quite sure what to look at. Sure, the view was nice as he took a seat a little too close to one of the poles, but he still couldn't get over the sight of his best friend. When Drazan came back, he hadn't skimped on the drinks. Jask snorted as he took two of the shots off the tray and tossed one back. "In a hurry tonight, D?"

"Making up for lost time!" Draz took one of the shots and held it up for a toast, which Jask met a little too eagerly.

They killed the entire tray before the end of the second song, and Jask felt more relaxed than he had in a long time. Jask nodded his head to one of the dancers and jerked it toward Drazan. "How about one for the grumpiest man in the room?"

"I'm not grumpy," Draz mumbled as the girl straddled his lap with a smile.

"You sure look grumpy." She leaned and motioned for another dancer to join. "But we'll fix it for you, handsome." Another dancer joined and for one song, the man and woman took turns dancing on Draz.

As the music died down, Draz pointed at Jask. "*He's* the one getting married tomorrow."

"Which means I'm the one that needs to behave," Jask reminded him. "I'm... probably *too* content with just watching this." He took another drink and shook the empty glass, then stood with a wink to the girl. "Time for refills, anyway."

"You said probably!" Draz called after him. "That means one lap dance for the groom when he gets back." The laughter of the dancers followed Jask to the bar, and he couldn't shake the feeling that Vince would forgive him for whatever happened. He had to, right? Draz was back.

He refilled the tray and carried it to the table, then sat back down with his legs splayed. "Well?"

"That's my boy." Draz grinned as he watched the two move from him to Jask.

The man straddled Jask first, rolling his hips to the rhythm as he smiled. "Congratulations on the wedding. This one's on the house," he said with a wink.

On instinct, Jask's hands found the man's waist right as the girl's hands snaked down his chest from behind him. She was warm, they both were, but his eyes found Drazan in the space between them. "Thanks, D."

"What are friends for?" Draz asked quietly before downing his last drink, an indecipherable look on his face. It cleared quickly and he waved at Jask before heading back to the bar for a third time.

The moment Drazan was out of sight, Jask felt out of place. The girl was whispering in his ear about some kind of private room, but all he could think about was Vince. This was fun, but he had a fiancé to think about. "No, no thanks," he said carefully. He dislodged the demon man from his lap and stood, glancing around to see where his friend went.

Draz was waiting at the bar for the next round, having a quiet conversation with the bartender. He frowned when Jask approached. "Aren't you supposed to be getting a bachelor party lap dance?"

"Sorry, was I interrupting? I came here to hang out with you, D. You know I can't touch them; I'm getting married. Vince would kill them both."

"You don't have to touch them. You just have to enjoy the dance. Even your hot-headed demon should understand that. Besides, I was coming right back. Just getting more shots." He takes the tray from the bartender and holds it up to prove his point.

Jask nodded but didn't make a move to grab one. "Yeah, would've been great if the chick was cool with keeping it like that. She offered." He slides his hands into his pockets and makes his way to a different table, a little further back. "Better to walk away."

"Alright, no more lap dances. You can't really say you blame her, though." Draz handed him a shot as they sat down, and the slight stroke to his ego had Jask shooting it back without a second thought.

"Missed you, D."

"I know. Me too." He takes another one. "But let's not focus on the past. We're here now."

The drinks flowed a little too easily after that, and toward the end of the night, Jask was undeniably drunk. He grinned at Drazan like he was the best thing he'd ever seen but sighed heavily as it faded. "I want Vince. We should go."

Draz shook his head. "We're just getting started. We can't leave yet. Besides, you can't even go back to Vince."

"How are you still so *sober?*" Jask asked. He swayed on his feet and gripped the other side of the short bar to steady himself. "And fuck the rules, since when have I ever listened to rules? Vince was right."

"You'll disappoint your mother, speaking like that. Not to mention, when has Vince ever been right?" He waved the bartender down. "One more for the road?"

He hesitated. He shouldn't, he knew he shouldn't… but it smells delicious to him now, and it's for Drazan. *Drazan.* The best friend he thought he'd never see again. "Only if you promise to come to my wedding."

"Wouldn't miss it for the world, babe." Draz turned his back to him to grab the drinks. Facing him once more, he smiled and held up his own glass. "To love."

Something jagged soothed — or drowned in booze — inside of Jask, and he drained his glass quickly. As he set it down, he could feel his heart rate speeding up and slowing back down, over and over again. He shook it off, taking a step closer to Drazan. "I'm… glad you fff—finally came home," he slurs out.

Draz put a hand on Jask's shoulder, pulling him in for a hug. This time he didn't hesitate, just held Jask tightly for a few moments before stepping back and smiling sadly. "For what it's worth, Jask… I'm sorry about this."

"Sorry?" The word sounded funny in his head, like maybe it wasn't a real word anymore. His vision blacked around the edges as he struggled to say focused, but with each second, he felt… heavier. "D?" he asked, his voice sounding far away. "Sorry about… about wh—"

Thud.

II

VINCE

Having the wedding in Athar's marble monstrosity of a mansion had been Jask's idea. He owned it and everything in it now, and they all found it fitting that they would cement their union in the former lodging of the angel that had so opposed it in the first place. The great hall of the home was quiet as the assorted guests shifted in their seats. There weren't many here, for safety as well as preference on behalf of the grooms. Strauss and a few of the ranch hands took up a row, looking around with wide eyes. Pattie sat behind them, his surprising plus-one — Kos — sitting next to him, fidgeting in his suit. Damien sent his congratulations in the form of a gift but was unsurprisingly not able to attend the ceremony. Edis and Leota sat near the front with Arro, talking quietly with smiles adorning both of their faces.

The blue and gold silk streamers looked perfect in the fading sunlight coming through the open windows above the hall, and the flowers had been placed strategically by Leota, Amaranth, and Astarte. The women *insisted* on decorating the area themselves, and the former mates had given in after a few not-very-vague threats from their mothers.

Looking out from his side of the hall, Vince couldn't complain. They'd strung white lights across the walls, and it gave everything it touched an ethereal beauty that had Vince squirming to find Jask and get this started. The demon scanned the small group again, and his gaze fell on the door opposite the one he was peeking out of now. Jask was behind that door, getting ready to exchange their vows. Was he as eager as Vince? Nervous? Perhaps he should go to check on him. They didn't have to look at each other just to talk.

He was opening the door to step out when the main door opened to admit another guest. Vince frowned as he ran mentally through the guest list. Who else could that be? Before he could see the new arrival, he was pulled back by his collar and the door slammed shut. He turned to glare at his mother before resuming the pacing he'd stopped to open the door.

"You'll wear a hole in the floor," Amaranth scolded with a shake of her head. "And you knew better than to peek. What if you'd seen Jaskian?"

"Oh no. What if I had seen the love of my life looking ravishing in a matching suit? The *horror*." Vince didn't try to hide his sarcasm, his pacing continuing.

"Can't even leave you alone for one minute. And to think I left to get you this—" Amaranth held out a glass of whiskey — "for your nerves."

"Bless you, Mother." The sarcasm left Vince's tone completely as he downed the drink in one shot, taking a deep breath after. "And thank you. For everything. The decorations look amazing, and I'm sure Jask will be just as pleased."

"That's better." Amaranth pulled her wrap around her shoulders and sat on the couch as they waited for the music to start. He and Jask had decided to exit their rooms at the same time, meeting at the altar instead of walking down the aisle as tradition demanded. They'd chosen to come out to the song Vince had sang to him when they'd first given in to each other what seemed like so long ago. At the beginning of the second verse, they'd be stepping out, getting their first look at the same time. Vince pushed his hair back and stepped up to the mirror, making sure to put his Stetson on straight. He was still staring at his reflection when the song started, and Vince turned to look at his mother, his heart suddenly racing in his chest. She smiled serenely and stood, coming to kiss him on the cheek before leaving the room.

Vince watched the door close behind her and swallowed. This was it. He was about to marry Jask. There was nothing and no one here to stop them. No one that could hurt them anymore. They had their friends and family here. They had a nice, simple honeymoon planned back at the home Jask had purchased for Vince and his family after the bond had been initiated. They'd be alone — blessedly and beautifully alone — for one full week. Vince listened very closely to the song, stepping to the door and wrapping his hand around the door-knob. He almost couldn't breathe with the way the excitement was coursing through him.

The part of the song that was his cue started and he opened the door quickly, his gaze immediately going to Jask's door. His heart stopped for a second when he realized it wasn't open. Jask *couldn't* have missed it. Vince was sure he was paying attention, too.

He took a quick look over the crowd to see if something had gone wrong, if anyone had any information. Astarte now sat with Amaranth by Leota and Edis, and they all looked concerned as well. Vince's eyes met Astarte's, but she looked away before he could read her expression. He frowned and kept searching the room, freezing when he saw someone that couldn't possibly be there. Drazan sat in the back row; legs propped up on the chair in front of him with his arms crossed across his chest. He grinned at Vince and tipped his head in greeting before looking over at Jask's door with a raised eyebrow. Vince couldn't help but look in that direction again. It was still closed, and his heart was pounding so hard he feared it might explode. Something was incredibly wrong. The song was almost over, and even if Jask had missed the cue, there was no way he didn't notice the song was soon to finish. Vince could worry about Draz later, right now he needed to check on Jask.

He was halfway across the hall when Edis stood and put a hand on his chest. "Wait here. I'll go." His brother-in-law tried to sound calm, but Vince could see the worry in his eyes.

Vince hesitated but nodded — maybe Jask was just in the bathroom or destroying the wedding cake so all that was left was the pie. He took his spot before the officiant and clasped his hands behind his back to keep them steady. He focused his gaze on the now-open door of Jask's room, digging his fingernails into his palms.

Edis shouldn't be taking this long. A cough echoed in the room, and Vince turned his head. Draz was watching him with a small smile on his lips. Vince's unease grew, and he glared at the angel until the sound of a door creaking took his attention. Edis was stepping out of the room, a piece of paper in his hand and a shocked look on his face. Vince didn't even register he was moving until he was snatching the paper out of Edis' hand.

"Vince... I'm sorry." The words were quiet, and he felt his blood turn to ice in his veins as he read the words on the note in his hands. This *could not* be happening. He pushed past Edis and ran into the room. It was completely empty, void of anything that might suggest anyone had even been in it today.

That couldn't be right. He'd *seen* Astarte bring in Jask's suit. Vince looked for the garment bag but couldn't find it. Hands shaking, he looked back down at the note in his hands. At the words written in Jaskian's handwriting, the letters looking like they'd been written in a hurry: *"I'm sorry. I can't."* That's all it said. No signature. No explanation.

Vince stormed back out to the main hall. The whispers and muttered conversations ground to a halt as Vince stood in front of the chairs. Draz watched him calmly from the back, that same smarmy smile on his face. *"You,"* Vince growled as he took a step toward the smirking angel.

"Me?" Draz stood and stretched, seeming like he didn't have a care in the world. "I'm sure I have no idea what you're insinuating."

"You show up and now Jask is missing?" Vince wanted to rip him apart.

"Missing? You were always so dramatic, Vincenzo. Seems to me that he just realized you weren't what he needed. You should respect his wishes."

Edis immediately jumped forward to physically stop Vince from lunging at Draz. Leota and Pattie stepped in next, as Vince was only dragging Edis with him. The three of them managed to stop Vince's progress and Draz left the house with a jaunty wave over his shoulder. "Have a good life, Vincenzo!"

"No!" Vince fell to his knees as the door closed. Vaguely, he could hear people moving. Conversations being had involving searches and reasoning behind Jask's departure. Vince felt Leota's arm around him. He heard the cry of a baby fading, his mother presumably taking Arro away from the commotion. This was another dream. Johnny was going to show up and tell him this was just an alcohol-induced nightmare. Because there was no way on earth that Jask had *left* him. Not again, and not like this.

The paper in his clenched fist caught his attention and he pulled it open to stare at it. A tear hit the page, and Vince angrily wiped his face, running his arm across his eyes as a sense of despair roared through him.

Jask wasn't here. No sign of him remained. Vince had been forsaken. He sank further onto the floor as the same phrase repeated in his head. He couldn't deny it anymore.

Jask had abandoned Vince at the altar.

~

Vince eventually came to his senses and demanded Edis take him home. There had to be *something* that would tell him where Jask was or why he'd made this decision.

As soon as they landed in his living room, Vince was running up to the bedroom. He stopped in the doorway and his heart fell to his feet. The closet door was open and all of Jask's clothes were gone. The drawers were hanging out of the dresser, and with one look, Vince confirmed only his things remained.

No second note, barely a trace that Jask slept here just two nights before. Vince walked into the bathroom next, laughing bitterly when he saw even Jask's shampoo and other toiletries had been taken. He couldn't even be that idiot that would spray Jask's cologne on his pillow for comfort. He walked back out into the bedroom to find Edis in the doorway. The pity in his expression was too much to bear, and he looked away.

He left their room and checked the others. Room after room, anything that had been Jask's was gone. How'd he do this in one day?

After Vince had checked everything he could, he found himself back in the living room. He sat slowly on the couch where he and Jask watched that stupid old car movie last weekend. Something about speed and anger? Vince shook his head at the inane thought and didn't look up when Edis sat with him. Vince didn't keep track of how long they sat there in silence, but at some point, he couldn't stand it anymore.

"Why, Ed? Why now? Why *today*?" Vince's voice came out as a whisper.

"I don't know, Vince. I don't really understand either. Jask was so happy about this just yesterday." Edis put his hand on Vince's shoulder, squeezing in what Vince assumed was supposed to be a comforting gesture.

"Did he say anything? Anything at all?"

"Not to me, but we only talked for a few moments before I left him to go back to Lee. He was with mom for the rest of the night," Edis replied, keeping his voice quiet as well. It almost seemed like if they were too loud, something would shatter. That *Vince* could shatter. Vince rubbed his hands over his face and then stood.

"Guess I need to talk to Astarte, then." Together, they headed over to the home Astarte lived in. Edis opened the door without knocking and they headed to where they could hear voices in the kitchen.

"What I don't understand is how Drazan fits into all of this," Edis was saying to Vince. "How did he even know where we were having the wedding?"

"I told him."

Vince turned slowly to Astarte, forcing himself to keep calm and crossing his arms. "I'm going to need more than that."

"He came here to see me. Told me that he was sorry for running out on Jaskian, that... that he wanted to make up for lost time. I told him a good way to start would be showing up and supporting him at his wedding," she said, shifting in her seat like she was already bracing to defend herself.

"And you didn't think to tell any of us that he was back?" Vince demanded. He knew it was unfair, but he couldn't shake the feeling that Draz held the blame for all of this.

She shook her head, but kept her gaze lowered. "I assumed it would be a nice surprise. You have to know how much Jaskian misses him. Truly, I don't see why it matters, anyway."

How much Jask missed Drazan was not something Vince really wanted to think about. He decided to change tactics. "Did he say anything to you this morning?"

"Who? Drazan? No, I haven't seen him since he stopped by

about a week ago. If you're asking about Jaskian, no... I haven't seen him since he went up to bed last night."

Vince frowned, because that didn't sound right. "You didn't come with Jask to the wedding?"

"Amaranth came and got me this morning," she said quietly. "I went to say goodbye to him, but his room was empty... I assumed he left without me or cheated and stayed the night with you."

"No. He wasn't with me. Did *anyone* see Jask earlier?" Vince looked around at everyone in the room. Every single one of them shook their head in the negative.

Edis took a step forward and placed his hand on Vince's shoulder. "Vince, I think we have to consider the possibility that he just... left. He took his things, left a note..."

"You can't be serious. Jask wouldn't do that!" Vince hated the fact that he sounded like he was begging someone to agree with him.

"I don't know, Vinnie." This time, it was Leota that spoke. "Without the bond..."

"The bond broke a year ago!"

"But this is the first time Drazan has been in the picture since a year ago." Edis said, not unkindly. "I've seen them together, Vince. Maybe... maybe he just realized..."

Vince stood abruptly, knocking the chair back. "No. *No.* That isn't what happened."

"We don't even know if Jask knows Drazan is back," Leota reasoned, and it was clear by the look on her face that she was simply desperate not to see her brother hurt. "Has anyone spoken to *him?*"

Another round of shaking heads from the somber group has Vince wanting to scream. "This *can't* be happening."

But it was... and the utter, absolute silence that met him proved it.

JASKIAN

"Ow!" Jask opened his eyes and glared at the woman in front of him. "Was that necessary?"

She shrugged as she stepped away from him to a nearby table. "Needs must and all that, darling."

"I don't know what that means." He spat on the floor and licked his lips, tilting his head back. "Who the fuck are you supposed to be, anyway? Drazan's new plaything?"

"If only," she muttered, separating what appeared to be spell ingredients into neat little rows. "I'm Zaepris. That's all you really need to know for now. As for Draz, he should be back by now. How long does it take to crash a wedding, anyway?"

Dread seeped through Jask's system as he pictured Vince standing up there by himself, waiting for a groom that wouldn't come. "Don't know, been years since I've crashed anything of the sort."

Whistling caught both their attention as Drazan strolled in. "Yeah, I remember that. The Butler wedding? Or was it the Bradley wedding? Something with a B, anyway."

"Bouden, actually." Jask tried and failed to crack his neck, then did his best to stretch against the restraints holding him down. "Gonna tell me why I'm here, D? And why you're letting Tall, Dark and Dangerous over here stick me with things?"

"Would you believe me if I said it was for science?" Draz sat something down on the table. "By the way, the cake was delicious. I brought some back if you want to try it."

Anger flared through him and he jerked, but Drazan knew what he was doing when it came to bondage. "You couldn't have waited one more fucking day?! And what's your plan, Drazan? Gonna kill me? For *what*? Do you think I wanted any of this to happen?!"

"What difference would one day have made, Jask? And despite the fact that none of us wanted any of it to happen, it *did*. Do you think it's fair that you and Vincenzo get a fairy tale ending while Johnny is dead?" Draz didn't look at him, his gaze was focused on a dark corner of the room.

And there it was — as close to an admission as he'd ever get. Jask wasn't making it out of here alive, and all because he'd tried to save his mate. "Then what are you waiting for, D? You want revenge that badly for a man you knew a handful of months? Do it. Prove to me I never meant a damned thing to you."

"You were everything to me for a long time. And then the moment you weren't, everything went to shit for me. Forgive me if I'm a little upset about it." Draz finally turned to face him. "And as far as getting on with it, there are still preparations to be made."

Jask snorted, then eyed his former best friend. "It didn't

have to go to shit, D. I looked for you for months... begged you to come home."

"You didn't need me anymore. You had Vince. Edis and his little family. Why even try to look for me?"

Blinking, Jask just shook his head. "You're my best friend, Drazan. I owe everything to you. I was *fucked* when you left, you know that? It took me weeks to even look Vince in the eyes because part of me thought it was his fault."

Drazan sighed. "We should have talked about this before I went to the wedding, then. I would've loved to tell him that. Add fuel to the fire."

"It wasn't, though. It was never his fault, it was mine. That's what all this is about, isn't it? Drugging me, kidnapping me before my wedding. Tying me down, letting someone else do whatever they want to me. You're punishing me because I used you and threw you out. Is that about right? Do I have that right?"

"Speaking of..." Zaepris came over again and stabbed a needle in Jask's arm, drawing more blood.

"No. You don't have it right. This honestly has very little to do with you, and everything to do with your blood." Draz watched Zaepris work, leaning against the table.

His eyes flashed with dangerous promise, but whatever Drazan was using to tie him down was severely limiting his powers. "The fuck does that even mean?"

"Oh, is it monologue time? Fantastic." Draz stepped away from the table and snatched a chair, coming to sit in front of Jask. "You know I've always had an affinity for magic? When I left, I couldn't help but think about all the things Ci had been able to do to us in that building. I went searching and found Zae. She's a necromancer." He smiled at Jask, looking more alive than he had the entire conversation.

"Necro..." Jask trailed off as the truth of that smacked him in the face. "No. Drazan, you can't be serious! No one can bring back the dead, not even me, and that's *with* Cidos' and Athar's powers! You can't fuck with this kinda stuff!"

"Bit too late for that. We're too far in it." Draz almost sounded apologetic, which would have been endearing if Jask wasn't abjectly terrified.

Tears pricked his eyes as he fought to keep his expression as neutral as possible. "You know how blood magic works, Drazan. A vial here, a pint there... it won't work. Are you really prepared to trade my life for Johnny's? You're the one that stole his body, right? For this? For her?"

"For her? She's doing this *for me*. And yes, I took his body. I'm surprised neither you or your fiancé figured it out."

Jask closed his eyes again, not wanting to watch whatever was going to happen next. "Sue me for wanting to believe better of you, D."

"Stop looking so sad, Jask. I don't want to kill you. We're going to take it one step at a time." Draz stood again. "You sure you don't want cake?"

"Well, if you don't feed me, I'm not gonna be much use to you, am I? I'm a little pissed you brought the cake and not the pie, but whatever. Feed me." He opened his mouth, sliding his tongue out with an annoyed expression.

"I'm surprised you even had cake." Draz brought the cake back over and put the fork in Jask's mouth, and Jask made an unsatisfied noise as he ate it.

"Vince insisted," he said as he chewed. "Didn't realize it was going to be used to further torture me."

"Maybe he doesn't know you as well as you think?" Draz raised an eyebrow as he offered him another bite.

"How cute you two are," Zaepris offered from her spot by the table. Jask ignored them both, keeping his eyes on the fork as he continued to be fed.

When the plate was empty, Jask risked another glance at his friend's eyes. "I'm thirsty."

"What can I get you? I only want you to be comfortable." Draz headed for the door, plate in hand.

That sounded like a joke to Jask given the circumstances, but he wasn't about to be stupid about this. "Some real food would be nice. Water. And if you're going to let your new girlfriend keep taking my blood, I'm going to need some blankets. I'm cold enough as it is, you know damned well I'll go into shock from the cold before she manages to get half of it out."

Draz gave a low bow before turning and leaving the room to gather the supplies.

"Is it all true? The stories Draz tells me seem a bit crazy," Zaepris said.

Not one part of Jask wanted to talk to her, but he also knew she was likely his only way out. "I guess it depends on what he's told you, then. But chances are, yeah... it all really happened." He paused for a moment, then decided to take a chance. "My turn. What's in this for you?"

"Other than Drazan's eternal gratitude? The spell. The things I raise are normally not very pretty to look at. If we can perfect this, I'll be a rich, rich woman." She came to sit in the chair Draz had vacated. "Since we're exchanging questions, how are you feeling about missing your wedding? That must sting."

The thought of Vince made his chest tighten, and Jask was thoroughly aware he couldn't afford to break down. Not then. So, no matter how sad he was, how much he missed his mate, he couldn't let himself drown in it. "Honestly, I'm just pissed that the *cake* of all things was the only part I got to experience. If you two manage not to kill me, I'll be marrying Vince soon enough."

"Oh. You poor thing. You don't know why Draz was at the wedding, do you? He convinced your lover that you didn't want him anymore." She shook her head sadly.

"He..." Jask swallowed, his eyes darting around the floor as he let that piece of information sink in. "No. Drazan... he wouldn't. He wouldn't!" he yelled, the restraints lighting up with what little grace he had access to.

"What the hell is going on in here?" Draz demanded as he returned with the things Jask had requested.

"Fuck you, Drazan. Wasn't bad enough to fucking steal me, you had to go make sure no one would even miss me?" He realized as he said it how selfish it sounded, but he was too angry, too hurt, too *scared* to fully articulate.

"Oh, I see you heard about Vince. I'm really, truly sorry but I couldn't risk him coming after you."

Part of Jask wanted to believe that Vince would still come for him — would realize that Jask would never leave, not like that... but as he thought back on the last year, he knew he was wrong. Vince would believe it without question, because Jask hadn't shown him anything different. The trauma he'd suffered after killing his father and brother, being indirectly responsible for Johnny's death, Drazan's departure, and everything else... he hadn't been a good partner. He hadn't shown Vince exactly how much he was really relying on him every single day, how much he really loved him, and now... Vince wouldn't think twice.

He said nothing as Drazan offered him something to drink. The only thing that stopped him from denying the water outright was the slim possibility that if he kept his strength up, whatever spell Drazan was using to hold him would eventually fail... and then he could go make everything right.

He just had to hold out and survive until then.

III

VINCE

"He's not coming back this time, Vinnie." The words hurt as much to think about as when he'd first heard them. His sister delivered the sentence quietly while holding his hand in both of hers. He'd clenched his jaw and took a deep breath before standing and shaking her off. Taking his keys and storming out of the house seemed dramatic at the time, but he'd desperately wanted a drink. He needed to get away from everyone telling him that Jask didn't love him anymore. Herchel was surprised to see him but with one pointed glare, Vince stopped the questions he knew the other man wanted to ask. After the fourth — maybe fifth? — whiskey, Herch just left him with the bottle.

Now he could hear the bartender telling him it was well past closing time, but all he could do was watch the feather on his wrist. He spun it slowly and let it remind him of the feeling of Jask's wings on his skin. He would never feel that again. All he had left was the one single piece of his mate. Jask gifted him with this feather as a symbol of his love. He wouldn't have done that if he was having second thoughts.

"Right?" He squinted at Herch, but the other man just

shook his head, obviously unaware of the questions flying through Vince's whiskey-soaked mind. Vince huffed and stood, letting Hersch lead him out the door and into the early morning air.

"Go home, Vince. Sleep it off and dry out. The whiskey bottle won't hold the answers." Herch closed the door and Vince stared at it long and hard before beginning to walk down the street. Something was wrong and no one could see it. Why couldn't anyone else see it? *Jask* would've noticed something wasn't right. That thought sent a fresh wave of pain through him. He stopped walking down the street as another thought occurred. Maybe Jask did notice, and something happened because of it. That didn't explain the missing clothes and items from the house. Or the note that Vince still had in his pocket. He'd tried to throw it away a few times, but it was the last thing he'd gotten from Jask. Now, coming up on the next day, he still couldn't bring himself to part with it. He watched the sun begin to rise in the distance and realized he'd spent his entire wedding night drinking whiskey at Herch's bar. The night that was supposed to be shared with Jask and only Jask.

Vince should be in bed with the angel right now, sleeping in without a care in the world. Instead, he was walking down the sidewalk of his town while normal people were just waking up, getting ready to start their days. Like he and Jask had been doing for the past eight months in this town. They had a life together; they'd built everything they had from scratch. Things were finally settling into a normal routine. Lee and Ed were even considering letting Arro go to school when he came of age. Things had been good. Better than good.

A car speeding past him shook Vince out of his own head and he realized he'd been standing at a crosswalk for longer than was normal. He blinked and crossed the street, turning onto the path that would lead him out of the city and toward his home.

Eventually the streetlights and apartment buildings gave way to trees and the sounds of birds chirping. Vince breathed in the fresh air as he continued to put one foot in front of the other. His brain was swimming with what ifs and conspiracy theories about what could have possibly happened to his fiancé. He was halfway to the plot of land they'd built their houses on when he remembered he'd driven to the bar. He reached into his pocket and pulled out his keys, staring at them like they'd betrayed him. Vince sighed and looked over his shoulder. Was the walk back to Herch's worth it? He was distracted by the sound of running water to his left and he stumbled into the woods.

A river flowed through the woods and Vince could see a small pool of water further down, a short waterfall bubbling down into it. Despite the fact that he was incredibly drunk and was in no condition to be doing so, Vince decided it was a fantastic time for a swim. Articles of clothing were left on the forest floor until Vince was standing on the bank of the pond in nothing but his underwear. With no hesitation, he stepped in. The water was cold, the area still clinging to the winter temperature even though spring had started a few weeks ago. It helped sober Vince up, so he pushed forward until he was chest deep in the middle of the body of water.

Vince's head cleared slightly, and he started to think back over the past few months, trying to find anything that could've warned him about what was coming. His dream with Johnny made him think of the night they'd found out his body was taken. The one-year anniversary of his best friend's death. Vince leaned back in the water and stared at the tree-tops as his mind took him back to that night.

Vince stood outside the old house and stared at the hole in the ground that was once his best friend's grave. The others had re-treated inside already, but he couldn't bring himself to go. What rea-son would someone have to desecrate the burial ground like this? He scrubbed a hand down his face and fought the urge to cry for what must have been the twentieth time that day. When would the hits stop coming?

Footsteps padded quietly behind him until he could feel Jask standing just to his right. He spoke quietly, like making too much noise would somehow further the damage done here. "We'll figure out who did this, Vin. I promise."

Vince grasped Jask's hand, needing the comfort Jask was there to give. "Why would someone do this? Who would even know to look here?"

"Other than us? I don't know. It's not like we took any steps to hide it, but... Vin, the possibilities here aren't good." He squeezed Vince's hand like it was a lifeline for him, too. "Do you remember anything about the magic that killed him? The color, smell... any-thing at all?"

"I wasn't with him." Vince hated saying those words. Hated knowing that Johnny's blood would always be on his hands. "Drazan was there, but I wasn't. I could've stopped it, Jask."

Jask moved until he was directly in front of Vince, blocking his view of the empty hole. "No, you couldn't have. Cidos was in-

sane, and even if you could've stopped him from killing Johnny... it would've been you in the ground, instead."

It should be him. Vince should've been the one buried or burned. He opened his mouth to say exactly that but looking into Jask's eyes stopped him. Speaking that out loud would only hurt Jask and he'd dealt with enough pain. Vince wouldn't do that to him. He couldn't. Instead, he just pulled Jask into his arms, dropping his head to his shoulder and holding him tightly.

"I should've killed him a long time ago. I'm sorry, Vin. I don't think I'll ever be able to tell you how sorry I am." He kissed the top of Vince's head and held there, exhaling slowly. "We'll fix this. We'll find him."

Vince didn't know how they'd pull that off. They had no leads, nothing to point them in the right direction. Even so, he knew Jask wouldn't stop until he found Johnny. Or what had once been Johnny. Vince pulled back from Jask and looked out at the lake. "Want to take a walk? I don't really feel like going back into the house right now."

"Sure," he answered softly. Their fingers laced together a moment after that, and Jask tugged him along. "We don't have to stay here if you don't want. Ed and Lee already went back home."

Vince smiled at his fiancé, trying to portray that he was fine. He could tell from the look on Jask's face that he'd failed miserably. He decided to try for distraction instead. "If I go home, I'm going to sit and think myself into a place I really don't want to be. Why do that when I can take a moonlit stroll by the water with the love of my life?" He raised Jask's hand to his lips and kissed it quickly.

"Smooth," Jask teased. "How am I supposed to say no to that?"

"You aren't. That's the point." Vince shrugged before pulling Jask

a little closer and wrapping an arm around him. "Let me know if you get cold."

That earned him a soft kiss to his temple. "I love you. You know that, right? And no matter what happens... we'll figure it out together. You're stuck with me."

Vince ceased floating immediately. His feet touched the bottom of the pond and his breathing sped up to match his whirling thoughts. Jask loved him. Jask said that Vince would be stuck with him. The demon's mind raced as he thought back to each and every time Jask said something similar. Back to the times Jask expressed it without verbally saying it. In the loving looks, quiet evenings, and soft touches they shared. The times Jask held him after each nightmare reliving Johnny's death, the times Vince reciprocated when Jask dreamed of his family. The family was wrong. All of them were *so wrong*. Jask wouldn't have left willingly. Vince scrambled out of the pond, snatching up his boots and clothes and running toward the road. The heat that he naturally generated caused the water on his body to steam in the cool morning air as he sprinted down the road.

In the back of his mind, something told him that he should probably be concerned that someone might see him running down the road in his boxers like a madman. But he didn't have time to put his clothes back on, he had to find a mirror. He spared a second to be thankful to Draz for showing him the transportation spell, wherever the angel may be. He came up to the cul-de-sac that he shared with his strange little family and to his door. Without pausing or thinking about his actions, he rammed the door with his shoulder and knocked it off the hinges. Why waste time finding his keys?

He dropped his clothes and his boots in the entryway and swiped a knife from the kitchen before making his way up the stairs.

He slid to a stop in front of his bathroom mirror and blinked as he took in his appearance. Water still dripped from his hair and his eyes were wild. His bare chest heaved with the force of his breathing and he looked almost psychotic holding the knife. He looked down at himself and put the knife slowly on the counter. He couldn't help Jask if he didn't calm the hell down. Stepping back into the bedroom he shed his soaked underwear and quickly redressed in clean clothes, putting Jask's note in his back pocket. He made sure he had everything he could possibly need before going back into the bathroom and picking up the blade. He sliced his hand with barely a wince and dipped his finger into the blood. He placed the spell design against the glass and waited for it to light up before climbing through, headed to the person that had helped the last time he'd lost Jask.

~

Vince looked up as Damian entered the bar and gave a small sigh of relief. He'd been waiting for half an hour for the man to show up. Damian sat at the table with a smile and ordered a drink with a wave of his hand, the waitress scrambling to obey his silent command.

"You look like hell," Damian observed once the drink was delivered, taking a small sip.

"I feel like hell." Vince didn't see the need to lie.

"Shouldn't you be off on your honeymoon?" Damian raised

an eyebrow. Vince ran a hand down his face and then re-counted the entire story to his former employer. He watched as Damian's eyebrows lifted higher and higher and then finished with, "And now... I'm here. I need your help."

"I think you're right. Anyone that would send a bodyguard with you to meet someone as harmless as me cares too much to leave on your wedding day." Damian ordered them both another drink.

Vince scoffed. "Yes. Harmless. Look, Damian, I need to find him. Something is wrong and I've already wasted almost two days."

Damian observed Vince for a moment before setting his drink down and leaning forward. "I have someone that can help. A witch I keep... employed."

"Why'd you say it like that? *Employed.*" Vince tilted his head.

"It's not an optional employment. When I started gaining influence and power, she was an asset. She wanted to leave after, and I knew I would still need her. I have her hidden in a swamp north of here. She's trapped by a warding spell. She can only get out if I allow it. And I haven't yet." Damian shrugged like there was no big deal to what he'd said.

"Great. She's your prisoner and you think she's going to willingly help me?"

"I'll give you something to take her. An appeasement. It'll be fine, Vinnie. Trust me." Vince finished his drink as his stomach sank with dread. He'd talk to the witch because he had no other choice. He only hoped it would lead him back to Jaskian.

~

Damian supplied Vince with transportation and the trinket to take to the witch. Driving down the mostly abandoned highway, Vince kept glancing at the wrapped-up box. Damian didn't tell him what was in it and Vince wasn't sure he wanted to know. Alnaess - the witch Damian referred him to – lived in a swamp not far from where Vince and his family had hidden from the Veris clan before. Even being away for the last year couldn't erase how familiar he was with the area. Vince's mind did what it was good at, wandering as the drone of the engine lulled him into a haze. He thought about the times he and Johnny came to hit the bars. Meeting Damian, all the things he'd done in his *employ*. Vince scoffed a little as he mused over what Damian mentioned about Alnaess.

Damian could've trapped him just as easily. Used him as another "asset." Vince might not have been the smartest demon around, but he knew what he was worth. He knew how strong he was, and he knew he was damn good in a fight. Why had Damian let him go? Could he be heading into a trap, or was Damian sincere with his offer of help?

The exit he needed was coming up and Vince pulled off the main highway. It didn't take long for the paved roads to give way to dirt and gravel. He could see the swamp in the distance and his anxiety over this entire situation worsened. Whatever the risk, he couldn't stop now. Of course, like everything else in his life, that mantra was proved wrong as he physically had to stop the vehicle.

Vince grabbed the trinket and stuffed it in his back pocket, exiting the car and stretching as he checked out the area. The note from Jask brushed his fingertips as he pulled his hand back out of his pocket and he ignored the urge to read it again. He knew now – he *hoped* – the note was fake. Keeping it didn't make sense, and he still couldn't bring himself to get rid of it. He rolled his shoulders and went over Damian's directions one more time. He had to cross the swamp to get to her and it did *not* look inviting. With a deep breath, Vince decided he'd been through worse and trudged forward.

He made it halfway through the swampy waters — jeans soaked, and his mood further soured — when he saw something ripple nearby. Vince stopped moving immediately, his instincts on high alert. What kind of terrible things could a witch have surrounding her swamp? He wasn't sure he wanted to know that any more than what was in the box. Slowly he continued forward, but he kept his eyes in the direction he'd seen the movement. Without warning, there was a burst of water and Vince barely dodged the gaping maw of an animal Vince had never seen before. He swam away and twisted just in time to avoid having his leg taken by a vicious snap.

The beast, what Vince could only assume was some type of mutated crocodile, made an unhappy noise indicating its frustration at missing its meal again. Vince waited for the next lunge and caught the monster, wrapping his arms around it's middle and squeezing with everything he had. Claws scratched down his arms and he cursed, forcing himself to ignore the pain as he tightened his grip. He held on until the croc's struggles weakened and then let go, stumbling back as the wounded reptile swam away, a sullen twitch to its tail.

"I see you met Betty." Vince whirled around at the voice;

hands raised in defense. Sitting on a half-rotten log was the most beautiful woman Vince had ever seen. She eyed him suspiciously, tapping her foot against the ground. "Why are you in my swamp?"

"Betty?" Vince knew he sounded like an idiot. "Wait. Your swamp? *You're* Alnaess?"

"Yes, Betty. She keeps unwanted visitors away. No one has ever gotten past her, and yet... here you are. How do you know my name?" She gave a head tilt that had Vince looking her over again. Her dark green hair cascaded down her barely covered body in luxurious curls. Her eyes were a dark grey that matched the water surrounding them and she stood slowly, walking toward him with a dangerous look. "I won't ask again."

"Damian. He... he sent me here." Belatedly, he removed the box from his pocket and held it out to her. "With a gift. I need your help."

"Mentioning Damian is the last way to get my help," she sneered, her beautiful face momentarily marred by the look.

"Yeah. He might've alluded to that fact but I'm desperate. I have this." Vince held the box out further. She took it slowly, her fingers dragging along his hand as she pulled it away. Opening the box and sniffing the contents made her relax incrementally, until she was watching him again.

"Finger bone of a disemboweled angel. Acceptable. Still not what I want." She crossed her arms.

Vince shivered and decided he absolutely did not want to know where Damian had gotten something like that. "Fine. I'll do anything. Name your price."

"You don't even know if I can help you." She raised an eyebrow.

"My fiancé is missing. I need help finding him."

"Easy enough. Are you willing to do what I need?"

"I told you." Vince was running out of patience. "*Anything.*"

"Good. Then you'll kill Damian."

JASKIAN

"I miss you." Jask pulled Vince a little closer, kissing him again to swallow any potential response. He knew this wasn't real — that it was just a dream, that he'd wake up soon back in that room. As much as he wanted to believe he was tangled up somewhere with the love of his life, there was one thing he couldn't deny: he couldn't feel Vince's heat. As their bodies pressed together, he felt almost nothing.

***Almost** nothing.*

But when Vince's hand snaked down and wrapped around his length, it drew a gasp from his lips. Over and over, he rocked his hips up into that hand until he was desperate for more, and with a low growl, he flipped them over to pin Vince to the bed.

"You're still mine, Vince," Jask whispered. "I'll find you again... I promise." His former mate spread his legs and Jask sent a tendril of grace through his body as he pushed in, the feeling overwhelming him even in sleep.

Vince either couldn't answer or didn't want to, and it tugged on something in Jask's chest. He bit and sucked marks into that tanned neck that disappeared instantly, like every part of Jask's subconscious was refusing to let him believe it was real.

He thrust in harder, faster, gripping Vince's cock and trying to elicit some sort of response — but nothing changed until Jask felt a sharp pain in his arm and sat bolt upright.

"Ow!" He blinked his eyes open slowly, ignoring the very real boner tenting his pants. "Fuck... even my sex dreams suck now. Thanks."

"Are you saying that's not for me?" Zaepris smirked, motioning toward his lap.

"Sorry," Jask said sarcastically. "'Crazy bitch' isn't really my type." He tipped his head back and tried to breathe. "Seriously couldn't even let me finish, huh?"

"Perhaps if you stopped calling me things like 'crazy bitch' I'd have let you. Maybe next time." She walked back to her table and then looked over her shoulder. "I could even give you a hand, if you ask nicely."

"Perhaps if you stopped trying to drain all the blood in my body, I'd stop calling you names," Jask countered. "And go ahead. Touch me. You won't like what happens when I get free."

"So dramatic." She sighed, shaking her head.

"Stop baiting him, Zae. You're only making things worse." Drazan stepped into the room, holding up a bag for Jask to see. "Breakfast?"

Whether he wanted to admit how hungry he was or not, his stomach betrayed him by rumbling loudly the second the scent hit his nose. "Yeah, I could go for some food. But D... tell me. What exactly *is* your plan for when I get free? You think I'm just gonna go home like none of this ever happened?"

Zaepris flicked a vial of his blood with her long, irritating nails. "Keep threatening him and you won't be going free, little angel."

"Why wouldn't you just go home? Once the spell is completed successfully, everyone will be happy. You can go back to your demon, and I get mine. Everybody wins." Drazan laid the bag on a nearby table and began taking out the food. He kept his eyes down.

Jask scoffed. "I'm tied to a fucking chair, Drazan. I haven't been allowed to get up for a shower... to use the bathroom..." His cheeks flushed as a particularly horrible memory from the day before flooded his mind. "But yeah, sure... everybody fucking wins."

"I know this situation is less than ideal," Draz continued despite the huff of laughter from Zaepris. "But think about how happy Vince will be if he gets to see his best friend again."

"It's not gonna work, D. It's just not. You can't bring people back from the dead, and even if you do... do you think it's really gonna be Johnny? What are you gonna do if he comes back but he's not all there, like some kinda demonic zombie?"

"That won't happen." Drazan leaned against the table. He seemed to be collecting himself and Jask could see that he was shaking. It only lasted seconds before he picked up a waffle and turned back toward him. Draz shook his head and spoke with more confidence, "We won't let that happen."

Don't think it's gonna be up to you, Jask thought. He took a bite of that waffle all the same, and it hit him how bland they really are without butter and syrup. It was a stupid thing to focus on all things considered, but what else was he supposed to do?

Zaepris used his temporary distraction as an opportunity to draw more blood, and for a moment, Jask couldn't even chew. He was lightheaded and frozen, his skin clammy. "D…"

Drazan frowned and put the food down again. He put one hand on Jask's chin and the other on his forehead. Concern was evident on his features as he searched Jask's eyes. "How much did you take, Zae?"

She shrugged, disappearing to the other side of the room. He was vaguely aware of the sound of mixing ingredients and a muttered incantation, but couldn't make the words out until she said, "Not enough. It's still not working."

Jask's body twitched violently as his grace tried and failed to replace the lost blood. Whatever measures they were taking to dampen his powers were working, especially now that he didn't have much strength at all. He used what little he did have left to try and fix his eyes in his former best friend. "I'd have… helped. If you'd have asked. Let me out, D. She's gonna kill me."

"We're almost there, Drazan. Don't listen to him, he won't help."

Draz looked closely at Jask before standing straight and turning to face Zaepris. "He can't help at all if he's dead. You're taking too much at once."

She stepped toward him and brought a hand up to his face. "Drazan… you need to prepare yourself for the fact that we're going to likely need all of it. Cidos was burned. We likely would've only needed a pint of his, but Jaskian? Most magic like this requires a life for a life. I thought that perhaps…

perhaps since we had a member of the murderer's family, we could make it work... but it's not."

Jask knew what that meant, and there were only two options. Either they killed him and hoped that the entirety of his blood would do the trick, or they did the same to Edis, who would be a closer — if not exact — match to Cidos' blood. He'd rather die a thousand deaths than be responsible for the death of yet another family member. "Do it," he said quickly. "Give me some of my powers back. Give me a day to try and heal... then take whatever the hell you need. You're right, D. This isn't just for you, it's for Vin."

"No." Draz shook his head. "This wasn't how it was supposed to go. We're not killing Jask."

Zaepris held her hands up. "Fine. Then let's let him rest for a bit. We'll try again tomorrow."

"Draz..." Jask croaked. "Water first? And maybe the... the rest of that fucking cardboard waffle?"

"Yeah. Yeah, of course." Draz grabbed a bottle of water and opened it, holding it to Jask's lips as he kept talking. "And maybe I can alter the spell on your cuffs to allow movement. Get you that shower you're complaining about. With supervision, unfortunately, but better than nothing."

"I volunteer to supervise." Zae eyed Jask's body with a hungry look.

Jask swallowed the water and narrowed his eyes at her. "I don't need grace to kill you. Just remember that." He turned his head to take another sip, then glanced up to his friend. "I'd be grateful, D."

Drazan nodded and picked the waffle back up. "Eat your cardboard and then I'll work on it."

~

Twenty minutes later, Drazan excused himself to do some research on altering the spell. Jask groaned when Zaepris didn't join him. "Thought you'd be sick of my company by now, Zappy. Rissy? Ape. There we go. Ape."

"Yes. Taunt the woman that holds your life in her hands. The way Drazan spoke of you, I thought you'd be smarter than that." She glanced out the door before picking up her syringe again.

Jask sat up as straight as he could. "He told you to stop. I've barely got anything left, if you keep going—"

"He doesn't know what he wants. He isn't thinking clearly and that's why I'm here." She stepped forward and took more blood, smiling at Jask's pained expression. "Did that hurt? It was meant to."

Refusing to give her the satisfaction, he shook his head and clenched his jaw. "Nope. You've taken so much I'm pretty much numb. And hey look, guess that took care of my boner problem... not that your presence didn't already do the trick."

She smiled almost ferally and gripped him by the hair, yanking his head back and stabbing a different syringe into his neck. "Cooked this one up just for you, Jaskian. Let's see if it doesn't take care of that mouth of yours."

For a moment, nothing happened. He was beginning to think whatever she injected him with was a dud, but the next — white hot fire raced through his veins. It was too much for him to even scream.

His body convulsed with the need to expel whatever it was as her icy hand closed painfully around his chin and jerked it toward her. "Traceless, that." She straddled his lap, and even the pressure from her slender frame hurt like hell. "Don't worry, it won't kill you. It'll just make you wish you were dead... it'll keep every single one of your pain receptors and nerve endings so sensitive that a light wind could bring you to your knees. Maybe if you beg Drazan hard enough, he'll let me finish the job."

"No," he choked out, trying to turn his face away from her. "I won't. I won't."

Her weight disappeared as his vision began to cloud, and this time, he could *feel* the blood leaving his body.

"Maybe not yet," she said with an amused tone. "But you will. No one can stand this very long, not even you."

But I'm not no one. I'm Jaskian Veris, and I... I'm...

IV

VINCE

Vince's knuckles were white with the force with which he was gripping the wheel. Alnaess' only request had been the death of the one man that was willing to help him since this nightmare began.

His sight was glued to the door of Damian's bar, and his current moral crisis lay solely in the fact that he wasn't *actually* having a moral crisis. He'd agreed to the deal. Vince was here to kill Damian. What did it say about him that he would willingly murder someone to save Jask?

After a brief internal struggle, he realized he didn't care what it said about him. He would burn the world down if it meant Jask being happy and healthy. The decision made, he released the wheel and opened his door. Enough time had been wasted and he needed this to be over.

Stepping into the dark room after standing in the sunlight made him pause. He let his eyes adjust as he scanned the room, looking for his target. That's all Damian could be to him now.

Damian was sitting with a woman who was wiping tears from her face, but Vince couldn't make out why. One look in his direction had Damian dismissing her and waving him over, having no idea what was coming for him. "Vincenzo! How'd it go?"

"She agreed to help me, but she had conditions." Vince didn't sit like he normally would, coming around to Damian's side of the table.

He shifted slightly. "Oh...? She didn't like her gift? It's very rare, certainly she must've known how difficult it was to come by."

"She liked it. She just wants something else more. Are you really going to make me say it?" Vince didn't want to do this in the bar — too many people that would see the next mark against his already-blemished soul.

Damian just shook his head. "She wants me, right? There are other ways to find him, Vincenzo. Other witches, other spells. Don't do this."

"Problem is that I'm out of time. And who knows what the next witch might want?"

His former boss stood slowly and took a step away from Vince, holding his hands out in front of him. "I helped you. I've always helped you, and I've hardly ever asked for anything in return. Just — just lie to her! Tell her you did it, I'll lay low. I'll let her go, just... don't kill me."

"You can let her go?" Alnaess had told him that only Damian's death could release her. Which one of them was lying? Did he dare risk it?

Damian scoffed. "Of course I can. It's just a binding spell, I can undo it with a phrase. If that's all she wants, I'll do it."

"She wants you dead, and I need her to get to Jask." Vince

ran a hand through his hair. "I can't fail him, Damian. Help me figure this out."

"Well, what kind of proof did she ask for? Between the two of us, I'm sure we can find a way to fake it." Damian's voice sounded desperate — which was something Vince had never heard from the man before.

"She just said killing you would break the spell holding her. If you can break it, and lay low like you said, maybe that'll be enough." Vince began to pace. If Damian was lying, as soon as Vince left, he'd run. He'd waste even more time hunting him down again.

The demon nodded and gestured to the back room. "I can handle that. Give me ten minutes to put my affairs in order, then I'll need to go home. I don't know the incantation by heart, and I keep the talisman somewhere safe."

"I'm coming with you."

Surprisingly, Damian didn't fight him at all on that request. When he entered the back room, he made two phone calls officially handing over control of his assets to people he trusted, then shredded an entire filing cabinet's worth of documents. "Never can be too careful."

"Is all this really that necessary? Can't you just lay low for a couple of weeks?" Vince watched everything curiously.

Damian snorted. "If you don't think she'll come here to burn down everything I've ever loved even after she thinks I'm dead, you didn't get a very honest first impression."

"To be fair, my mind was rather occupied." Vince helped Damian finish destroying what was probably valuable evidence against him, and after they were sure everything was done, Vince drove them both to Damian's home. After all this time, Vince realized he'd never actually been to his former employer's house.

If he expected a warm welcome, he didn't get one. They went straight down into the cellar and Damian moved an old shelving unit out of the way to reveal a safe. His body blocked the combination as he opened it, and after some shuffling, he pulled out a chain with some kind of ram's head bauble at the bottom. "Just need my book, one more moment."

"This is taking too long." Vince frowned.

Rolling his eyes, Damian disappeared for a moment to grab his spell book and came back, flipping through the pages. "Aha," he muttered, then held the talisman out in front of him as he read the incantation.

The talisman began to glow and broke apart, the pieces scattering on the floor around his feet. "There," Damian said bitterly. "It's done. Take the witch the heart of a cow and tell her I'm dead. I need to leave now."

"I need to know where you're going," Vince demanded in case he had to track him down and kill him. He left that last part unsaid, but the look on Damian's face suggested he caught the drift.

Damian showed him a spot on the map not all that far away. "It's a safe house. You can drive me there yourself if you'd like, since you don't seem to trust me anymore."

"Don't whine. It doesn't look good on you." They took a few moments to grab the necessities Damian insisted on bringing before Vince once again became his unwilling chauffeur.

The drive to the safe house took longer than Vince would've liked, but that had less to do with the distance and more to do with the fact that his skin was itching with the need to get to Jask. Over three days he'd been gone now. Anything could've happened in that time, and Vince spent the entirety of the drive torturing himself with grim scenarios.

When they finally arrived, Damian grabbed his bags. "Are you going to come tuck me into bed, too?"

"You literally owe me your life," Vince pointed out before opening the door and checking the house. After giving it the all clear, Vince took Damian's car once again. If he needed to get somewhere, he could walk.

The drive to the swamp took even longer this second time, and Vince was vibrating with a nervous energy he couldn't shake. Vince hadn't taken Damian's advice about the cow heart. If Alnaess could determine what the finger bone had been with a sniff, he didn't want to out himself with a fake heart. He drove up to the edge of the swamp and waded in, keeping an eye out for Betty. Halfway through he saw her, eyes trained on him from a close distance.

"Remember last time?" he asked, raising an eyebrow. She disappeared under the water and he continued his trek to find the witch.

As the swamp recessed to slightly more solid ground, he spotted a shoddily built cabin about fifty yards in. The walk up to the door was soggy at best but the door was already ajar when he approached.

"Come in."

Vince stepped in with only the slightest hesitation. "Lovely place you have here."

"I make do," she replied. "Is it done?"

Vince didn't trust himself to lie out loud to the witch, so he gave one short nod before actually looking around the room. It looked like she planned to keep her end of the bargain if the bowl of spell ingredients on her table was any indication. He turned back to face her. "What now?"

"Now... I find out if you're lying or not." She stood and headed for the door, throwing a "stay here" command over her shoulder.

She was gone for a full twenty minutes, leaving Vince plenty of time to panic and talk himself in and out of bolting a dozen times. He'd just decided to run for it again when she finally returned with a smile on her face. "I just left this swamp for the first time in almost seventy years. You did well. Did he suffer? Tell me he suffered."

Vince thought back to how irritated Damian acted at having to give up most of his life and going to the safe house. He nodded with confidence. "He absolutely suffered."

"Good. Then let's begin... I would like to take Betty and move to... greener swamps." She crowded the bowl of ingredients and fixed dangerous eyes on Vince. "Talk to me about him. His likes, dislikes, his desires. What he looks like in the morning. I don't care what it is, just talk."

Vince smiled for the first time in days, because this — *this* he could do easily. "In the morning? His hair is the most prominent thing to mention. It's just... everywhere. Sticking up in all different angles and he gets this adorable glare when I laugh at him for it." Alnaess nodded as she added something to the bowl, measuring with her eye. "And his likes? Well, me. Dislikes, also sometimes me. He's got this tell, though, when he's done being mad at me. No matter where I am or what I'm doing, he'll run his hand over the back of my neck and scratch. Just lightly. Won't say a word, he just keeps his hand there." Vince trailed off a bit as he started feeling the grief of not having Jask with him hit hard.

She hummed, adding a last ingredient that made the whole thing emit a puff of ice blue smoke. "Well, wherever he is, it's heavily warded. I can give you a vague area, maybe down to a ten-mile radius or so... but not any closer. You'll have to do the rest on your own."

"Okay, so, where is he? What do I need to do?" Finally, he had a direction, a solid lead.

Alnaess sucked her teeth. "I need a possession. Something touched by him, at least. Normally, words, thoughts... intentions... can do the trick, but not with warding that strong. Short of his blood or hair, I need something he physically came in contact with."

"I knew this would come in handy." Vince reached into his back pocket and pulled out the note found by Edis at the wedding. He handed to her quickly, eager to be on his way.

She hissed the second it touched her skin, then set it on fire. "There's dark magic in that. It's soaked with it... who exactly are we looking for, again?"

Vince watched as the paper turned to ash, floating to the floor. "My fiancé. He's never used dark magic in his life."

"Then that did not belong to him," she said flatly. "Whoever touched that letter had vile intentions, so unless your fiancé had a change of heart..."

"He wouldn't." Vince ignored the small seed of doubt in the back of his mind that suggested otherwise, instead focusing on the task at hand. "But that's all I had that he's touched." He waved a hand in front of him, and his eye caught on a flash of black. He stared at the feather on his wrist with a sinking heart. "What about an actual piece of him?"

Her eyes narrowed. "That would get you the closest, yes."

"Fuck." Vince didn't want to do it. This was the last piece of Jask he possessed. If he did actually change his mind — if he didn't want Vince anymore — this feather would be the last tie to his former mate. His heart made it all the way to the bottom of his feet as he pulled the feather off his wrist. "Here."

Alnaess spared one, single moment to give him what appeared to be an apologetic look, then set about starting another spell. Vince lost himself in thought until she was done and handing him a map with a circle on it. "I got you within six miles. Either he really doesn't want to be found... or someone really doesn't want him to be found. Look for areas where wildlife tends to shy away... they don't like warding that powerful."

"Hot damn. I could kiss you for this." Vince studied the map.

"You murdered the beast that kept me captive here for twice as long as you've been alive. That is enough thanks." She tapped her finger impatiently for a moment and then cleared her throat. "Well? What are you waiting for? Go find him!"

Vince grinned and took the risk of kissing her on the cheek before running out the door. There was an angel in need of a rescue, and he was the perfect demon to do it.

JASKIAN

"He's in shock," Drazan hissed. "Look at him. What the hell did you do? He was fine when I left."

Jask thoroughly begged to differ about being fine at any point during this, but he was too hazy to do anything at all but listen to them argue.

A palm smacked loudly against the table, making him flinch. "I didn't do anything," Zaepris lied. "He's just *weak*."

"Weak? He's barely breathing, Zaepris! Don't lie to me." Drazan sounded dangerous, a word Jask barely would've used to describe his friend before this.

Holding his head up was an effort, but through blurry vision, he could just make out her silhouette backing up. *Good, bitch. I hope you're scared.* She took a step closer to her table full of ingredients. "He wasn't going to cooperate, Drazan. I did this for you. It won't kill him, you have my word... you said yourself that if he dies, he's no use to us."

"Fix him. Now," Drazan demanded. He took a menacing step forward and watched closely as Zaepris put together the ingredients she would need. Draz stayed close to her as she administered the antidote and then he knelt in front of Jask. He put a hand over Jask's in what would appear to be a comforting gesture, but really, it just pissed him off.

"Oh look, now he cares," Jask said quietly. The relief came faster than the pain originally had, but he still ached all over. "Did you figure out a way to let me move? I'd like that bath right about now."

"Yeah, I did. Just..." Draz shifted his hands to the cuffs and muttered an incantation too quiet for Jask to hear. There was a small tingling feeling over Jask's wrists and then Draz was untying him. "Can you stand?"

Nodding, Jask rubs his raw wrists and pushes himself to his feet. The rush of blood had him lightheaded and dizzy, so he held on to Drazan as he tried to catch his bearings. "Guess not. Who'd have thought cake, a single waffle and barely a half a bottle of water wouldn't be enough to sustain me?"

"You've been around Vince too long." Drazan shook his head as he led him out of the room, and the reminder of his mate had Jask scouring the place for a possible exit. He knew he still didn't have access to his grace, but if he could get out... maybe he could find a way to call Vince to him.

The bathroom was even colder than the room he'd just been in, and he started shivering almost violently as Drazan turned the water on for him.

"Make it h-hot, D," Jask said. He didn't strip yet — he caught a glimpse of himself in the mirror, and all he could do was stare. His eyes were purple and sunken, and honestly, he looked like hell. "How long have I been here?"

"Little over three days." Drazan turned the water on as hot as it would go, and the steam wrapped itself around Jask like a blanket.

"Huh." He turned away from the mirror, finally stripping his dirty clothes off. "Three days and I already look like this... can't wait to see how good-looking I am in a month." He stepped forward, bracing his hand on Drazan's shoulder and slowly lowered himself into the water. "Don't look, I'm naked," he deadpanned.

"I've seen it all already." Draz tried to smile but then shook his head. "And I'm hoping this won't take that long."

Jask chuckled darkly as he reached for the soap. "Got news for you, D. I'm gonna be in here all day. Feel free to leave though, not like I can turn into a fish and swim down the drain."

Draz put his hands on the sink counter and lifted himself to sit there, leaning back against the wall. "I know you better than anyone in the world, Jaskian. You find the exit when we left the room?"

He knew better than to lie. "Yep. But something tells me you wanted me to find it, D. Cause you're right, you know me better than anyone. No way you'd have let me outta that room without a blindfold unless you wanted me to see it — or you're *actually* going to kill me soon."

"I don't want you dead, Jask." Not a reassurance that he wasn't going to, just that he didn't want to. Draz let his head fall back. "And you're as weak as a newborn kitten, not like you'd make it far."

The warmth of the water on his skin temporarily distracted him, and he let his eyes flutter closed as he cleaned himself. "No offense, but you severely underestimate my desire to get the fuck away from you right now. Vince would find me. Soon as I'm clear of whatever wards you've put up."

"He's not even looking for you. Last I checked he was at some bar. Herchel's. Drowning in whiskey and crying over the note I left," Draz informed him.

Knowing Vince was hurting didn't feel good, but Jask knew it was based on a lie. "Guess you don't know him at all, then. Cause see... at some point, he'll stop crying... and he'll come find me just to kick my ass. And when he finds out I was taken from him? Phew, I almost feel bad for you guys."

"I'm not scared of Vince." Draz sounded like he almost believed that. "None of that matters as long as the spell works."

Arguing seemed futile, so Jask laid back in the bath until he was fully submerged. Without access to his grace, he couldn't hold his breath for very long, but still... drowning out the rest of the world felt nice. He stayed there as long as he could and then sat up again to rinse the last few days from his hair. "I hope it works, D. I really do."

"It will. And then you can go home. I promise." Draz' voice was quiet.

"You still haven't told me what happens if it doesn't, D. Where's the line? When do you say enough is enough? When I'm already dead?" Jask bit his tongue to try and stop himself from saying more, but he couldn't help it. "Don't let me die here with Vince still believing I don't love him. Can you... can you just get a message to him? Then I swear, I won't try to escape."

"I can't, Jask. If Vince thinks for one second that you didn't leave willingly, he won't stop looking for you." Draz finally looked at him, his eyes sad.

Exhaustion and pain — both physical and emotional — made it hard for Jask to keep a straight face as he gripped the washcloth rod and pulled himself to his feet. "What makes you so sure he'll keep believing the lie, anyway? He loves me, Drazan. And he knows I love him. Get me a damn towel."

Draz didn't answer right away, instead stepping out of the room for a moment and coming back with the requested towel. He handed it to Jask and sat a folded bundle of clothes on the counter he'd vacated. "I made it believable. Spoke to your mother. Left a note in your handwriting with a small spell. Took all of your clothes out of your house," he said as he motioned to the outfit he'd brought in.

Each one of those admissions felt like an extra nail in an already-shut coffin. He dried off and dressed in slow, careful movements, then straightened up. "I'm not going to give up hope," he said, but based on the look on Drazan's face, it came across as a lie. He *would* lose hope, and probably quickly. "Can I get a real meal and maybe a chance to sleep before you tie me up again? And I need to use the toilet, so... you might wanna stand outside the door for that."

Draz nodded and stepped outside. "When you're done, I'll make you something to eat. You can sleep in my room." He pulled the door closed behind him, but already, he could hear Zaepris arguing with him.

He took his time in there, not having any motivation at all to even get off the toilet. Why should he help them? Why should he make any of this easy? Drazan obviously decided he cared more about Johnny than he did about him, and Zaepris wasn't exactly on his holiday greeting card list.

But eventually, the smell of real food coaxed him out of the bathroom, and he sat down at the table without making eye contact with anyone.

Draz watched him for a moment before pushing his plate closer. "You asked for real food and now you look like eating it is the last thing you want to do."

The truth was, he still just felt out of it. He picked up the fork and dropped it twice from not having a good enough grip before finally taking a bite, and Zaepris actually grimaced.

"Maybe that poison had a couple of side effects."

"Which is why we won't be using it again." Drazan's tone of voice didn't invite any arguments from his fuming companion, and Jask nearly smiled from the dissension.

The food was good but tasted a little off. It didn't stop him from clearing the entire plate and asking for seconds as he chugged the glass of water. When he was finally full, he glanced around. "So... I'm taking it you don't sleep in the room you're torturing me in?"

"No, I don't sleep in the lab," Drazan answered dryly.

"Well, at least I can add 'lab rat' to my resume. Where am I going then? You know how cranky I get when I don't sleep."

"Of course. Follow me, please." Draz put their dishes away and once again took the lead, leading him to a decent-sized bedroom.

The bed honestly looked incredibly comfortable, so Jask crawled right in, wrapping the blanket tightly around himself. "Come back in like four hours. Maybe nine."

"You think I'm leaving you alone in here?" Draz removed his shirt and pants, standing in only his underwear before pulling up the blankets and sliding in.

Jask narrowed his eyes but saw an opportunity to spread around some of the misery. He wiggled closer, throwing his arm around Drazan's bare chest and settled in. "Fine, then the least you can do is hold me."

Draz doesn't move. "You don't want that."

"You're the one that got in almost naked. C'mon. You kidnapped me, let that crazy bitch torture me, and you ruined my almost-marriage." Jask fully expected him to say no or push him off, but to be honest, part of him hoped that he didn't. Not because Jask genuinely wanted to cuddle with him, but because it might mean there was some, small trace of his best friend still in there.

After a moment of complete silence — Jask wasn't even sure Draz was breathing — Draz' arms wrapped around him. Not wanting to say anything to throw either one of them back to reality, Jask simply shut his eyes *and* his mouth for once. He'd take the kindness where he could get it... for as long as he could get it.

DRAZAN

Drazan stayed there, holding the man he once considered his best friend. In a lot of ways, he still did — but none of that could compare to how important it was to bring Johnny back. He felt Jask shift in his sleep and tightened his hold. Draz would comfort him in any way he could.

A few moments later, Jask sighed out a word. A name, actually. Even unconscious, he couldn't stop bringing up Vincenzo. Draz slowly rolled Jask to the side, giving him a pillow to hold. He climbed out of bed and snatched up his pants before leaving the room completely. Jask called out for Vince the way Drazan's entire soul called out for Johnny.

"Tell me you didn't sleep with him," Zaepris said from the kitchen with an eye-roll.

"Fuck off. You know I didn't. That's not what he's here for."
He went straight for the liquor cabinet.

"I don't know why he's here; you don't seem willing to
do what needs to be done anymore. You're too close to this,
Drazan." She tapped her long nails on the table and watched
him like a hawk. "I can have Johnny back in your arms by
nightfall."

Every muscle in Drazan's body froze. Johnny back in his
arms. That's all he wanted, *that's* what would fix everything.
Johnny would fix everything. All he had to do was drain his
best friend dry. His oldest, most trusted companion... but
he'd have his love back.

She stood, walking closer with measured, patient steps. "I
can make sure he won't feel a thing, Drazan. It'll be painless...
like falling asleep... and Johnny will finally wake up."

"And if you take it all and it doesn't work? I lose them both
and we don't get a second chance." Despite how tempting the
thought is, if the spell doesn't work Drazan isn't sure what
he'd do. How he would cope.

She shook her head and brought a hand up to his face.
"Oh, sweetie. If you think that boy or his demon will forgive
you after this... you don't know either of them as well as you
think. Your best shot to bring Johnny back is to let me do this
as quickly as possible before he gets enough strength back to
break out... or his brother comes looking."

Draz had barely spared a thought to Edis. His concern was
mostly Vince. He knew the stubborn demon would stop at
nothing to get Jask back, but would Edis really be a threat?
He had a family to worry about now. Drazan rolled the pros

and cons in his head as he replied, "Regardless, Jask is in no shape to continue."

"Exactly. Draining him slowly isn't going to get us anywhere. You need to decide before whatever is left in him shrivels up. Johnny? Or Jaskian? You let me know when you decide." She tapped his cheek and sidestepped to move past him, heading back to the lab.

Drazan took a deep breath through his nose and let it out slowly. Wanting Johnny back was now a physical ache as well as emotional. He hardly slept anymore, ate only to keep healthy. He needed to be in good shape to take care of Johnny since he was sure to be disoriented after the spell.

Before he realized it, Drazan finished the walk to the liquor cabinet and took out the last unopened bottle he had, the rest finished long ago. He sat at the table and took a long drink before sinking further into the chair. *Was Johnny worth Jask's life?* The thought hadn't finished before there was a voice whispering the affirmative in the dark recesses of his mind. He was finding it harder and harder to fight against that voice. The price he was paying for the darker blood magic, perhaps? And now, he had Edis to worry about on top of Vince, thanks to Zae's words. He didn't think Edis would actually come looking this soon, but he couldn't leave out any variables. Could he defend against both Vince *and* Edis? Having that direct link with Jask helped, but Vincenzo was stronger than Draz, and with Edis' help... Draz froze for the second time in the short period since he'd left Jask alone. He didn't need to defend against them both. He needed to take Edis, too! *How have I been so blind?* He stood so abruptly the bourbon he'd been nursing fell to the ground and shattered.

Cidos' twin along with Jask should be more than enough to complete the spell, and hopefully no one needed to die. Drazan looked at the broken glass in his kitchen as that train of thought turned dark. *Hopefully*, no one would die, but if they did? Well, at least he'd have Johnny to comfort him.

V

VINCE

Vince watched, enraptured, as Jask slid down on him inch by torturous inch. He ran his hands up his lover's thighs and gripped his hips and he fought the urge to thrust up, to rush this. He heard Jask's deep moan as he took Vince's length to the hilt and Vince's eyes moved up to his face. Jask's hands were braced on Vince's thighs and his head was thrown back in pleasure. He urged Jask to move with the hands still holding tightly to his hips, biting his lip as Jask obliged. For a moment – one blissful moment – everything was alright again. Except... it wasn't. Something nagged at the back of his mind and he couldn't put a finger on what.

"Jask, sweetheart. Look at me." Vince slid one hand up to Jask's shoulder, trying to pull him down. Jask stayed in the same position, slowly rolling his hips in circles. Vince frowned and propped himself up on an elbow. "Jask, please." Nothing changed, Jask's movements were almost hypnotic in the slow and steady pace.

"He's not real," a voice interjected. Vince jerked so violently that Jask disappeared, and Vince fell off the bed. He scrambled to his feet, spinning to see Johnny sitting at the edge of the bed. It was another fucking dream. Despite knowing that, Vince still grabbed a sheet *and wrapped it around his waist. Johnny raised an eyebrow. "Modesty? That's new."*

"Shut up. I'm a married man, now. Well... Almost." He rubbed a hand over his face and sat. "Are these dream visits going to be a normal thing? Not that I'm complaining."

"Time is running out." Johnny stated instead of an answer.

"That's super cryptic. Got anything else?"

"He's hurting him for me. You have to stop it." Johnny stood and began to pace, and right before Vince's eyes, his form flickered — as if his agitation was affecting his ability to stay there with Vince.

"Who's hurting who, Jay? Are you talking about Jask? Someone's hurting Jask?" Vince demanded.

*"You're wasting time! Wake **up**, Vince!"*

~

Vince shot up in Damian's bed, heart pounding in his chest. He'd stopped here after realizing he'd been going on two days with no sleep. With the understanding that passing out on the road was the last thing he needed, he'd come to the only place he knew would be empty. It wasn't like Damian was using it right now.

After a moment, his breathing and his heart calmed down and he threw the blanket off his legs. He had no way to know if these dreams were real, but he knew he needed to get moving, real or not. Damian's home was well-stocked in both weapons and rations, so Vince grabbed a duffle he found in one of the closets and packed up. Checking the map from Alnaess one more time, Vince hit the road.

Jask was being held in a completely different state. A

long drive awaited him with nothing to accompany him but his thoughts. If the dream held even a grain of truth, Jask could be in more danger than Vince originally thought. He no longer thought Jask left willingly, not even that small doubt remained.

Someone had *taken* Jask from him.

An unknown enemy currently held his mate – Vince still considered Jask that and would until the end of time – and Vince was still hours away. The steering wheel under his hands began to smoke as the anger rose. Whoever dared put their hands on Jaskian was going to suffer. Vince let the thought of his vengeance get him through the first two hours of the drive. He imagined ripping the faceless idiot apart, piece by bloody piece.

Vince took the next exit, the conventional travel no longer satisfactory. His need to get to Jask was now priority over anything else. He found the first gas station on the road and slammed the car into park. The door to the bathroom wasn't open and Vince looked around for witnesses before kicking it in. Taking a knife out of his pocket, he checked the name of the town on the map and looked up the names of local businesses near the area. Vince sliced his hand open and began to trace the symbols on the mirror. The drawback of traveling this way was that he didn't really know where he might end up, or who might see him magically step through the mirror.

The wards keeping Jask hidden would probably keep him from popping into that building, so at least he wouldn't be heading into enemy territory unprepared. He waited for the spell to take hold and stepped through. A quick look told him he was in what appeared to be a dressing room. The floor length mirror made stepping through easier than crawling off a sink or something equally as uncomfortable, which was the first positive thing to happen to him since before the failed wedding.

He pushed open the door to the surprise of an elderly woman carrying a bundle of clothes over her arm. She blinked at him and Vince tipped his hat to her. "Ma'am." With no further explanation, Vince stepped around her and out into the store — a store that apparently catered to feminine apparel only.

Trying to avoid suspicion, he grabbed the first thing he saw and took it to the cashier. The last thing he needed was for someone to call the cops or security on him. He paid for the garment and practically ran out of the store when she handed him the receipt with a confused look.

Exiting onto the sidewalk, Vince finally looked down at the thing he'd impulse bought. It was a pair of emerald green, satin panties. What the hell was he supposed to do with those? He shoved them in his back pocket and took the map out instead.

Twenty minutes later, he knew he was about half an hour away from the radius Alnaess gave him. His car was back at that gas station and Vince groaned as he realized he'd left the duffel with all the weapons and food in the back seat.

He looked up to the sky as he collected his thoughts. He would be going into unknown territory, facing a nameless nemesis, and rescuing Jask with his fists, wits, and maybe a couple of fire balls. All in all, it could be worse.

DRAZAN

Drazan entered his bedroom quietly. He didn't want to wake Jask or give him any indication of what he planned. He collected his shirt from the floor and pulled it on before slipping back out and locking the door. As an extra precaution, he took a knife from the kitchen and pricked his finger. One containment ward later and he was content Jask wouldn't escape. The cuffs would keep him from teleporting and Zae would still be here as well.

Speaking of his partner, he quickly made his way to the lab. "Zaepris! We've been doing this all wrong."

She looked up with an innocent expression. "I've been trying to tell you that, love. He's almost bled dry and... well, no Johnny. Have you decided to let me kill him?"

"No, for the last time, you cannot kill Jask." He frowned in thought. "At least not on purpose. Anyway, the spell calls for the blood of the murderer. Cidos was a twin. Edis is still alive. Between Jask and Ed, we should have enough Veris blood without killing anyone else."

Zaepris smiled, leaning forward and showing off her low-cut shirt. "Two Verises for the price of one? My, my, I'm a lucky girl."

"I need to go and... collect him." Drazan didn't like to think of himself as a kidnapper. What he did for the spell was necessary, and it wasn't his fault Jask and Edis wouldn't see it that way. "Can you stay and keep an eye on Jask?"

"Of course," she said, standing up and walking around the table. "I'll take excellent care of him, and I'll strengthen the warding to make sure it's enough to hold two Veris princes." She paused, pursing her lips for a moment. "Actually, Jaskian killed his daddy... I suppose that makes him the king."

Drazan gave her a small smile. "He'd probably like that." Another blossom of guilt in his chest made the smile fade, and he cleared his throat. "Do we need anything while I'm out? Are we still stocked?"

She huffed, gesturing to the table. "If I'm going to have to keep trying this over and over again, we're going to need some more of everything."

"I'll take care of it." He took a mental note of what he would need and nodded a goodbye before heading to the bathroom. He *could* use Jask's teleportation ability, but Draz didn't want to make it harder on the other angel. Jask was weak enough as it was.

He did a quick mirror spell into the bathroom of a shop not far from them and grabbed most of the ingredients they needed, then walked until he located the rest.

Drazan's next stop was Astarte's home. He was grateful she didn't seem to be around, giving him a clear shot to climb out the window he'd knocked on a few days ago. It felt like a lifetime ago now.

After making sure no one noticed a fully grown man sneaking out of the house, Drazan straightened his clothes and knocked on Edis' door.

Leota answered with a baby on her hip, and the second she saw Drazan's face, her jaw went slack. "What are *you* doing here?"

"Leota. It's nice to see you, too." Drazan smiled with all the charm he could muster. "Is Edis home?"

It took her a second to recover, but she nodded and stepped aside to let him in. "He's upstairs fixing Arro's crib. I'll go get him, just wait here." She disappeared up the stairs, and a few moments later, Edis was standing in front of him.

"Drazan."

"Ed. I see you've settled in nicely," Drazan said, keeping up the same smile.

He laughed a little sarcastically. "Yeah, after moving what felt like a dozen times. What can I do for you? If you're looking for Jask, no one's seen him in almost a week. He's not here."

"Actually, that's what I'm here about. Jask is with me," Draz admitted, belatedly realizing Leota might run and tell Vince. Immediately on damage control, he tried to look sheepish. "I just left him in bed, actually." It was vague enough he knew they'd make their own assumptions and there was no lie for Edis to sense.

"Wow. I gotta say, I'm surprised by that. It's good to know he's safe, but... I thought what you guys had was just for show."

"It was." Another truth, it *had* been for show. They didn't need to know it never went past that. "But Jask isn't doing well with this entire situation. Leaving Vince at the altar affected him badly. I was wondering if you'd come back with me? I could use you."

Ed shifted on his feet. "If it affected him so badly, why'd he do it? Why hasn't he come home, called me? At least apologized or tried to explain? He left a lot of damage behind him, Drazan."

"We're fairly remote. Phones don't work where we are, and like I said... we were busy. And I think he'd like to explain it to you himself." Drazan shrugged and gave Leota an apologetic look. He hadn't missed the very angry glare she was giving him.

"Right." Ed looked a little uncomfortable but nodded to Lee. "I suppose I need to go save my brother... again. I'll be home as soon as I can, okay?"

She bounced Arro on her hip but didn't take her eyes off of Drazan. "Don't be late for dinner, Ed. Mom invited us over, remember?"

"I won't be late."

"Thank you, Edis. I know this will mean something to Jask. Do you have a mirror you don't mind getting a little dirty? Quicker that way."

Ed nodded to the guest bathroom and shot his mate an apologetic look. "I'll clean it when we get back. Unless you just tell me where it is, I can just teleport us there?"

"Wouldn't even know how to direct you. No official address." Draz led the way into the guest bathroom and pushed on his palm to get his original cut bleeding again. He made quick work of the spell and motioned for Ed to precede him.

He looked uncharacteristically nervous like he knew something wasn't quite right, but climbed up onto the sink and through the mirror without any further protest.

Draz waved merrily at Leota and then followed, putting a hand on Ed's shoulder. "This way, I'll take you right to him."

Immediately, Edis tensed. "What's with all the warding? It's so strong it's making it hard to breathe," he said.

"I was worried about Vince." Drazan walked straight to the bedroom and opened the door, again letting Edis take the lead.

When they walked in, Jask was still out cold in the bed. Ed's shoulders relaxed at the sight, having the story he was told confirmed right in front of his eyes. "He looks like hell, Drazan."

"I *told* you, the situation is not ideal." Draz nodded and stepped forward to tug the blanket up over Jask, hiding the cuffs on his wrists.

"Well, wake him up. You heard Lee, if I don't straighten his ass out in time for dinner, she'll kill me."

Zaepris took that opportunity to lean against the doorframe. "You got him. Good."

Drazan sighed, because now the secret was out. "I did. Do you have that other set of cuffs? I haven't had a chance to distract him properly."

"No need to worry, he's harmless now. Go ahead, Edis. Try something. Anything at all." She gave him a smug smile and held out her arms. "Hit me with your best shot."

Edis' eyes flashed and he threw out his arm, but nothing happened. Not an ounce of power left his palm. He tried again, but to the same end — Zaepris was still standing unharmed. "What the hell did you do?!"

She walked closer to him. "Oh, took the liberty of devising a little spell while Drazan was away. Few hairs here, a couple of pints of Veris blood there... and poof! The Veris graceline is completely useless inside these four walls. I didn't want to take the chance that you'd somehow get the drop on us."

"Impressive. You used the blood we already collected?" Drazan ignored Edis' outrage in favor of making sure Zae obeyed his commands to not injure Jask further.

"I took what I needed and not a drop more. He's... basically in the same condition you left him in," she said flippantly. "Here." She tossed him the cuffs, and though Edis tried to squirm out of the way, Drazan managed to get them on him.

"Sit, please." Draz didn't wait for Edis to comply, he pushed him into the chair by the bed before kneeling to check on Jask. Close up, Drazan could tell how shallow Jask's breaths were, and it became clear that he wasn't sleeping at all — he was unconscious.

"The fuck did you do to him!" Edis yelled, trying and failing to break free.

Drazan took a deep breath to quell his anger before putting a hand on Jask's forehead. Without the link to the Veris graceline, Drazan was no match in strength for Edis or Jask — but he was still an angel. Though... in his opinion, not a very good one. He healed Jask as much as he could before standing and stalking toward Zaepris. "We need to talk."

No fear flickered in her eyes as she stepped out of the room, and when the door closed behind Drazan, she crossed her arms. "He's alive. You told me not to kill him, I didn't kill him. What's the problem?"

"He's *barely* alive! We don't have Cidos. Edis is close, but having them both is our best shot. I will *not* have you jeopardize this for me."

Zaepris took a dangerous step closer. "I'm just as invested in this as you are, let me remind you. They'd both be bled dry already if it were up to me, but I'm holding my end of this bargain. I made a decision while you were gone to make things easier — do you realize that the two of them together could kill us with the blink of an eye if those cuffs failed?"

Draz pinched the bridge of his nose. "You're right. I'm sorry. I just... really need this spell to work."

"So do I. Now, bring them both back to the lab. We've got work to do."

JASKIAN

Jask came back to reality slowly. Everything was fuzzy, everything hurt, but he relaxed when he opened his eyes and saw Ed staring down at him. "Oh, you found me. Gotta be honest, bro... figured it would've been Vin."

"Hopefully it still is, because I didn't find you." Edis held up his hands to show the matching cuffs, and dread pulled in Jaskian's gut when he realized he was still in Drazan's bed.

"Ed — Ed... you have to run. I don't think they lock the doors, run."

Edis shook his head before Jask even finished talking. "Drazan and another psychopath are right outside that door. What is happening, Jask?"

"She's a necromancer," he said quietly. "Drazan is the one that stole Johnny's body. They're trying to bring him back."

"Fuck." Edis leaned back in the chair, staring at his brother. "She did something. A spell. We're powerless here."

It slowly hit Jask that the spell was probably the reason he passed out. The extra blood she'd taken had sucked, but it hadn't felt like something that should take him out like that. But a spell that cut off whatever dregs of his grace he still had access to? That would've done the trick, no doubt in his mind. "Imagine that. The last remaining Veris men, crippled by a psycho and his pet zombiemaker."

"What a pair we make, eh? But at least now I know you didn't abandon us. That's something."

Jask scowled at his brother. "I can't believe any of you bought that. Like I'd *ever* leave Vince willingly, especially after all the shit I went through just to have him."

"He made it look convincing!" Ed argued. He looked down at his bound hands. "The note was in your handwriting. All your things were gone. Vince, he tried to tell us something was wrong, but we didn't listen."

That news relaxed him again when it probably shouldn't. "At least he knows. The worst part of being here was thinking Vince really thought I didn't love him. I know I haven't been the best to him since..." Jask clears his throat. "Well, you know. We gotta get outta here, Ed. *You* have to get outta here."

"How much of this place have you seen? What are our chances?" Edis stood and began to check every corner of the room, and Jask let him go for a moment.

"Ed. Stop. Look at me. I can't even sit up right now. I'm not going anywhere, but you? I can distract them. If you can get far enough away from the warding, you should be able to break the cuffs and go get Vin."

"I'm not leaving you here." Edis turned to frown at him. "If I go, they could kill you."

Jask chuckled darkly, but the effort hurt his chest. "He's not gonna kill me. She wants to, but he won't let her. They want you, Ed... the spell to bring him back requires the blood of the murderer. Draz thought mine would be close enough since we cremated Cidos, but it isn't. I guess that's why you're here."

"I don't even know where we are. I don't know where Vince is either. We've been trying to call him, but he's been gone for days." Edis looked like that was the last thing he wanted to tell Jask, but honestly, it filled him with hope.

"That's good news, Ed. Means he'll be here soon. He'll come; all we have to do is try not to die before then." Jask smiled weakly, but when the door opened again, it faded instantly. "What, you want a kidney now, too?"

Draz' face showed a brief hint of pain at Jask's words, but he appeared to shake it off. "What would you do if it were Vince?" Before an answer could be made, Edis stepped between Jask and Draz.

"You have to stop this, Drazan. It's not right."

They argued as Jask suddenly realized what a hypocrite he was being. Everyone in that room knew exactly how far Jask was willing to go to save Vince, because he'd already proven it. "Stop. Just... stop. Ed, he's not going to let us go."

"How do you—"

"Because *I* wouldn't have let you go."

They both turned to him, Ed in shock and Draz in relief. "You understand it now?"

"No. Because I've lived with the guilt of what I've done every single day." He sighed, letting his body droop into the mattress as things began getting hazy again. "But hear me, Drazan. If you hurt my brother... I'll kill you if it's the last thing I do."

"Guilt will be preferable to this grief, Jask. I will do my

best to keep you both as comfortable as possible," Drazan promised as he grabbed Edis' arm to pull him from the room.

Jask tried to get up and follow, but he barely managed to haul himself up and walk three feet before he was falling to his knees and gripping the door frame for support. "Damnit, Drazan, don't!"

Edis stepped toward Jask in concern but didn't make it far before Draz pulled him back and slammed him into the wall. He turned his gaze to Jask. "Don't make me hurt him. If you both cooperate, this will be over soon."

Nothing but that could've made Jask stop. "Please, D. He's got a kid. A family. I can't... I can't lose another brother, not now." Tears threatened to spill out as he crawled forward. "Don't hurt him."

Something softened in Drazan's eyes. "I'm not planning to. All I need is a little blood."

Ed jerked out of Drazan's grip and kneeled down to help Jask to his feet. "We've been in worse spots, Jaskian. Come on." He slung Jask's arm over his shoulder and helped him forward, turning his angry gaze back to Drazan. "Well? Where are we going?"

Draz pointed at Jask. "He needs to go back to bed. You're going to the lab."

"Very funny," Jask said. "You wanted the Veris brothers, you've got us. Together or not at all. I go where he goes until we're both home safe."

Drazan mumbled something under his breath that sounded suspiciously like "stubborn assholes." He eventually nodded his head and motioned forward. "You know the way, Jask."

He knew he should've listened and gone back to bed, but Ed was there now, and there was no way in hell that Jask was going to leave him alone. He'd protect his brother until he died... and find a way to do it after death, too.

The lab was just as cold and unwelcoming as Jask remembered, and he fought the urge to headbutt Zaepris in the face when she led him and Edis to matching chairs. The needle hurt worse going into the side of his neck this time, but he tried not to let it show — his concern was for Edis. "Listen, lady... that's my baby brother over there. He's Cidos' twin, so you shouldn't need more than maybe an ounce or two. Take more, and I'll find a way to kill you slow."

"You're being so incredibly dramatic." She answered, not bothering to even look in his direction. "Wake up on the wrong side of the bed?"

"Can we please just focus on the plan?" Drazan looked tired as he finally followed them in, a bag slung over his shoulder. "I got the refills."

Ed laughed at Zaepris. "Sounds like this is your first time with Jask. He got all of the intensity and absolutely none of the good looks," he teased, but Jask could see his face. He was scared, and this was just his way of covering it.

"Aww, shucks, Ed. You're just saying that cause I finally look worse than you do."

"Damn it, you're both going to talk the entire time. How did I not realize that?" Drazan spoke so quietly it was obvious he wasn't expecting an answer.

Jask chuckled — actually chuckled. "Seems like a stupid thing to be concerned about, all things considered... but if you don't like it, you can always let him go."

"*If* I let anyone go, it would be you. While Leota looks like she can be a handful, she doesn't worry me nearly as much as Vince. And Ed's blood is a better match for Cidos, I'd imagine. In reality I should've taken him in the first place. Hindsight and all, I suppose." Draz realized his monologue was now rambling and shrugged.

He squinted at that ridiculous logic. "So, you'd rather let me go and risk me, Vince, and Lee coming after you to free him? You know I'd get my strength back eventually."

"That's why I said if. Neither of you are leaving until we're successful."

The small flicker of hope that had kindled in Jask's chest fizzled out. "His body hasn't even twitched, D. What makes you think you're ever gonna make this work?"

"It will work. There are no other options." Drazan continued refilling the bowls as Zaepris approached Edis again.

"Stay still, pet. This shouldn't hurt... much."

Jask's fists clenched as he watched the syringe fill with his brother's blood, and for the first time, he truly hoped it worked. The less they needed to take from Ed, the better... and the nagging voice in the back of his mind kept reminding him that Vince really would want Johnny back.

Ed winced as she finally stopped and pulled back, then fixed his eyes on the coffin she was walking toward. "That's..."

"Yeah. I try not to look at it too much."

"I see it even when I'm not looking at it." Drazan finished with the ingredients and watched Zaepris closely. The look of hesitant hope on his face was almost heartbreaking, and Jask wished he had the strength to go hug his friend, even if he didn't understand.

Zaepris took what she needed and tried again, with everyone around her watching. But still, even with Edis' blood, nothing changed. Johnny was still dead, Drazan still looked unsatisfied, and they were still prisoners.

If it didn't work then, it would never work, and Drazan wouldn't stop trying until they were both dead.

Jask just had to hope Vince found them first.

VI

Three. *Fucking*. Hours. That's how long the walk from the town to this isolated structure in the middle of nowhere took. The original estimate of a half an hour was based on the assumption that Vince would be driving, which he'd thoroughly fucked up in his haste.

Luckily, once he'd hit the woods, it was hardly any trouble to find the spot Alnaess told him about. The area surrounding it became increasingly quieter the closer he came — no birds chirping, no leaves rustling. There wasn't even a breeze in the air.

Vince stood behind a line of trees and eyed the building that hopefully held Jask. Wards and runes were painted across the entire front and the windows were boarded up. It definitely looked like the kind of place someone would hold a person captive... especially an angelic someone.

Seeing no one outside, Vince walked forward toward the entrance. He didn't know who or what could be in there, but he'd decided "guns blazing" was an appropriate plan. The wards made his skin crawl as he approached, and with one last fortifying breath, he kicked in the door. The door breaking in two caused quite a bit of noise and Vince heard something clatter as if it were dropped. He immediately headed for the sound.

What he never would have expected was Drazan rushing out of a door at the end of a long hall. The door behind him swung open further and there sat Jask. The angel's head hung low, and Vince's blood ran cold as he took in Jask's pale appearance. Even from where Vince stood, his trembling was evident. His gaze returned to Drazan and a small part of him was satisfied with the fear he saw in the other man's eyes.

"You son of a bitch. I'll kill you." Vince ran for him, but Draz jumped back through the door, screaming for someone.

"Zaepris! The Veris spell, break it! Break it *now!*"

He heard another crash as a woman shouted it was done, and the moment Vince broke through and entered the room, he was dropped to his knees by a crushing force. Drazan's eyes were wild as he kept one hand firmly on Jask's limp body and the other pointed at Vince. "Leave. Don't make me do this, Vincenzo. Think of how upset Jask would be if he woke up and found out his own powers killed his former mate."

Vince struggled to stand but he managed, his limbs shaking from the effort. Briefly he noticed Edis by Jask and a woman standing behind them. Her eyes were curious as she watched the scene unfold. "Get your hands off of him, Drazan. What the hell is even going on?" A brief glance around the room made it obvious a spell was in the works, but he couldn't tell what kind. That's when his eyes fell on the table in the back of the room. A sheet covered most of the body, but Vince could see enough. Suddenly, everything clicked into place. "Drazan... tell me that's not Johnny."

"I told you to leave, Vince." Drazan clenched his jaw but didn't attack again just yet. "I'm bringing him back. We're bringing him back, and I won't let you get in the way."

Vince stepped forward and kept his eyes on the angels as he fought to push past whatever hold Draz had on him. "You know I won't leave without them. Not unless you kill me. I don't understand how you could do this. They're your friends! Not to mention, Johnny wouldn't want this." Vince's words were labored as he continued his advance. If he could just get to Jask — if he could get Drazan *away* from Jask — he could end this.

"They're the reason he's dead," Drazan growled, his eyes glossing over. "You *all* are!" Another powerful wave of Jask's stolen power hit Vince square in the chest, sending him flying backward into the wall. It crumbled around him and buried him briefly, but the second he fought his way out, Drazan was on him.

The impact knocked Vince on his ass again and he watched a fist come at his face almost in slow motion. Reacting mostly on instinct, Vince blocked the hit and bucked Drazan off of him. They were barely standing again when Drazan actually landed a punch this time. Vince staggered back and cursed as his head swam. In a normal fight, Draz wouldn't be a match for Vince, but with him siphoning Jask's power this fight wasn't going to end well.

One look at Drazan's face confirmed he wouldn't listen to reasoning, either. His eyes were filled with determination and something else Vince almost didn't want to identify — an unholy light that Vince could only describe as crazed. Drazan came for him again and Vince stepped into the hit, tackling Draz with a shoulder to his midsection. He lifted the angel and slammed him into the wall, but a second later Draz slammed his elbow straight into Vince's back, dropping him to his knees.

"Draz," Vince tried again. "You have to stop. You'll kill them both, and even if it works... Johnny will *never* speak to you again. You *have* to know that."

The angel gripped Vince by his throat, nothing but hatred and insanity on his face. "He'll forgive me. He loves me, and he knows whose fault this is. Zaepris... do it. Take it all."

She giggled with delight and hurried to toss some ingredients in the bowl on the altar as Vince tried to get Drazan off of him. "Who first? The king or the prince?"

"Just *do* it!" Drazan screamed.

Vince watched in horror as the sadistic bitch chose Jask as her first victim. He pulled against Drazan's hold on him, but when the angel didn't budge, Vince did something he rarely did and began to pray. He prayed for a miracle, for Jask to wake up, for his ancestors to give him the strength to break free. *Anything.* Just as he began to lose hope, a new voice interrupted the bloodletting.

"Well, this is... interesting. What have you gotten yourself into now, Vincenzo?"

Recognition sparked on Zaepris' face first, and she grabbed Drazan, bolting toward Johnny's body. In the blink of an eye, Drazan used Jask's powers one last time to teleport the three of them out of there and out of reach.

Later, Vince would think back and realize he should've stopped them, but in that moment all he was worried about was Jask. He used the surrounding rubble to climb to his feet and stumbled over to the chair, falling to his knees in front of his love. Vince put his hands to Jask's neck, almost sobbing with relief when he felt Jask's pulse still going. "Sweetheart, wake up. I'm here now."

The sound of metal being broken caused Vince to look to the side. Riskel held the remnants of Edis' cuffs in his hands. That was something Vince would worry about later, right now he just needed Jask to wake the hell up. "Jaskian, open your fucking eyes!"

He still didn't, not until Riskel also broke the cuffs binding Jask. And even then, it took almost two full minutes for his grace to work enough for him to accomplish it.

"Vin? Fuck. I'm so tired of having this dream," he mutters, tipping his head back with a ragged breath.

"Not a dream. I'm here, just fashionably late." Vince couldn't stop touching Jask. He checked for injuries, ran his hands over the marks from the cuffs, and then finally pulled Jask into his arms. He didn't care that he was sitting on the floor or that Edis and Riskel were watching. All that mattered was Jask.

Jask let out a heartbreaking noise as he hugged him, then kissed all over his face. "You're warm. You're actually warm this time."

Normally, Vince would complain about Jask's need to kiss him like that — but he couldn't bring himself to do it this time. When Jask slowed down, Vince kissed him properly before pulling back to look into his eyes. "I was so fucking worried."

"I knew you wouldn't believe I left on purpose." Jask kissed him again, but Riskel cleared his throat to interrupt them.

"Does anyone care to explain why I had to leave my perfectly comfortable bed for this? One of *you* gets to explain it to Veris."

"How the hell are you even here?" Vince frowned at him.

Riskel looked at him like he was an idiot. "You prayed to me. You needed help, so... here I am. Good thing, too... or all three of you would be dead by now. That spell was bad news."

"I absolutely did no—" Vince's frown intensified as he remembered doing almost exactly that. He looked back at Jask. "You get to tell Veris. He's your grandfather, he likes you better."

"Add about twelve greats to that and yeah, he's my grandpa."

Edis walked over and smacked Jask in the back of the head. "That's for getting fucking kidnapped."

"Hey! Don't blame him. For that matter, aren't you here too?" Vince glared at Edis before looking back at Riskel without waiting for an answer. "What did you mean about the spell?"

Riskel gave him that same look as before. "She's a necromancer. She's figured out how to keep herself from dying since back in the day of the original wars, but there's something different about whatever she's trying to do here. It's no good, the place reeks of bad magic. You guys should probably clear out of here before she comes back, I'm just saying."

Vince stood slowly and pulled Jask up with him. He kept his arms around him as he looked around at the destroyed room. "Yeah. Ed, can you get us home?"

"I think so." He nodded his thanks to Riskel and gripped

both Vince and Jask, then squeezed his eyes shut as he teleported them all back to his living room.

Leota was on them in an instant. "Where the *hell* have you been?"

Edis hugged her instantly and began explaining quietly. Vince ignored them both in favor of looking at Jask. "Stupid question but... are you okay?"

"I feel like I got hit by a fucking truck, but yeah. I'll live now that my grace is no longer cut off. Hungry enough to eat one of you, though. Pretty much the only thing the bastard fed me was cake and waffles."

"What an asshole." Vince kissed Jask's head and laced their fingers together. "Come on, I'll take you home and get you fed. Then I'm going to find Drazan and murder him." Vince began to walk towards the door, but Jask didn't budge.

He shifted on his feet and shook his head. "No, you won't. The killing has to stop, Vin. It has to. That's what got us here, we got our freedom, but we *destroyed* Drazan. It came at a cost so high, I..." Tears welled in his eyes as a look of hopelessness crossed his face. "It has to stop."

Vince couldn't stand seeing Jask hurting like that, so he did the only thing he could: he agreed. "Yeah, of course, sweetheart. I won't go after Draz." He left the word "immediately" unsaid and continued on, "Let's go home so I can take care of you."

JASKIAN

Being out of that room felt surreal. He allowed Vince to lead him home, bathe him, feed him, and get him in bed — but he still felt like he was in a dream. The only thing that told him it wasn't was Vince's body heat.

Truthfully, he felt fine physically. His grace had plenty of time during that to replenish the blood he lost and all the negative effects that came along with it had already faded, but something still felt... wrong. Off. Like there was something broken inside of him that not even his grace could fix.

Maybe nothing could.

Astarte was only allowed in long enough to confirm that her son was alive and hadn't abandoned them, then Vince kicked her out and insisted Jask get some rest. He didn't even know what that looked like anymore if he was being honest. Sleep? A vacation? A lobotomy?

Vince returned with the blanket he'd given Jask the night before the wedding. The one that didn't actually happen. Vince distracted him from heading further in that line of thought by literally tucking him in. "You want me to stay?"

"Where else would you go?" Jask asked, suddenly concerned that maybe the note did more damage than he thought. "You know I didn't leave on purpose, right?"

"Yeah, I know. Just didn't know if you wanted me here bugging you while you tried to sleep." Vince shrugged.

Jask deflated against the pillow and pulled the blanket up around his shoulder as he rolled onto his side. "No, you don't have to stay."

There was a sigh and Jask felt the bed dip as Vince laid behind him, wrapping his arm around Jask's waist. "If I leave, I'm going to sit right outside the door so I can hear everything that happens. I just didn't want to smother you." He placed a gentle kiss to the back of Jask's neck. "Thank you, by the way. For letting me take care of you."

"Feels a hell of a lot better than what Drazan and that crazy bitch were doing," he admitted. "And it's nice to not be freezing to death anymore."

"Then I'll stay and resume my duties as your personal space heater," Vince agreed, throwing a leg over Jask's for good measure.

Being surrounded by Vince was the best he'd felt in a while, and it didn't take long for him to fall asleep — but it also didn't take long for him to wake up in a cold sweat begging Drazan under his breath to stop. He waited until his heart rate calmed down and turned his head to see if Vince was awake or not, and the sight that greeted him was that of one dead-to-the-world demon, complete with drool and quiet snores.

He slid out of bed as carefully as he could and stepped out of the room, then out of the house entirely. Part of him knew that walking around was dangerous because Drazan *was* still out there and hadn't gotten what he wanted yet but being cooped up in a bedroom was making him antsy all over again.

It didn't even occur to him that he was walking around the neighborhood half-naked until one of their neighbors came out to ask what the hell he was doing. "Sorry, Miss Hasi. Just... got lost, I guess."

"Lost? In your own neighborhood? You feeling alright, boy?" the elderly woman asked with a suspicious squint.

No, he thought. *I've never been less alright in my life, thanks for asking.* "I'm okay, ma'am. I was sleepwalking, thank you for waking me up."

"That's dangerous, waking up sleepwalkers." It looked like she'd continue her lecture, but they were interrupted by a frantic scream of: "Jask!" Jask and Hasi turned to the sound to see Vince running down the street, also wearing nothing but a pair of boxers. As soon as Vince caught sight of Jask, he tripped over his own two feet. He fell to his knees and slumped forward, hands on his thighs.

"Oh, thank fuck. I thought... I woke up and you were gone... and then I..." He stopped talking and dropped his head, panting.

As if Jask needed to feel any lower. He whispered a quick apology to Hasi for disrupting her evening and went to Vince, helping him back to his feet. "I'm sorry."

"It's fine." Vince waved it away, even though it was clear he was anything but fine. "Just, maybe, next time you can leave a note?"

Hasi went back into her home, mumbling about half naked idiots causing scenes and Jask ignored her, blinking at Vince. "You mean like the note that was left last time? I thought it would be in poor taste, all things considered."

"Good point. Okay, next time take me with you." Vince looked down at them both and then around at the houses, many of which now were full of curious spectators. "And now maybe we can go back."

It was strange. Jask never cared much for what people

thought, but now, he cared even less. He didn't want to go back, he wanted to keep walking until he outran his own memories. Yet... he couldn't bring himself to do that to Vince, not with the look on his face being what it was. "Okay, Vin. We can go back."

To spare them the awkwardness of being gawked at the entire walk back, Jask teleported them to the bedroom. He didn't realize until after they landed that there were a multitude of witnesses that just saw him use a power most angels don't have, but again, he couldn't find it in him to care. If a few of them figured out there was a Veris on the block, what would it matter?

"Should we talk about that? I mean... you were just kidnapped. You can't be walking around naked." Vince stepped away and grabbed his jeans from the floor, slipping them on.

Jask watched with a pit in his stomach. "I'm sorry. I needed some air, and I guess I just wasn't paying attention to how far I'd gone. It won't happen again."

Vince ran a hand through his hair and sat on the edge of the bed. "You still want to walk? I don't think I could go back to sleep now if I tried. Oh, we can head out to the woods. I found a waterfall recently," he rambled.

"Sure." Jask tried to smile, but he knew it ended up looking more like a grimace. He was still tired, more emotionally than physically at that point, but the thought of letting Vince down more than he already had gave him the motivation to stand. "A waterfall sounds nice."

"Come on, I'll drive." Vince found a shirt and finished getting dressed quickly. He tucked his keys into his pocket and then stopped moving, giving Jask a sheepish look. "Actually... my truck is at Herch's."

Of course it was. Jask forced a smile as he dressed, and then teleported them once again to get Vince's truck. The effort took more out of him than normal, so he gladly climbed into the passenger seat and leaned against the window. "Thank you. For... coming to find me. I don't think I said that yet."

Vince took his hand and brought it to his lips. "I'll always come for you, Jask."

The cheeky reply was right there for the taking, the double entendre clearly laid out for him — but Jask let it be, let it pass by with nothing more than a brief, fleeting smirk. "To the waterfall, then?"

Vince kissed his hand once more and then focused on the drive, leaving Jask to try and wade through his muddled thoughts. Before Jask noticed any time passed at all, the truck was being pulled over onto the side of the road.

"Are we here already?" he asked, honestly not sure how much time had passed.

"Yeah. Turns out it's a lot closer when you're not drunk and walking aimlessly." Vince opened his door and then walked around to open Jask's, and he got out unceremoniously to look around.

So far, all he could see were trees. "Wanna just... teleport us there? If Drazan still has a strong enough connection to me to steal my powers, you should be able to pull it off."

Vince's face fell and the hand he'd been holding out to Jask dropped to his side. "I'm sorry I'm not..." He looked to the side and then back to Jask, a smile on his face. It looked forced, and it definitely didn't reach his eyes. "It's not far. Promise."

"Okay." Jask slid his hands in his pockets and started walking. He felt badly about that — he hadn't intended it to be an insult toward Vince, just Drazan, but everything he did felt wrong. He was saying the wrong things, doing the wrong things, having the wrong reactions. He should be thrilled he's free — thrilled that Vince cared enough to risk his own life to come and find him, and the same with Edis — but instead, all he felt was an unbalance he couldn't shake.

They traveled to the waterfall in silence, Vince not looking at him once. He spoke when they finally reached the destination. "What's going on, Jask? You know you can tell me anything. I can't fight if I don't know what it is I'm fighting." Vince walked to the edge of the pond, but Jask stayed where he was.

How to even explain it? Why should he *have* to even explain it? To Jask, it was obvious... or should've been, anyway. He simply shook his head, choosing not to burden anyone else with the weight he carried. There was nothing anyone could do about it, anyway.

It was his turn to force a smile as he joined Vince. "Sorry, I think I'm just... kidnap-lagged. Do you think that's a thing? It feels like a thing. I'm okay." He looked around, taking in the crystal-clear waters and the brush surrounding it, then marveled at the waterfall. "We should swim down that," he said suddenly.

"Right now?" Vince looked between the waterfall and Jask.

Not seeing a valid reason why not, Jask nodded enthusiastically. "Yep. Right now."

Vince reached over his shoulder and grabbed a fistful of his shirt. Seconds later, Jask got an eyeful of the gloriously tanned and muscled torso of his fiancé. Vince's pants followed quickly and soon he stood naked in the middle of the woods.

The sight actually calmed Jask but didn't make him any less eager to throw himself over a waterfall. "Have I told you lately how beautiful you are?" he asked, using his grace to undress himself instantly. "Hope the fall doesn't cut you up too bad."

Vince didn't respond to Jask's compliment, but the blush covering most of his body made it clear the words were heard. He shrugged and began his climb to the top of the waterfall. "It'll heal."

For a moment, Jask simply watched the muscles of Vince's body work as he scaled the side of the fall. It was a sight to see, and once he was up, Jask teleported next to him. He held his hand out with a small grin. "Together?"

"Always." Vince smiled back at him and accepted his hand, entwining their fingers.

Originally, Jask wanted to swim down — but he hadn't expected Vince to come with him and he wouldn't risk him getting hurt like that — so instead, he jumped, pulling Vince with him.

The free fall was incredible. For a glorious moment, Jask felt nothing at all but the wind and water spray hitting his skin. Even the smack of pain when they hit the water was welcome, and he let the current drag him deeper, deeper down until everything was lost.

Jask lost all track of time until Vince dragged him back to

the surface with him, his eyes concerned as he studied Jask's face.

"What?" Jask asked, a little defensively. "You're okay, right?"

"Sassy motherfucker," Vince sighed before pulling Jask in for a heated kiss.

The distraction was perfect — not one part of Jask wanted to explain why he felt better jumping off a cliff than he had in weeks, maybe months — so he slid his hands down Vince's body and laid back until they were flush. His hands gripped Vince's ass and spread his cheeks as Vince hummed into the kiss and rocked his hips, showing him exactly how much he enjoyed the touch. He ran a hand through Jask's hair and tilted his head back so he could kiss down his neck, and for once, Jask was content to let him do whatever he wanted.

"Feels good, Vin," Jask mumbled.

"I almost lost this. Lost you. *Again*," Vince whispered into Jask's skin. The words were spoken so quietly that Jask wasn't sure he was meant to hear them. Vince didn't stop, trailing down his lover's body. Occasionally Vince paused to suck a mark into Jask's skin, but never stopped long, continuing his journey mapping out Jask's body with his lips and hands.

"He wouldn't have killed me." Jask didn't know why that bothered him so much — but this was Drazan they were talking about, and no matter how desperate he got... Jask had to believe he wouldn't have actually done it. He rocked his hips up to chase Vince's tongue and regretted saying anything at all, but it was too late.

Vince sat up, pulling away completely. "He was literally going to kill you in front of me. How can you still believe that?" Vince closed his eyes and shook his head. "Never mind. Don't answer. I don't want to talk about Drazan when I have you naked in front of me." He covered Jask again, kissing him with a hint of desperation that wasn't there before, and Jask tried to return the sentiment.

Tried.

"Vin..." Jask said quietly, running his hands down his almost-husband's back. "Can we just go home?"

Vince's forehead dropped to Jask's shoulder and he didn't speak for a moment. When he lifted his head — an obviously forced smile plastered on — he kissed Jask once more. Just a chaste peck of the lips. "Of course, sweetheart. Whatever you need." He rolled off Jask and stood, holding out a hand to help him up.

The look of disappointment in Vince's eyes made Jask feel like shit, but there wasn't much he could do about it as he took Vince's hand and got to his feet. "I'm sorry. I'll make it up to you later, I promise. I'm just tired," he lied. It wasn't a *complete* untruth, but after everything, he felt... spent, in ways he couldn't even begin to comprehend. "Let's get some food and you can make me watch another marathon of those movies you like."

The smile on Vince's face was a little more genuine this time. "Deal. What do you want to eat?"

"Believe it or not, I'm actually in the mood for sushi." Jask dressed again and handed Vince his clothes as he added, "Sound good? Or maybe I'll whip up some food related to whichever trilogy you want to watch."

Vince dressed quickly, hopping on one foot as he adjusted his jeans. "Nope, you said sushi. We can stop by that place on the edge of town and then I'm making you sit through four hours of badly-budgeted martial arts films."

"Martial arts films, sushi... want me to just take you to Japan?" Jask asked, hoping to make up for the fact that he couldn't get himself in the mood. "There's not much left there, but we could always squat in one of the old minka house things."

"Absolutely not. You've been through hell, Jask. The last thing you need to be doing is carrying my heavy ass across the world," Vince argued as he laced up his boots.

It was true and Jask knew it, but the reminder that he couldn't pull it off stung a little, nonetheless. He waited until Vince was fully ready to go before scratching the back of his neck. "Can we uh... try to be quiet when we go back? I'm not in the mood to deal with Ed... and maybe if you could keep the whole jumping-off-cliffs thing between us, that'd be cool."

"Like I said, whatever you need." He shrugged and took Jask's hand to walk back to the truck. "We don't even need to go home, technically. The old house is still set up for our honeymoon."

Something about going there before their actual wedding didn't sit right with Jask, particularly because he feared being there would remind Vince that they *didn't* actually get married. "Nah, we can go home. I like our couch."

"Your wish is my command." Vince opened the door to the truck, holding it for Jask, and he got in without complaint.

The ride back was silent, almost eerily so, and unfortunately for Jask, Edis was waiting for them in the driveway when they pulled in. Jask knew he had to be more careful about what he said around Ed than Vince thanks to his particular sense of lie-detection, so he kept his excuses short as he denied the request to come to family dinner.

For the second time that day, he was met with a look of disappointment on the face of someone he loved — but Jask simply apologized this time and shoved his hands in his pockets as he headed for the front door, trusting Vince to grab the sushi they'd picked up.

Sometime soon, he'd have to deal with his family and figure out a way to move on, but for now, he was reserving the right to just... be.

VII

Vince closed the door to the laundry room and kicked the dryer. The resounding boom caused him to freeze as he waited to see if Jask would come to investigate. When a few quiet minutes passed and his fiancé failed to make an appearance, Vince didn't know if he felt relieved or disappointed. Jask staying away meant Vince didn't have to burden him with his frustration. Jask coming to investigate meant they'd finally have to talk about the aforementioned frustration. It's not like Vince could think of another excuse for abusing their appliances. Nothing believable at least. Vince hopped up to sit on the dryer and leaned against the wall, letting his head fall back so he could examine the ceiling.

Three weeks they'd been home with Jask barely leaving the couch or bed. Vince tried to be supportive. He knew that Jask needed them to be understanding and patient. Every single member of the family seemed to be walking on eggshells around the angel, waiting on him to be ready to talk. The problem being that Jask wasn't talking. He wasn't doing *anything*. Vince pushed a hand through his hair and jumped back down. He'd wasted enough time and didn't want to explain to Jask that he'd been pouting. Despite his earlier hope of a conversation, he didn't want to put any more weight on Jask's shoulders.

He opened the dryer and grabbed the basket. He filled the basket with the clothes and took a step toward the door. A flash of emerald green caught his eye and he pulled the fabric out, the panties from the store unfolding in his hand. They'd been in the back pocket of those jeans for the last three weeks. The dryer must've shaken them out, finally. He'd forgotten all about them until now.

An idea popped into his head and as ridiculous as it sounded, he couldn't shake it. Jask needed something new to get him out of his head, and this was *definitely* something new. Vince tucked the underwear in his back pocket and hurried into their room. Closing the door behind him, Vince dropped the basket and sprinted into the bathroom. He looked at himself in the mirror and wondered if this idea spoke of brilliance or stupidity. He grinned at his reflection, thinking to himself, *or maybe it'll be stupidly brilliant.*

He stripped out of the shorts and t-shirt he wore for lounging around the house. Once he stood naked in front of the mirror, the doubts returned. Could he pull this off? Only one way to find out.

With a shrug, he pulled the satin up his legs, adjusting himself to his satisfaction. The front was a little snug but the feeling of the satin along his length was actually pleasant. He twisted and looked over his shoulder. His ass looked incredible. Facing the mirror again, his thoughts battled against each other.

This could work.

You're an idiot.

Shut up, brain.

Vince took one last look at himself, spinning to get the full effect. He'd never done anything like this before but deep down he believed Jask would like it — or at least... he hoped.

One fortifying breath later and he exited the bathroom. His steps became less sure as he approached the sitting room where he'd left Jask, and by the time he reached the love of his life, his body trembled with nerves. He almost didn't want to see how Jask would react.

"Um..." Jask sat up slowly from his permanent spot on the couch and eyed Vince like he'd never seen him before. "You... those... I... fuck."

It wasn't often Jask was rendered speechless when he actually wanted to say something, and Vince resisted the urge to fidget under his gaze. "Surprise?" He grinned, hoping it came off as confident.

Finally, *finally* Vince saw that long-forgotten look of lust on Jask's face. "That's a good surprise, Vin." Jask leaned forward and mouthed over the bulge, then yanked Vince down onto his lap. "Did I forget my own birthday again?"

Relief surged through him as he straddled Jask. Vince reached between them to adjust himself again, the fabric of the underwear tightening over his rapidly thickening cock. "No, I just wanted to do something different for you." He rolled his hips down to grind against Jask, and this time, Jask didn't try to pull back or say no. He reached around and ran his hands over the satin until he was tugging it to the side and biting his lip, and Vince could feel the evidence of Jask's arousal underneath him.

"Gonna ride me wearing these, Vin?"

Having Jask inside him hit the top of Vince's "very favorite things" list, so he was nodding before his lover even finished the question. "Fuck yes. Why are you still wearing clothes?" He leaned back just enough to pull off Jask's shirt, but every piece of fabric on Jask's body disappeared before he could even get it over his messy hair.

A second later, Vince could feel Jask's power coursing through his body and easing the way as he guided himself down, and as soon as he made it halfway, Jask growled and thrust up to bury himself deep.

Vince cried out Jask's name as his grip tightened on his shoulders. He vaguely recalled he was supposed to be riding him, but after roughly a month of not having this he realized he didn't want to rush. Slowly, he circled his hips, keeping Jask deep and letting his head fall back.

"Good, Vin... fuck..." Jask palmed him for a moment then pulled the head of Vince's cock fully out of those panties, rubbing and teasing the head. "Just like that."

Vince thrusted forward, trying to get more of Jask's hand on him. The new angle caused Vince to see stars and he moved in the same way again, his body shaking with the effort to keep going slow and steady. Some part of Jask must have taken pity on him, because a couple of rough movements later, Jask had Vince pinned to the couch and was fucking into him like he was trying to make up for every single time he told Vince no.

"Ah, fuck!" Vince wrapped one leg around Jask and planted his other foot on the couch, lifting his hips to meet each thrust and moaning as the satin rubbed against his cock.

He suddenly regretted never trying this before. "Don't fucking stop, Jask." He gripped Jask's hair and pulled him in for a kiss which was met feverishly, and another wave of grace pulsed through him as Jask drove himself deeper.

"So damn tight," Jask grunted, his movements becoming erratic. "Gods, I missed you. Come for me."

Jask's voice sounded so deep, so *wrecked* that Vince could do nothing but obey. His back arched as he let go, making a mess of them both. "Missed you, too." Vince's hands moved from Jask's ass — he didn't remember putting them there — and up to where he knew Jask's wings were hidden. He kissed Jask one more time before flattening his palms and sending his own wave of pleasure through his former mate's body.

They were plunged into total darkness as Jask's orgasm hit him strongly enough to knock out the power to the whole house. Even the windows shook with the force of it, and those giant wings expanded out from his body as Jask filled him up so much he could feel it spilling out around his cock. He collapsed a moment later with heavy, sated breathing, caging Vince completely against the couch.

"Son of a bitch," Vince huffed out a laugh and kissed the side of Jask's head. He wrapped his arms more firmly around Jask and buried his fingers in the now-available wings. He smiled as he felt Jask shudder above him. "Guess the panties were a hit, then?"

"*You* were a hit, Vin. The panties were just a plus." Jask kissed all over his face and finally his lips, and the power slowly came back up around them. "I'm sorry I've been so distant. You don't deserve that."

"I get it. I do. You've been through some shit. I just wish

I could help more." He moved one hand to Jask's cheek, running his thumb over it lightly. "Wish you'd talk to me about it."

Before Jask could answer, there was a knock on the door, followed by Edis' voice. "You guys okay in there? Power went out on the whole block for a couple of minutes."

Jask tossed his head back and barked a laugh, and his face lit up after. He slid out and dressed them both with a blink, then opened the door with another. "Guess I was a little backed up. Sorry, Ed."

Vince sighed and sank further into the couch, unhappy with this development. At no point were clothes or family members supposed to enter the equation.

"Backed up?" Edis took in the scene and the look of realization on his face may have been hilarious, but Vince was content to continue pouting.

"Yeah, it's uh... been a while. Anyway, power's fixed and we're good, so..." Jask trailed off, shifting on his feet and giving his brother an expectant look.

"Yes. Yep. I'll just..." Edis pointed over his shoulder in the universal "I'm leaving" sign before disappearing completely. Vince pulled Jask back on top of him immediately.

"I believe we were having a conversation before the ginger interrupted."

Jask chuckled and kissed him, settling in after and closing his eyes. "You're right. It's naptime, isn't it?"

Vince couldn't even deny that sounded amazing. "Yes. I imagine knocking out the power on the entire block probably took a good chunk of energy. So, I'll happily nap with you, *af-*

ter we talk." He kept his arms around Jask and his eyes on the ceiling, waiting patiently.

"I knew this was a trap," Jask said lightly. "I just want you to know that I know that." He paused long enough to kiss Vince's cheek, then sat up with a sigh. "Okay. You want me to talk? Ask questions."

"I don't know what to ask, honestly." He reluctantly sat up as well, taking Jask's hand. "How'd you even end up with Drazan in the first place?" Even as the words left his mouth, Vince wasn't sure he wanted the answer. Did Jask plan to meet up with Draz that night without telling him?

He squirmed a little like he didn't want to *say* the answer, either. "He knocked on my window the night before the wedding and we went to the bar. I was just so fucking relieved to see him I didn't think it was weird, but... he drugged me."

Vince relaxed, nodding. "Okay, I can understand that. I would've gone if it'd been Johnny." He ignored the familiar ache of grief as he pressed on. "How did Edis fit into all of it?"

"Draz needed the blood of the one that killed Johnny. He wanted to use mine since he couldn't get Ci's, but it wasn't working no matter how much he took. Eventually, he remembered that Ci had a twin, and lured Ed there." Jask frowned deeply, curling one wing forward so he could pick at the feathers. "I couldn't stop it."

"That's not on you, sweetheart. You were drugged, chained, and bled. Magically chained at that. The only one to blame here is Drazan. That bastard would've *drained* you! Nothing is worth that." Vince hoped Jask could hear the sincerity. No matter how badly he wanted Johnny back, sacrificing Jask would never be an option.

It was clear by the look on his face that Jask didn't hear anything of the sort. "Where would you draw the line, Vin? If it were me that died, and you thought you could bring me back? Where would you say enough is enough?"

"Are you asking me if I'd be willing to lose Johnny to keep you? Seems to me I've already done that." Vince looked down at the floor, his voice quiet. He knew that wasn't fair, he knew the situation wasn't the same. That didn't stop the guilt. Because deep down there was a little voice. He tried not to listen to it very often — nothing good ever came from that voice — but it made him very aware that if the choice came between Jask and Johnny, he'd choose Jask. Living without Johnny hurt in a way that he could bear. Living without Jask simply wasn't an option. If Jask wasn't alive, Vince didn't want to be, either.

They may not have been bonded anymore, but when Vince pulled himself out of his thoughts, he swore he could feel the shame coming off of Jask. "I've apologized more times than I can count, Vin," he mumbled. "I never wanted him to die for us. I never wanted anyone to die, yet I'm a murderer. My own mother won't look me directly in the eyes anymore." He huffed with a pained smile and stood up, rubbing a sore spot from one of Athar's attacks that never quite healed. "Can we take that nap now? I think I've had enough talking."

"I have one more question and then I'll do whatever you want." Vince needed a break from the heavy conversation. They both did. He stood with Jask and gently tugged him back into his arms. "Do you still want to get married?"

Jask squinted. "Seriously? What kind of a question is that?"

"The kind that I would like answered." Vince replied with a cheeky grin.

"Yes, I still want to marry you. You know I didn't miss our wedding on purpose, right?"

"I do, but we haven't really talked about it and I want to do it as soon as possible. Now I can start arranging things." He kissed Jask quickly before leading him to the bedroom. "Plus, I like hearing you say things like 'I want to marry you' or 'Vin, you're so handsome.' Oh! Or 'your dick is perfect, best I've ever had.' You know, the really romantic shit."

Jask shook his head with a quiet laugh as he laid down on the bed. "Just tell me when and where, you... handsome, excellently-endowed almost-husband of mine. Did I cover it all?"

"Yeah, sounds about right. We can get t-shirts made that say that for the night before." Vince slid under the blankets next to Jask. "Which you will be spending here. In this bed. With me."

"I figured that was coming, and you won't hear any complaints from me." He wrapped Vince up and kissed his neck, then settled and huffed a laugh. "But you get to tell our moms."

"Deal. Also, you owe me a pair of panties, pretty sure these are ruined." Vince settled into Jask's arms and fell asleep, feeling better than he had in weeks.

DRAZAN

Drazan took a slow sip of his drink and stared at the glass coffin holding Johnny's body. Without the Veris brothers, they had nothing — no chance at all to bring his love back to life, and now they were on the run from Riskel, too.

"We shouldn't have pushed so hard," he said bitterly. "Now everything's fucked."

"This is only a setback," Zaepris soothed as she refilled his glass. "We'll get it done."

He huffed, no longer believing her. "You said that when we kidnapped Jask, when we nearly killed him, when we took Edis, when we nearly killed *him*. I'm starting to think you're not much of a necromancer."

She arched a perfectly sculpted eyebrow at him. "Excuse me? If I recall, *you* decided to not kill them outright. I told you numerous times we should've drained them both."

"You couldn't guarantee success, and if we would've killed them and failed, I would've killed *you*," he leveled back.

"You can't make an omelet without breaking the eggs, Drazan. You knew from the beginning sacrifices may need to be made." She tossed a cover over the coffin, breaking his stare.

The loss of visual didn't do much for him. "You're a walking fucking cliche, you know that, Zaepris?" He stood, draining the last of his whiskey and setting the glass down. "Whatever. I know Jaskian better than anyone else on this damn planet. Mark my words... he'll be back by the end of the week."

"You think his demon will let him come back?" she asked curiously.

"I don't think Vincenzo will have a say in it. I was with Jask every single day during his relentless search for Johnny — well, Pavo as we knew him then. He tried so damn hard to save him. Give Jask a few minutes to stew over the fact that he walked away from a chance to bring Johnny back... and he'll come running. It's just who he is."

"And Riskel? What precautions can we take against Vincenzo calling grandpa back into the mix?"

He paused, then let out a sigh that made him look like he was deflating. "Short of hoping Veris shows up to help a nobody like me — which seems unlikely given his relationship with Riskel — there won't be anything we can do to stop that other than to try and stay away from Vince."

"I'm sure that will be doable. It's not like he traveled across the country to find his lover last time," she said, the sarcasm dripping from her words as she stole his discarded glass and poured herself some whiskey. "Nothing could go wrong."

Anger surged through Drazan as he smacked the glass from her hands, not flinching in the slightest as it shattered against the wall. "What do you suggest we do!" he screamed. "All you've done is fucking complain and repeat what *should've* been done before!"

Fear shone in her eyes as she looked over the glass now glittering on the floor, and Drazan watched as Zae forced herself to compose her features back into nonchalance. "You're right, of course. No point in dwelling on failure. I'll look for a spell to hinder the Ancient one from interfering again."

"That's better," he said coldly. "And this time, try not to underestimate what you'll need." Drazan stormed out, slamming the door and leaving Zaepris — and her failures — behind him.

JASKIAN

Seeing Vince happy was nice, but only served to accentuate how badly Jask was slipping. He should be right there with him, putting the finishing touches on their wedding and making plans for that long-awaited honeymoon, and yet...

"Whatever you need, Vin," Jask said quietly.

"Jask, I asked if you were hungry. What does that have to do with my needs?" The room slowly came back into focus and Jask realized the notebook Vince kept for the wedding laid closed on the table.

Shit, he thought. "Uh... you need me well-fed?"

"You weren't listening." There was no questioning lilt, only a stated fact filled with barely contained sadness. Vince dropped his pen to the coffee table on top of the notebook and stood. "I'm gonna make dinner. Burgers sound good?" He didn't wait for an answer, walking away from Jask and into the kitchen.

Instinct told Jask to follow but his limbs wouldn't get on board. Not even his fingers twitched when he tried to tell himself to stand, to follow Vince and apologize for the fifth time that day alone. He just... didn't have it in him.

Two days prior, he'd managed to track down Drazan's phone number. It hadn't been a difficult task thanks to his previous profession but deciding what to do with it was an entirely different story. Should he call and yell at him? Somehow trap him or get revenge? To ask why over and over again until it made sense?

He knew he'd never figure it out until he called, so he

stood and walked toward the corner of the room as far away from Vince as the layout would allow and tried to reach Drazan. It rang a few times and went to a full mailbox, so Jask tried one more time before giving up and joining Vince in the kitchen. "Hey, I'm—"

"Sorry. Yeah." Vince kept his back to Jask, adding spices to some meat in a bowl in front of him.

Of all the things that Jask had ever done, disappointing Vince felt the worst. He stepped up behind him and wrapped his arms around him, kissing the back of his neck. "I'm trying, Vin. I'm sorry."

Vince leaned back into him. "I don't want to fight. I get that you're upset about Draz going psycho and I *know* this entire thing brought back all the guilt of Johnny, Athar, and Cidos. I understand all of that. That's why I asked if you still wanted this. If you don't, just say the word. I'll stop."

"I want to marry you, Vin. But fuck, it seems like I can't do anything right." He took a step back and rubbed the stubble on his chin. "I need you to be here for me, but it feels like you're mad at me for hurting."

Vince dropped his hands to the counter and bowed his head before turning to face Jask. He crossed his arms and nodded. "You're right. I'm sorry."

"Even now you look defensive." Jask sighed, wondering if that was just what being with a demon was like. "Maybe we should just... take a few days? I can try to get my shit together and you can keep planning our wedding."

"You mean separately? You want to leave?" Vince's arms fell to his sides, his shock evident.

Truthfully, Jask didn't want to leave, but he also didn't

know what else to do. If he stayed it would just be more of the same... and the plot already forming in his mind would be a lot harder to pull off with Vince around. *I wish I could trust you to go along with it.* But as he took in the hurt on Vince's gorgeous face, he knew he couldn't do it. "No, that's a stupid fucking idea." He stepped forward and gripped Vince's face, kissing him softly. "Just forget I suggested it."

Vince wrapped his arms around Jask's waist and dropped his head to Jask's shoulder. He adjusted until the space between them disappeared and they were touching from head to toe. "I'll stop pushing. Just don't go."

"I won't." Jask held him a little tighter and let out a slow, measured breath. He'd lost enough already without losing Vince too, but the fact remained that things weren't working the way they were going. "How do we find a middle ground here?"

"Run away to Alaska." Vince joked; his voice muffled by Jask's shoulder.

Somehow, Jask didn't think that would help. "Then we'd be dealing with the same shit, but I'd freeze to death."

"I'd keep you warm, sweetheart." Vince lifted his head to flash a grin at Jask before sobering. "You tell me what you need, and I'll do it. Whatever it takes."

He shifted his weight as he looked into Vince's eyes, searching for any sign that he didn't mean it with all of him. When he found none, he took a chance. "I want to find Drazan. To help him, not to kill him."

Vince stayed quiet long enough to make Jask uncomfortable and when he opened his mouth to speak, Jask expected a rejection. Vince's next words shattered that delusion. "Okay. I'll help."

For a few moments, Jask couldn't say much of anything. He was flooded with emotions — relief, happiness, and fear for what would happen when they actually found him — but most of all, he was grateful. He kissed Vince again like he hadn't in a long time, then shook slightly as he pulled him into a tight hug. "Thanks, Vin."

"You know I'd do anything for you." Vince's words were sincere. "So, how do we do it? Finding him shouldn't be that hard for you, right?"

"I've tried calling him a couple of times, but he won't answer me," he admitted with a frown. "I haven't tried to get his address, but you're right. Shouldn't be too hard. Do you think they went back to the place you found me?"

"You tried calling him *before* we had this little heart to heart?"

Jask deflated. If that's what Vince was latching onto... this discussion was far from over.

VIII

VINCE

"No, don't do that." Vince pointed at him. How could Jask not see how dangerous that was? "You hid that from me, which means you were planning on going alone. I am one hundred percent behind helping Drazan, but I draw the line at your safety!"

Jask squinted. "I called twice and didn't get an answer, Vin. Like twenty fucking minutes ago. I didn't even know what I wanted when I called him, I just knew I couldn't keep sitting around doing nothing."

"Okay." He pushed down the irrational over-reaction. "*Okay.* That's fine. I'm fine."

"Are you sure? You look constipated," Jask pointed out. "I wanna see if Ed's on board, too. If he'll help too, Drazan might be more willing to just work together instead of repeating what happened last time, and we'll have a better chance of success. I just can't sit around if there's really a chance we can save him, y'know? He didn't deserve to die."

"He didn't, but neither do you or Edis. If the answer is your life for Johnny's, we aren't doing it. He wouldn't want that. Can we just agree on that?"

Jask frowned, and for a heartbeat, Vince thought he was going to say no. "Yeah. I can agree to that."

All of the tension Vince didn't realize he'd been holding onto melted out of his body. "Good. Then what's the next step, boss?"

"We talk to Ed, see if he's on board... then I was thinking maybe we should talk to Veris? I feel like he'd know if it's even worth it or not." He suddenly became very interested in his hands, sucking his teeth and fidgeting. "I just don't wanna go near Draz if we can't actually help. I can't do it again."

"That makes sense. You still have to apologize to Veris anyway so two birds one stone, right?"

Jask put on an adorably innocent expression. "Who, me? Apologize for what?"

"Cute. Keep that up when he's around and he may not stab me for praying Riskel out of bed." Vince couldn't resist kissing Jask before turning back to their dinner.

"Ah, so you want me to apologize to him for something that wasn't my fault? That's pretty on brand," he laughed. "Here's me thinking I did something I forgot about."

"I'm sure you did. Let me think about it." He began making the patties and setting them to the side. "What about that thing with the pumpkin? Pretty scandalous if you ask me."

Jask snorted. "Hey, we agreed to never talk about that again. That was a one-time thing." He shuddered, stepping up beside him to help with the food. "With our luck, we'd apologize for that and they won't have even known about it. I'd rather not have to explain to them what our thought process was there."

"Pretty sure no thinking happened that night, Jask. Fine.

We won't bring up the pumpkin incident." Vince grinned at him. "One of the best nights of my life, though."

A soft smile spread across Jask's face, and for the first time in a long time, he looked like himself again. "Mine too. Probably the worst night of that pumpkin's life, though. Certainly the last."

"He died with honor." Vince finished the last burger. "You want to invite Ed, Lee, and the hell spawn to dinner? Talk it all out in one go."

"Nah. Ed won't listen with Lee and the kid around. It's better to get him on his own, let him make his own decision and let him deal with your sister."

"If you think Leota isn't going to blame us for this in some form, then you're delusional." Vince hoped she wouldn't, but if Ed agreed then it really would be their fault if something happened. He tried to think positively about the situation, but the bad outcomes outweighed the good.

Jask stalled by taking a bite, chewing slowly and pinching his brows together. "It's our fault no matter what, Vin. Don't you get it? All of it. It *all* happened because you and I couldn't stay away from each other. Everything that happened was just collateral damage, and it's apparently not over yet. Drazan, Ed, Johnny... they're all just notches on the "people we fucked over to be together" bedpost. Sometimes I just wonder how long we're gonna let that list get, y'know?"

Vince put his barely touched burger down and looked out the kitchen window. "Way I see it, everyone that helped wanted to be there. Drazan and Johnny are the ones that brought us back together. Ed got a family out of the deal. Do I wish things happened differently? Absolutely. Does the guilt of Johnny's death eat at me? Yes. Every damn night. Which is why I'm going along with you to help Draz. But I can't find it in me to feel bad or apologize for wanting to be with you, Jask. For wanting to do what it takes to keep you. Probably makes me a selfish bastard, but..." Vince shrugged and picked his burger up, keeping his gaze on his plate and chewing without tasting.

"I'm not saying I regret it, Vin. We helped a lot of fucking people. Generations of people. And I'm not saying you don't see what I see, I just mean... we're getting the blame no matter how this ends. Might as well go all-in." Jask stood, kissing the top of his head and wiping his hands. "I'm gonna take a shower, babe. Come find me when you're done eating."

His footsteps echoed as he walked away, and Vince dropped the burger and stood. If the choices were naked Jask in the shower or food, he'd choose Jask every time. He cleaned the kitchen up in record time before making his way to the bathroom. He found Jask standing under the water, letting it curve over his strong shoulders and slide down the dip in his back.

Eyes glued to the play of Jask's muscles, Vince leaned against the door frame with his arms crossed. He watched as the angel's shoulders flexed and as Jask's arms lifted to run his hands through his hair. The water trailed down the exposed skin and accented the cut of Jask's toned form. Vince would be happy standing in that doorway for eternity. He retrieved his phone from his pocket and snuck a photo before fully stepping into the bathroom. "Want company?"

"Mmm. Always." He turned, giving Vince a much different view that confirmed his words.

Vince immediately lifted his phone back up and took another photo before Jask could object, then dropped it back to the sink counter and tugged his clothes off. He stepped into the shower beside Jask with a smile. "Hi."

"Hey." Jask pulled them flush and kissed him softly, then reached around him for the shampoo. "Want me to turn the temp down a bit?"

"No, it's fine." Vince leaned in to lick a drop of water off Jask's chest, which earned him a low hum.

As the kisses turned more heated and the touches a little more urgent, Jask lifted Vince from his feet and pivoted to pin him against the shower wall under the shower head. "I should know better than to use one of these to actually get clean," he teased.

Vince happily wrapped his legs around Jask's waist. "You're right, it's all your fault. Can't blame me. It gets hard for me when I see you all wet and naked." Vince rolled his hips to show Jask exactly how hard it was for him. "Get it?"

"Yes, I get your terrible innuendo." Jask chuckled and nipped at his pulse point, and with that bite came a flood of power that made Vince shudder. "Hang on tight, Vin," he breathed, then gripped his ass and spread him open to slide in, pressing them both against the wall.

Vince did exactly as ordered, his arms tightening around Jask's shoulders as he let his head fall back against the tile. He shifted down until every inch of Jask's impressive length was buried deep and sighed. "I could stay like this forever."

"Yeah? Good." He pinched his tongue between his teeth as another wave of grace washed over Vince, then leaned back to grab the soap without Vince moving at all. "You can just stay right there until I'm actually clean, then."

Riding on that second wave, Vince dragged his hands down over Jask's chest. He thumbed over his nipples before continuing down to his abs. It took a second for Jask's words to pierce through the fog of arousal in Vince's brain. "Wait, what? You're not serious."

"Dead," Jask said with a nod. He soaped up his gorgeous body and scrubbed, swatting Vince's hands out of the way as he playfully smirked. "You can do it, babe. Just hold still for me, I'll be done soon."

"Your faith in me is misplaced," Vince mumbled. He decided to play along with it because Jask always made it worth it in the end when Vince acted the part of a good boy, but he couldn't resist reaching between them to stroke himself as he kept his eyes on Jask's hands. He bit his lip to keep in the moan, rocking his hips just an inch and clenching around Jask. Maybe his good boy act was a little rusty.

"Apparently." Jask frowned, dropping the soap and the pretense. "Hop down, we'll just go to the bedroom."

Vince matched the frown, not moving. "I'm enjoying the show. I can be good, promise." He tried to look innocent but the look on Jask's face suggested he wasn't succeeding.

Two blinks later, the water was shut off and they were dry on the bed, Jask still buried deep. "You don't have to pretend for me, Vin. It's okay." He kissed him deeply and rolled onto his back, dragging Vince with him. "You want it that bad... take it."

The new angle caused Vince's vision to go blurry as Jask's cock hit that magic spot inside him. He planted his hands on

Jask's chest again and ground down to get him there again. "Fuck, sometimes I forget how big you are." He lifted himself slowly before slamming back down and Jask rolled up to meet it, burying himself deep.

"Guess that means I don't fuck you enough, huh? Can't have you forgetting." He held Vince in place and started an unrelenting, almost brutal pace. The sudden speed caught Vince by surprise, and he pitched forward from his original sitting position. His hands found the headboard while his knees tightened against Jask's hips, and words seemed lost to him as a particularly deep thrust caused stars to burst behind his eyelids.

For the first few moments, it was all he could do to hold on and enjoy the ride. As his brain function began to come back online, he dropped his hands from the headboard onto Jask's shoulders and sent a pleasure pulse. Jask's original order had been to take what he wanted, and he planned to do exactly that.

"Not... fair," Jask breathed, his eyes closing on their own and rhythm faltering. "Nothing should feel that damn good."

Vince smiled and kissed Jask quickly before sitting straight. He scratched his nails lightly down the angel's chest, circling his nipples once before he reached where his name sat carved into Jask's stomach. He traced the letters slowly, keeping up the tiny pulses as he started a slow grind designed to drive them both a little crazy.

"Vincenzo," he groaned, planting his feet and rocking up, his breathing becoming a little ragged. "Don't tease me."

"Wouldn't dream of it. I'm just committing this image to memory." He began to ride Jask faster as he looked him over one more time. The contrast in their bodies always fascinated Vince. Almost every inch of Vince's body sported a scar or ink of some sort, whereas Jask's only displayed only Vince's name. No other marks marred his flesh and Vince couldn't help the shiver that came every time he thought about it.

He shifted to get better leverage and set about riding Jask in earnest, and it didn't take much after that to have the angel tipping over and barely containing the collateral damage. The house around them shook and Jask began stroking him, sending dual waves of pleasure through him.

Vince cursed and braced his hands behind him on Jask's thighs. His orgasm hit him hard as Jask's waves brought him over the edge. His vision went white, and he may have chanted Jask's name, but he couldn't be sure. Coming down from the high happened slowly and he slumped down over Jask, uncaring of the mess. "That felt nice."

"Nice?" Jask laughed, rolling them again and pinning Vince to the bed. "You always were an awkward demon." He kissed him once then climbed off the bed, stretching his arms out and shuddering as his wings followed, then nodded to the door. "I think I'll finish that shower now."

"You like how awkward I am. If I promise to behave and keep my hands to myself can I join you?" He motioned to his body. "I seem to have made a bit of a mess."

A grin flashed across his face. "I kinda like you like that, but if you insist..."

Vince grinned and stretched in what he hoped conveyed a seductive pose. "You can take a picture if you want something to look at later. Capture the moment for eternity." He winked and waited as Jask did exactly that before jumping out of bed to enjoy a relaxing shower.

Drazan

"I don't understand why we're still here," Zaepris said coldly. "You're wasting your time, my time, *and* valuable resources trying to keep his body from decomposing. Don't you think enough is enough?"

"No. There is no 'enough' in this situation. I will do whatever it takes until he's back." Drazan continued working on the preservation spell, but Zaepris' mood visibly soured further.

Her nails clacked obnoxiously on the table until Drazan was ready to put her in a matching coffin, but one sharp glance had her curling her fingers into a fist and sighing deeply. "You need to move on. I'm telling you that as a friend *and* a colleague. He's gone, Drazan. You should be focusing on other things... other... people."

"I'm not interested. Which I've repeatedly told you. My focus needs to remain on the spell - on *him* — so that I can understand what we've been doing wrong."

She rolled her eyes, frustration etched in her features. "You're wasting your life, Drazan. He wouldn't want that."

Draz slammed his hands down onto the table. Those empty platitudes always made his blood boil. People who didn't know better said those things. Statements along the lines of "they're in a better place" or "time heals all." Drazan *hated* those asinine responses. He took a deep breath before replying. "You don't get to say that. You didn't know him like I did. What Johnny would've wanted is to *live*. To be here with me."

"I don't think he'd have wanted you sitting here wasting away in front of his enchanted corpse," she shot back. "But fine, waste your time. When you decide to give it up... let me know." Zaepris flashed him a sarcastic smile and headed for the door, throwing a bitter "I'm done wasting time" over her shoulder on the way out.

"You weren't much help in the first place," Drazan mumbled to himself. He didn't need her. He knew the spell well enough by now, and lately she'd been nothing more than a distraction. He finished the preservation spell and sat down, his eyes on the coffin.

He could do this alone.

JASKIAN

"So... how do we do this?" Jask asked, straightening the tie he'd donned. "Do we just... pray or something? Should we go pick a fight and find ourselves in another near-death situation?"

Edis shook his head as he picked Arro up. "I think you're both insane and I wish you wouldn't do this at all, but if you're insisting... just ask him to come. Don't do anything additionally stupid."

Jask grinned cheekily. "Who, me? I never do anything stupid, it's Vince that you wanna lecture."

"Vince," Ed started, but sighed and pivoted to head out.

"Never mind, I'm not going to waste my breath. Tell Veris we said hello."

"Well, at least he knows I can't be talked out of doing anything stupid." Vince waved as their nephew and Edis left the room, and Jask just rubbed his jaw.

He still wasn't convinced this was the best idea, but he was out of options — tracking Drazan had proved to be an impossibility despite his considerable skills, and if he didn't go to him with some sort of a plan, he'd probably end up being a blood bank again. "Okay. Uh... Veris? You... busy? Got time to come see your favorite grandkid?"

Vince huffed a small laugh. "Favorite? I don't think I've ever heard either of them say that."

"Just because we don't say it doesn't make it untrue, Vincenzo," Veris intoned from what had been an empty spot on their couch moments ago. "Why am I here?"

"Would you believe me if I told you we missed you?" Jask asked, knowing damn well that not one person in that room believed it. "It's Drazan. He's... well, he's trying to bring Johnny back. From the dead," he added, as if that needed restating.

"So I gathered. And you want me to stop him?"

"Not exactly," Vince offered with a smile.

Veris looked between them until Jask finally got up the courage to spit it out. "We want to help him, as it were. Just maybe not in his current methods," he explained. "He tried to kill me and Ed. I'd rather not swap my life for Johnny's... though, yeah, I realize how selfish that sounds."

Vince opened his mouth — presumably to argue some

more with Jask — but Veris held up a hand to stop him. "Why would you need to trade your life for his?"

"Some crazy necromancer told Draz that the only way he could bring Johnny back was with the blood of his murderer, which was Ci. Obviously, *he* doesn't have any blood left, so he kidnapped me and... yeah. Let's just say it's not the most fun I've ever had with Drazan while strapped to a chair." Jask pointedly ignored the look he got from Vince but made a mental note to make that up to him later, then added, "He took Ed too once he remembered they were twins."

Veris stood. "Do you mind if I take a look at those memories?"

"That's kinda kinky, grandpa, you sur— oh, you meant the ones where he kidnapped me. Yeah, go for it." Jask shifted uncomfortably as Veris came forward. He wasn't sure what that was going to feel like or exactly what they would see, but he also wasn't in a position to say no when Veris placed his hands on Jask's head and began to sort through his memories. Amusement swirled in Jask's thoughts as Veris obviously sped through his fresh memories of Vince and the green panties, but soon enough Veris reached the time with Draz. All amusement fled while he examined them. After what felt like an excruciating amount of time, the elder angel stepped back. "That absolute *idiot.*"

"Honestly, I'm surprised Riskel didn't tell you." Jask rubbed his temple and tried to shake off the lingering feelings of sadness that resurfaced, then pulled Vince close to him for comfort. "And yeah, I agree he's a fucking idiot, but why do *you* say that?"

Vince kissed Jask's forehead and wrapped his arms around

him as they watched Veris pace. "He told me that you two had gotten yourselves in trouble but that he handled it. Then I proceeded to distract him with what we'd *been* doing before he left to play hero." He sighed and turned to face them. "And he's an idiot because he almost killed you both for nothing. He doesn't need more than a pint, at most."

"No, he took way more than that, but it didn't work," Jask countered. "I didn't exactly have a measuring cup handy, but I promise it would take more than a pint to get me in the condition I was in."

"It didn't work because he didn't use the right ingredients. Granted, it's been ages since someone successfully completed the spell, but they still should've clarified they were properly prepared before starting out."

"Wait." Vince looked at Jask, his eyes full of hope before he turned back to Veris. "You're saying we can do this. We can bring Johnny back?"

It was clear that Veris' first instinct was to leave and pretend this conversation never happened, but one reminder from Jask that they wouldn't stop until they figured it out loosened his lips. "It's not easy. If you want to overcome death, you have to... undercome life."

"That's not a wo—"

"I'm older than you and it's a word if I say it's a word," Veris warned. "Now, the point stands. If you want to bring someone back from the grave, you need to put someone else *in* a grave. Demons can't exist without their essence — hence why severing yours would've killed you, Vincenzo. Angels can't survive without their grace, either. However, under the right circumstances, and with the right spell... it's possible to replace that essence or grace."

Jask blinked. "You're saying we'd have to steal a demon's essence?"

"That's the ingredient that he's missing. It's the only way to complete the spell," Veris said, sounding apologetic.

"Jask... if they need a demonic essence..." Vince didn't finish his thought as he sat down, running a hand over his face.

There were only two reasons that Vince would even say that: either he was pointing out that they'd need to become murderers — again — or he wanted to volunteer. "It won't be yours, Vince, and I swear to Veris who is standing right in front of me that if you're suggesting Drazan uses yours, I'll kick you in the mouth."

Vince raised his hands in surrender. "Fine. You're the boss here."

"So... that's it then?" Jask asked Veris. "We kill a demon and use a pint of... Ed's blood? My blood? Say a creepy incantation and Johnny's home for dinner?"

"Edis' blood would be best, but yes. That's it," Veris agreed. "You'll need a special container." He disappeared out of their sitting room and appeared a moment later with a small flask in hand. "Here. Do the ritual, then use this to collect the essence." He handed the container to Jask as Vince frowned at them both.

"We aren't *actually* considering murdering someone?"

Veris raised his eyebrows as Jask tucked the blade away. "Are you getting squeamish all of a sudden, Vincenzo? I'd have thought you'd be the one talking Jaskian here into it, not the other way around."

"Enough people have died because of us — because of me. Who are we to decide who deserves death so Johnny can live?" Vince asked quietly.

"The same people that decided my father and brother needed to die so that you could live," Jask reminded him, irritation causing his skin to prickle. "The same people that decided it was okay for Johnny to die for the same cause and the same people that let Drazan walk away when it all fell to shit."

Slowly, Veris stepped back. "Well... it sounds like you two have some things to discuss, so... bye." In a blink, he was gone, but Jask knew the conversation was far from finished.

"You know that isn't what I meant. Who are we picking, Jask? Herch, maybe. He's been nothing but kind to us since we got here. One of the neighbors? Our co-workers? How do we choose?"

Whether Jask wanted to admit it or not, he already had a demon in mind... and he knew Vince wouldn't like it. For once, he chose to keep that information to himself and simply step in to kiss his former mate, hoping the distraction would be enough to put off that conversation to another time.

Chances were good that Drazan would either handle it himself or finally realize it wasn't worth the cost — so if they were lucky, they wouldn't have to choose, anyway.

But when are they ever really lucky?

IX

A dejected sigh from the bedroom reached Vince's ears and he opened the bathroom door just a little more. He wrapped the towel he'd grabbed before his shower around his waist and looked out through the barely open crack to see Jask tossing his phone on the bed, and the frustrated look on his face told Vince they'd hit another dead end. Finding Draz seemed to be harder than either of them realized. They'd both agreed after Veris' visit two days ago to find Drazan first and to make a decision regarding the rest later.

Vince still had reservations about killing another demon, but the need to bring Johnny back slowly smothered those thoughts. Vince knew that should probably worry him, but he shoved that down with everything else he didn't feel like dealing with. If he didn't think about it, it didn't exist. He took one last look at himself in the mirror before stepping out of the bathroom. "No luck?"

"No. He's completely hidden himself from me, which I didn't even think was possible. I guess he spent too much time as my partner... he knows all my tricks." Jask sat down and tapped his fingers incessantly on the desk. "I need to try something he won't see coming."

"Like?" Vince asked as he opened the drawer. A new pair of silk panties caught his eye and he blinked. Apparently Jask made good on his promise to replace them. Vince pushed them to the side and grabbed a pair of boxers to slide into.

"If I knew, I'd be doing it already," he deadpanned. "There has to be something he didn't anticipate. Do you have any ideas?"

"I'm the pretty one, Jask. You're the brains," Vince tried to joke as he finished getting dressed. He sat on the bed across from Jask and shrugged. "We could go back to their hideout. Look for clues of a second location. Or what about the girl? Sassafras or whatever her name is. Maybe we can find her."

Jask looked up abruptly and grinned — not the kind that lights up his face, but the kind he once flashed right before trying to kick his ass the first time. "Zaepris. She won't know enough to hide from me. You're a genius, Vin."

Vince couldn't stop the pleased smile on his face. Hearing things like that from Jask always made him feel all tingly inside, which meant he decided to joke about it to hide the small swell of embarrassment in his chest. "Yes, so I've been told."

"Now, we just have to hope she leaves him for supplies or something. Can't find her if she's in the same room as him, but the second she steps out, I'll have her." He stood, making his way toward the door but stopping when he reached it to toss a smirk Vince's way. "Should've gone with the panties, babe."

Vince's attention stayed focused on Jask's ass until he couldn't see him anymore, so it took a moment for the words to register. A quick glance at the clock confirmed he could waste some time before heading into work. A few moments later and Vince's undergarment situation was now drastically different.

After a second check in the mirror, he deemed himself worthy to leave the house. He'd stolen one of Jask's shirts so it would hang a little lower on his hips, so as long as he didn't disrobe on the jobsite, no one would know he now sported a pair of soft pink panties under his jeans. That secret was for Jask to find and no one else. He snatched his hat off the dresser and left the house with the truck keys in hand. Any other day would find him starting up the old beast and driving to the construction zone. Today, however, his feet decided to do something different. Vince found himself in front of his mother's door and she opened it before his knock even ended.

"Vincenzo, is something wrong?" Amaranth looked concerned. Vince never showed up this early without premade plans.

"No. Maybe?" He looked down at his boots. "I think I may be making a mistake, Ma."

"Come in. I'll feed you and you can tell me all about it." He followed her to the kitchen, shooting a quick glance at Astarte's door. Their mothers shared the third home in the cul-de-sac so that each couple could have their privacy — decision made unanimously after a few awkward encounters at the lake house they'd shared for a while. His mother caught his look and shook her head. "Don't worry about her. She hardly comes out before ten anymore." Vince sat at the seat his mother gestured to and accepted the mug of coffee she handed him.

"Still adjusting?" he asked quietly. No need to disturb his future mother-in-law intentionally.

"You could say that. Now tell me what's got your panties in a bunch."

Vince coughed out his first sip of coffee and barely stopped himself from dropping the mug entirely. His mother patted him on the back as her look of concern grew, but he waved her away and cleaned up the mess with a dish towel.

The smell of bacon and eggs began to fill the room and Vince leaned against the counter, watching her work. Some of his best memories growing up were of his mother cooking while he and Lee studied or played, or while she listened to him complain about work or whatever drama his love life endured at that time. If anyone would listen and not judge, it was her. She knew how much losing Johnny hurt him. How much it hurt everyone.

He couldn't get her hopes up if this didn't work. He gazed down at the pan as she stirred the eggs and decided to keep it vague for now. "Recently an opportunity arose for Jask and I to do something that would make some people very happy. But to accomplish it I may have to do something questionable and I'm trying to decide if it's worth it."

Amaranth nodded as she transferred his food to his plate, then shooed him away and back toward the table. He grabbed a fork on the way and poked at the food as she crossed her arms.

"And what did Jask say?"

"That's complicated. I think he feels kinda like I do? But

this thing is a big deal. Ends justify the means kind of big. This thing is something I want too, though. So, I can't help but think maybe I'm being selfish. Then on the other hand, this thing may help Jask and isn't that reason enough?" He shoved eggs in his mouth to stop the babbling.

"There's a lot I could say, Vince. Millions of questions I can ask. Is this thing harmful? Is it illegal?" She sat next to him and placed a hand over his on the table. "But I know the man I raised, and I know the man he chose to marry. You'll make the right decision – whatever that may be." She smiled at him and he could see the trust on her face. She really believed what she was saying.

Vince chewed thoughtfully on a piece of bacon as he gazed out the window. He didn't know how much he needed to hear that until she said it. This decision made sense. It was the right thing to do.

His eyes landed on the clock and the time reminded him that he needed to be at work soon. He finished the food on the plate and stood to drop it in the sink. On his way back he leaned down to kiss his mother on the cheek. "You always know what to say, Ma. Thank you."

"It's what mothers are for." She smiled and walked him to the door. "Let me know how your thing goes."

"You'll know if it goes well," Vince assured her as he jogged to the truck, and the roar of the engine helped him further relax as he backed out of the driveway. They'd find the necromancer, get Drazan, and Johnny would be back. Vince hummed along with the radio the entire way to work.

JASKIAN

The prospect of finding Drazan through Zaepris filled Jask with a little too much hope. He wasn't sure why that wasn't something he thought of himself, but if he were being honest, he'd have had to admit it's because he wasn't completely sure what he was doing was right. Still, not doing anything at all wouldn't help, so some action was better than none.

He wasn't stupid. It was clear there was something wrong with Drazan — something beyond grief, beyond the pain of losing someone, particularly when that someone wasn't around for very long. Jask would never discount the power of instant attraction even amongst non-bondmates, but the level of Drazan's desperation reeked of magical influence. The only question Jask had was whose influence? Zaepris? Someone else? Or was it a legitimate possibility that he simply never knew Drazan as well as he thought he did, and this type of behavior was always there, just hidden from him?

Questions like that would drive him nuts, so he took off toward his old office instead of dwelling. From there, it didn't take long to employ some of his old methods of tracking, and he had two different programs and a spell of his own creation seeking her out. To his surprise, the spell found her almost instantly.

That doesn't make sense, he thought. *Unless I'm the luckiest bastard in the world and happened to catch her on a supply run... but no, she's...*

He squinted at the location and blinked several times as though it would suddenly change. She wasn't at a market or in a forest somewhere digging up roots, she was at a residential address. One glance at the clock confirmed that Vince would be at work by now, so he decided to go check things out without him. More than likely it was a fluke — from what he'd seen, Zaepris didn't leave Drazan's side.

Indecision gripped him the moment he stepped outside of his office and spread his wings. If she *were* with Drazan, he could be walking into a trap. Even if she wasn't, there was still a good chance it was a trap. Maybe they were trying to draw Jask out to take him again. Though, maybe they weren't thinking about him at all, and this was simply a good idea that Drazan had overlooked. In the end, he convinced himself that his hesitation was nothing more than a knee-jerk effort to protect himself after what happened the last time he saw the necromancer, and kicked off from the ground to go find her.

The flight was shorter than he expected it to be but chalked that up to nerves, and when he landed on the front porch of a quaint but run-down little cottage, he didn't hesitate much before knocking. He heard a cat screeching in response and the clatter of something made of glass a moment before the door swung open and Zaepris' angry glare looked him over.

"What the hell do you want?" she demanded.

Jask shifted and tried to flash her a friendly smile, though the sentiment was hard to muster. "I need to see Draz. Is he... in? Is this your new hideout?"

"No," she scoffed. "Your little friend isn't here, now get off of my porch."

Not one to disobey, Jask took two steps backward until

he was safely on the cobblestone pathway leading up to the porch. "Did you two have a fight?" he asked with no small amount of amusement. "Happens to me all the time. He gets bitchy, but if you feed him and rub his head, he'll quit whining."

"I wasn't talking about your demon."

"Neither was I," Jask countered. "Turns out I have a type. Now, can I come in? It's rude to make your guests wait outside."

There was a moment when Jask genuinely thought she'd smack him, curse him, or both — but the fiery redhead sighed heavily and took a step back to let him in. "My time isn't free, Jaskian. What are you offering?"

He regarded her as a whole new creature. Gone were the cocky expression and long, painted fingernails. She looked almost haggard, like she'd been used up and tossed to the side. It gave him an idea. "Oh, the usual. Revenge? My guess is that Drazan offered you the same shitty treatment he gave me, maybe plus or minus a little bloodletting. He used you and when you weren't useful anymore —" he flicked his fingers in the air — "poof. Am I close?"

Every line in her face deepened as she screwed her face up. He could practically see the word "no" on her lips, but to his surprise, she deflated before letting it out. "Yes. You think you're doing a guy a favor by telling him it's a worthless cause, and what does he do?"

"Little shit kicked you out, didn't he," Jask placated. "What a nob."

Her back straightened. "I left; he didn't kick me out. Not even *he* is that stupid."

No lie prickled his bones, so Jask took that to be the truth. "Well good for you, standing up for yourself. I'm proud of you, Zae."

"Don't mock me, Veris," she warned. "I might not have been able to raise Johnny from a grave, but I'll have no trouble putting you in one. Now speak or *get out.*"

Fear spread through him despite the easygoing expression he held on his face. "Oh, right. The revenge. Yeah, me and the old ball and chain want to stick it to Drazan for what he did. We just... can't until we know where he is."

"You want Drazan's location? Fine. I don't owe him anything at this point, but it *will* cost you, in case you've already forgotten."

Jask nodded once. "I figured. What did you have in mind?"

"Five of your feathers," she said instantly. "Primary ones. They're incredibly useful if you know how to use them."

"I use them to fly," he joked. "Does that count?" Plucking wings was a horribly painful business unless done carefully and only on feathers needing to be removed, which he didn't have any. It hadn't been that long since the last time Vince helped him preen. Nevertheless, he needed Drazan's location and knew the necromancer wouldn't budge on her price, so he sucked in a breath and reached up to fist his hand in his own wing. "Don't ever say I didn't do anything for you," he hissed, yanking hard enough to make him yelp.

Once he handed the feathers over, her demeanor changed almost completely. For the first time, she looked like someone that could *pass* as decent instead of the raging lunatic he'd known her to be. She busied herself with pressing the feathers and tucking them away, then turned to Jask with a genuine smile. "Now. You wanted the little idiot's location? Fine, I'll take you there. I want to see the look on his face when you kill him."

"Uhh..." Jask coughed, caught off guard by her calling his bluff. No matter what, he didn't plan on killing Drazan. A plan formed quickly in his mind. "Yeah, totally. Just have a question first. Are you a demon? I can't really tell."

Zaepris laughed loudly. "No, I'm not a demon. I'm not an angel, either, before you ask. Don't worry about what I am. Are we going or not?"

So much for my plan to kill her and use her essence. Jask didn't dwell on the possibilities — the simplest explanation was that she was a human, and he didn't have time to wonder if there were other races he didn't know about. "Fine, let's go."

He stepped up to her and put a hand on her arm, giving her just enough access to his power to teleport them to Drazan. The second they landed, he knocked her out and dragged her body around to the side of the house, then took care to try and arrange her comfortably. "Sorry about this, Crazy. I can only handle one wildcard at a time," he whispered.

Part of him wanted to go home and get Vince. To his surprise, his former mate had been on board — more or less, anyway — and leaving him out of things now would only lead to trouble. But Jask hoped that he'd be able to appeal to whatever humanity Drazan had left and get him to stop all of this nonsense once he knew the cost, and if that ended up being the case, he wouldn't need Vince as backup. He'd simply be able to return home with good news and finally put some effort into helping Vince plan the wedding.

Knowing that Vince would prefer that to just about anything else, Jask decided to get it over with and knocked on the door, once again bracing himself for the possibility of a trap. Though he hadn't sensed any lies coming from Zaepris, he knew better than anyone how easy it could be to speak around the truth or suppress the body's innate reaction to lying. Anything was possible, and he'd be a fool to let his guard down now.

And Jask didn't take himself for a fool.

DRAZAN

The moment Jaskian stepped foot on his property, he knew. The problem was he didn't know what to do about it — did he risk letting him in after everything, try to pretend he wasn't home, or tell him to leave and hope he listened? Somehow, he didn't think any of those options were great.

He ignored the first knock as he threw the sheet back over Johnny's coffin. The second knock went unanswered as well as he tried to tidy up, and the third he ignored simply on principle. Nothing good would come of this visit.

By the time Jask knocked for the fourth time, Drazan understood he wouldn't be leaving without some sort of nudge. He tried yelling through the door that he wasn't home, but all that did was make Jask laugh. With a defeated sigh, Draz opened the door and stepped aside. "Come on. But if you're going to kill me... just be warned I've learned a thing or two about the afterlife. I'll never let you be in peace."

"Why would I expect anything else, D? You haven't let me live in peace since Johnny died. I wouldn't think death would deter you." He made himself at home on the sofa and looked around the house, then clicked his tongue. "You need a decorator."

"Did you just come to insult me?" Drazan asked, irritation making his fists clench.

Jask grinned. "Course not. I came here to stop you from being an idiot," he clarified. "I had a little chat with Veris the other day. Thought maybe you'd find the information interesting."

"I doubt it."

"You're fighting a losing battle, Draz. You have to know that." Jask leaned forward, concern almost concealing the fear on his face.

Flashbacks of a similar conversation with Zaepris invaded his mind until he was nearly growling. "Don't tell me how to spend my time, Jaskian. You lost that right a long time ago. I don't work for you anymore. If you don't like it, go join Zaepris. You two can start a club."

"Oh, she's here. A little unconscious, but... here," Jask said flippantly. "I needed her to lead me to you since you seemed hellbent on avoiding me."

Draz paused. "Do you blame me?"

"Uh... yeah, kinda. Actually, I blame you a lot," Jask agreed. "But that's not why I'm here, so should I get to the point or do you wanna wait until Vince works out where I've gone and comes after me again?"

He closed his eyes and tried to steady his breathing. "The two of you really need to work out your communication issues. Yes, get to the damn point."

"You can't bring him back with just blood," Jask said simply. "You need something else, something I guarantee won't be worth it."

There wasn't anything in the world Drazan wouldn't give to get Johnny back, so already, Jask's statement rang false. "Try me."

"You need a demonic essence. And as we learned from the whole bond business, you can't strip a demon of his essence without killing him. You're not willing to kill someone just to bring him back, or else I wouldn't be sitting here."

Oh, I would've killed you if given the time, Drazan thought bitterly. "Ah, well... you're right," he lied, not caring if Jask picked up on it or not. "Wouldn't do such a thing, I suppose I'll just... bury him again and call it a day."

Jask was on his feet in an instant and gripping Drazan by his jaw. "You'll never pull it off on your own. It's not just that, and I'll never tell you what the spell is to make it work. Veris won't either, so don't even try." Pain shot through Drazan's jaw as Jask sent a wave of his grace through him, but his grip didn't loosen in the slightest. "Do you understand me, Drazan?"

"Yea," he choked out, pushing Jask's chest to little avail. "Let me go."

"No." He pushed forward until Drazan's back was hitting the wall hard enough to crack it. "You're not killing anyone else. *We* aren't killing anyone else. I'm willing to look past the kidnapping and torture. I know you're hurting; I get it—"

"No, you *don't!*" Drazan screamed, letting off a blast of his own power that finally forced Jask back. "You got to keep Vince. Edis got to keep Leota. Everyone came out of this happy except for Johnny! And... and me," he finished lamely, most of the frenzied rage he'd felt just moments ago dissipating already. "You don't get it because you got what you wanted. You all did."

Jask shook his head. "Yeah, you've played that card before and it's not working now, either. Being sad doesn't give you an excuse to become a murderer, Drazan. I did what I had to do in order to *protect* the people I love and the ones that'll come after us. It's too late to protect Johnny, and you know that."

"So, what would you have me do, Jask? Just stop? Walk away and pretend like he didn't die for you? For *Vince?*" he spat the name like the curse it was. If not for Vince, Johnny would still be alive. He chose not to dwell on the fact that he'd never have met Johnny without Vince. "I can't do it. Just tell me the spell, I'll leave you out of it this time."

"You can't leave me out of it. It's not just the essence, D. That's what I keep telling you. You need that, blood from Ed or me, and a spell I'm refusing to give you. It's over. No one is going to tell you how to do this. Just... come home with me."

Drazan laughed bitterly. "I'm not coming home to play house with you, Jaskian. This is your last chance to leave."

He plopped back down on the couch and kicked his feet up on the table. "You won't be able to drug me this time, Drazan. And we both know you'll never get the upper hand with me conscious, so... I think I'll stick around until we figure out what the fuck is wrong with you."

"There's nothing wrong with me," he said defensively."

"Oh," Jask said, "D, there's absolutely something wrong with you. Not to mention, if you're dead set on doing this, I might as well help you. Keep the collateral damage to a minimum this time."

The sudden shift had him blurting out "yeah, and well did that work last time" before he could stop himself. The look of determination on Jask's face had him confused more than anything, but if Jask really *was* offering to help... it wasn't something he was willing to refuse. "You serious?"

"You're not going to stop, are you?"

"No."

"Then yeah, D. I'm serious. But I want you to look me in the face and tell me you truly believe Johnny will be okay with you killing someone else to bring him back. If you can do that, you've got my help. I'll bring you a demon, give you Ed's blood, and even do the damn spell for you."

Drazan just stared at him without being able to answer. Logically, he knew that Johnny *wouldn't* forgive him for such a thing — at the very least, he'd say no if given the choice himself — but the desire bubbling in his chest had him believing the words as he spoke them: "Yes, he'll forgive me. Now tell me. What do we do first?"

X

VINCE

In a way, working at the construction site always helped Vince focus. It reminded him of his time on the ranch back home. Being able to be productive and creative – instead of destructive as people expected – always led him to a sense of calm. This type of thing is what he understood. No magic, no death, no high stakes. Just good, honest work that made him feel like he contributed to something greater than himself. The school being built here would be open to kids of all lifestyles. A safe place for angels and demons to learn together and hopefully bridge the divide much of their continent still suffered from. He stepped back from inspecting the foundation of the gymnasium and checked it off on his list.

A text alert from his phone distracted him from getting to the next item and he retrieved it from his back pocket. He expected something from Jask in an update on the necromancer, but the text that came in showed Leota's name. The contents of the message sent a chill down his spine and he hit the call button immediately. It didn't take more than a few seconds for Lee to answer, and Vince wasted no time. "The fuck do you mean there's someone on my porch?"

"What else could I mean, Vincent? There is a man on your porch."

"That isn't my na—" he stopped and pinched the bridge of his nose — "You know what? Never mind. Is he delivering something?"

"No. He's just sitting there looking sad." Lee sounded sympathetic.

"Have you tried *asking* him why he's on my porch?" Vince tried not to sound frustrated.

"No, I'm not taking Arro over there and I'm sure as hell not sending Ma or Astarte. You can either wait until one of the angels get back or until you come home yourself."

"Yeah, thanks." Vince hung up before Lee could comment on his sarcasm and tucked the phone back in his pocket. It looked like it would be a short workday for him. No way he could allow some stranger to just sit that close to his vulnerable family. Lee could take care of herself, but not with Arro to worry about. He tossed the clipboard to his assistant and waved down the foreman. After a quick discussion and a promise to work a Saturday shift soon, Vince ran to the truck to find out just what fresh hell waited for him.

~

The entire drive back the thoughts in Vince's head caused his worry to grow. Lee knew what Drazan looked like, so it obviously wasn't him. Neither Veris nor Riskel would bother waiting outside, having no qualms about popping in uninvited. That ruled them out. Someone from the fights years ago? An old client of Jask's? Maybe someone from Jask's job?

Vince shook before he even finished the thought. They would've called him if something happened to Jask. Herch didn't make home deliveries, no matter how much Vince begged. Anyone else Lee would've recognized, and Vince still didn't know who it could possibly be by the time he entered the neighborhood. He parked the truck at the front and made his way around to the back of Leota's home. He didn't know what he may be walking into so better to do some investigating first.

He leaned around the corner of her house, trying to get a glimpse of the mystery stranger. The only thing visible from this angle happened to a shoe on his bottom step. Leaning any further would likely land him on the ground and explaining to Jask the grass stains on his shirt were from Vince's amateur spy attempts didn't sound appealing. He almost ended up falling anyway when Leota's voice appeared suddenly from behind him. "What in the seven hells are you doing, creeper?"

"Son of a bitch, Lee! I'm trying to find out who the fuck is at my house.," he whispered, ushering her inside her house and closing the door.

"So, go over there and ask him." She crossed her arms and raised an eyebrow.

"No, going in guns blazing is a terrible idea. I don't know what that person is capable of." Vince mimicked her stance.

"Who are you and what have you done with my brother?" she asked with suspicion. "Guns blazing is kind of your thing, Vince."

"I like to think that I've grown, thank you." He stepped around her — ignoring her snort of disbelief — and headed to the front of the house.

"I must've missed that growth period because you're still the same dumbass I know and love. I'm assuming you're holding back because of Jask?" Leota stooped to pick up Arro out of his play pen.

"We recently had a mutually beneficial discussion on the health and wellness of the other. Basically, he said if I were to deliberately get myself hurt or killed, he would 'kick me in the mouth.' His actual words, I'm not paraphrasing." Vince slid open one of Leota's blinds and squinted out the window.

"How romantic," she stated dryly as she joined him at the window.

"I know, he makes me all tingly." Vince leaned closer to get a better look and cursed when he realized who sat on his steps.

"What? Who is it?"

Instead of answering, Vince yanked open Lee's front door and headed directly for the last person he should be seeing. "Damn it, Damian, what the hell are you doing here? You're supposed to be hiding!"

"I was! She found me. Somehow, she knows you lied, and she's been after me ever since." Damian stood and crossed his arms, looking defensive.

"And you decided to come here? Endanger my entire fucking family?" Vince pointed to where Lee stood in her doorway and narrowed his eyes at his former employer. He watched as Damian's shoulders slumped and his hands fell to his sides. The demon exuded an air of defeat and it caused Vince to look a little closer. Damian's normally pristine tailored suit appeared wrinkled and frayed. His eyes were red, and his hand shook as he ran it through his slightly overgrown hair. He looked like he hadn't slept in days.

"I had nowhere else to go, Vince." The dejection in his voice caused Vince's anger to subside slightly and he shook his head. He looked over his shoulder at Lee and gave her the all clear. She hesitated only a fraction of a second before closing her door. He motioned for Damian to join him as he unlocked his own home and dropped his keys on the table in the hall.

"Come in, make yourself comfortable." Vince played the part of proper host as he gave a small tour of the home. He stepped into the kitchen and grabbed a beer. "Here. You look like you need this," he popped the top and offered it to Damian. He waited as Damian downed half before asking his question. "How'd she find you?"

"I sent Geoff on a supply run. We were running low on food at the safe house. We'd worked out a system. Schedules, special knocks, sleep shifts. Geoff's return time came and went with no sign of him. We searched the property and found – "Damian paused to finish the rest of his drink – "we found a pile of flesh. Bones and organs and blood. Geoff's shoes were placed neatly beside it. Not a spot on them."

"How'd you get away?"

"As soon as I saw... *that*, I ran. I've been running for weeks but she always seems to find me. I keep finding dead animals or notes in my bed." Damian leaned back on the couch, his eyes closing. Vince couldn't help but feel responsible for this. Damian sending him to the witch saved Jask and Vince repaid him by forgetting all about him as soon as Jask was home safe.

"Alright, I'll help you with her but I'm dealing with another situation right now. You can stay here until that's resolved and then we'll take care of your witch." The look of relief on Damian's face was immediate. He murmured a thank you as Vince took out his phone to update Jask on their new guest.

"What situation are you dealing with now?" Damian inquired as Vince's call to Jask went unanswered.

"A missing person one. That is, a new one. I found Jask." Vince frowned down at his phone. Logically, he knew Jask would call back when he wasn't busy. Illogically, he was now worried all over again. What else could happen today?

He didn't have to wonder long — a crash from the next room set Vince's teeth on edge, but Jask and Drazan appeared in front of him before he could jump into action.

"Hey, I f— what the hell is he doing here?" Jask asked, his attention snapping to Damian. "Go away."

Damian sent a fearful look to Vince, but he held up a hand. One thing at a time. "Hold on a second, you went after Draz alone? We *just* talked about this."

"I didn't hurt him," Drazan argued. "Not this time, anyway. We just talked."

Jask shrugged. "Your idea worked. One thing led to another, and... shit. We left Zaepris outside."

"I can see you didn't hurt him." Vince replied to Draz, uncaring about where Zaepris was or wasn't left. "Jaskian, can we continue this conversation in the kitchen? Please?" This conversation needed to happen without bystanders.

His fiancé shivered with a grin. "You never call me by my full name, I feel like I'm in trouble." The smile disappeared completely when Jask realized he was absolutely in trouble, and he cleared his throat. "Uh... I'd love to, Vin. But it's probably not a great idea to —" Vince's glare caused Jask to abruptly stop — "yeah, okay."

Once they were in the kitchen and away from Damian and Drazan, Jask rubbed the back of his neck. "Just didn't want to waste time. And I brought him here, it's not like we killed a demon already."

"That isn't the issue. He could've taken you again and thanks to recent events—" he pointed toward Damian through the door — "I don't have a witch to track you. What would've happened if he didn't listen to reason?"

Jask didn't miss a beat. "Then I would've killed him. He only got the upper hand last time because he drugged me. Conscious, there's no way in hell he overpowers me."

Vince ran a hand through his hair. "Yeah, okay. You're right. I'm sorry I—" His apology cut off at the sound of a shout in the other room and Vince bolted through the door, expecting to see the witch in their home. Instead, he found Drazan pinning Damian to the ground via a knife to his throat. "Good job, Vincenzo," Drazan praised without looking up. "You found me a demon. Not even I expected you to work so fast."

"Shit," Jask whispered from behind him. "Drazan, that's... probably not what this is. Let him go."

"No. Tell me how to do the damn ritual." He pushed the knife a little harder into Damian's throat, making him yelp.

"Do something!" Damian hissed.

"I didn't find you a demon," Vince argued, but he couldn't make himself move in Damian's defense. The more he thought about it, the more it made sense. Damian's entire life revolved around death and crime. He'd trapped the witch for his own selfish reasons. He'd kept Vince as an attack dog for months. Countless demons lost their lives because of him. Was this the break they'd been waiting for? Could he let Drazan do this?

"Vince!" Damian's voice cut into his inner monologue and he glanced at Drazan. Their eyes met and an understanding passed between them. This needed to happen because this was how they got Johnny back. Vince nodded slowly, his resolve strengthening with every moment. "I'm sorry, Damian. Draz, the spell. It's the same one." He lifted his shirt to point at the scarred runes on his abs. "The only difference is that the essence is transferred to a container instead of an angelic vessel."

Drazan rolled his eyes. "A fucking container. I should've guessed as much." He grinned a little ferally down at his captive and took a deep, satisfied breath. "Say goodnight, demon. Don't worry... this will only hurt a lot."

JASKIAN

Nothing about the situation felt good. Killing Damian had been high on Jask's priority list since the moment he'd first found out about the demon, but this? This seemed cruel and unusual. Even still, Jask stayed quiet as they journeyed back to Drazan's hideout, and continued that way until Drazan cut Damian's shirt off and started carving the runes into his skin.

"Vin," he whispered, pulling him back a few paces. "Look at me and tell me you're sure about this."

Vince watched Drazan work for a few more seconds before turning to Jask. "I am. We have to do this."

"Okay. Then I'm with you, you know I'm with you. I'm sorry it's come to this." He grabbed Vince's face and kissed him, holding for as long as he dared before darting over to help hold Damian down. The addition of his grace made it so the demon couldn't move a muscle, and while it was hard for Jask to look him in the face... he at least did what he could to make sure Damian didn't feel the pain that Drazan promised.

The sound of Draz reciting the spell transported Jask back to the day he almost lost Vince. The day he *did* lose Vince, if he was being honest with himself. Something changed that day when the bond broke. Sure, they were still in love and would do anything for the other — but it was muted now, and the security he once felt was long gone.

Flashes of that fateful day continued assaulting him. Athar's laugh. Johnny's body. The absolute wreckage they left behind. And Cidos' face when Jask finally caught up with him... the spells that nearly unraveled it all.

"Jask!" Drazan yelled, snapping him out of it. "I need you, get the damn container! I'm almost done."

He didn't end up having to move. Vince was there in a moment shoving something into Drazan's hands, and Damian started bucking wildly and fighting Jask's grip and his grace. It took all of his focus, all of the strength he'd inherited when his brother and father died to hold him steady — to keep him down until Drazan was finally crying out in triumph.

Tears ran down Jask's face as Damian went lifeless under

him, his body dripping blood and face permanently contorted in fear. Over and over, the faces of those he'd seen the end of berated his mind: Cidos, Athar, Johnny, Damian, Cidos, Athar, Johnny, Damian, Cidos, Athar, Johnny...

"Fuck!" he screamed, clutching the torn, sliced remains of Damian's bloodstained shirt. "Fuck, fuck!"

Vince's hands hauled him to his feet, but he barely noticed. He couldn't bring himself to regret the action, but there was no way he'd ever let himself live it down. This was too much, too many people dying for a cause he thought was long put to bed. "Jask?" His former mate's voice cut through and caused him to start breathing again, if for no other reason than he had to. Even if their lives weren't tied by fate anymore, they were tied by something tighter.

"I'm okay," he rushed out, checking Vince's face for any signs of distress. "Are you? I know you cared about—"

"Hello!" Drazan yelled. "A little help over here?"

The essence Drazan and Vince managed to wrangle into the container was glowing and angry, like the last existing part of Damian was railing against what they'd done. It looked almost beautiful. "Whoa," Jask whispered. "I think we pissed him off."

"You think?" Vince scoffed, stepping in to check it out. "What's gonna happen if we try to put that thing in Johnny? Is he gonna be... like that?" He gestured broadly to the swirling, screaming essence, and Jask realized he didn't have a clue what the answer was.

Veris didn't prepare them for this part. He wasn't sure Veris expected them to do it at all, but from what he knew of the ancient angel, he was smart enough to figure it out. "Uh..."

Jask said lamely. "Throw a blanket over it or something, I can't concentrate with it doing that."

"A blanket," Drazan deadpanned. "We need to finish the job, Jaskian. No time to get squeamish now."

Part of Jask balked at the insinuation that any part of him was squeamish given all that he'd done to get them there, but he knew arguing with Drazan was futile. "Do you have a pint of Ed's blood? Cause I don't. This won't work without it. Cover the damn thing, don't cover it, I don't care. You two need to see if you can find anything out about calming it down before you put it in *anyone,* and I'll go see about that blood."

"And how do you expect us to do that?" Vince asked, and his mortified expression would have been adorable if it weren't for the horrible situation.

Again, Jask didn't have the answer, but he was decent at bluffing. "I don't know, read it a bedtime story while you try and get ahold of Riskel. I have a feeling Veris won't be much help in this department, though, now that I think about it... he managed to calm Riskel down, so..."

"Jask."

"What? Yeah, it's not the same thing. I don't know, does it look like I've ever done this before? Just do *something* while I'm gone." He sidestepped around the two and nearly got away with simply disappearing, but Drazan threw something at him.

He turned to see an expectant look on Drazan's face. "Um... the body? You're not just gonna leave it here, are you?"

"Me? Wait a minute, why is this my problem?" Jask asked, wrinkling his nose.

Drazan waved his hand a little erratically over Damian's body. "We're a little preoccupied with the essence, get it out of here."

Just as he was about to argue, Vince uttered his name so quietly he'd have missed it if he weren't standing right next to him. One look at Vince reminded him of exactly how hard it must've been for him to see Damian like that, to know he traded one friend for another. It was a pain Jask knew all too well, and he'd have done anything to save Vince from it. "I got it, Vin. Be careful, okay?"

He planted another quick kiss to Vince's lips, then scooped up Damian's heavy body and teleported away. The effort left him panting — he knew he couldn't take the body anywhere near their little cul-de-sac oasis, so he opted to take Damian to the same place they'd burned Cidos, buried Johnny and where he'd lost Drazan to begin with.

Being back there was odd. It didn't incite the emotions he expected it to; instead, all it did was make him set his jaw and construct a pyre as quickly as he could. He wanted out — out of that yard, out of the situation — out of any situation that would require him killing someone else. The only way out was through, and to get through, he had to keep moving.

He stayed long enough to ensure Damian's body was burnt enough that no necromancer or witch could resurrect him and cause more damage, then wiped his brow and tied his hair back before teleporting once again to Edis' front door. Jask knew he was sweaty, dirty, and reeked of burning flesh, so the last thing he wanted to do was drop in on family dinner and traumatize Arro, which meant his only option was to knock.

He stood there shifting his weight from foot to foot until

the door swung wide, and Leota's smile faded instantly when she took in his appearance. "What the hell, Jask? Where's Vince? Where's that guy that showed up?"

He held up a hand to stop her questions. "Damian's dead. Vince is fine. Is your man home? I have a favor the size of the Grand Canyon to ask of him."

She opened her mouth and closed it twice before finally getting out, "Yeah, I'll go get him. You're going to explain at some point, right?"

"Of course, I'll tell Ed everything and he can fill you in." He spotted Arro coming up behind Lee and realized this wasn't the place to do what he needed to do. "Have him come to my house; it'll be better if Arro doesn't see."

Before she could protest, he teleported to his own kitchen and opened the fridge, pulling out the half-empty gallon of milk and dumping the rest down the drain. Just as the last of it was disappearing and he was rinsing out the jug, Ed let himself in.

"Jask? You get drugged again or something? Lee said you were acting weir- what the hell is that smell?" Ed covered his nose as Jask turned slightly to face him, still rinsing out the jug.

"I need your blood," he said quickly. "Not all of it. Just like... a pint or so."

Ed's jaw went slack. "*Just* a pint? Jask..."

"I know, okay! I know. It's a big ask. I'll heal you after and mow your lawn for the next forty years, I just... fuck, Edis. I need you to do this. I need this shit to be over."

He set the cleaned-out jug down on the table and turned to face his only brother properly. "I'm not doing a damned thing until you tell me what this is about. Is it that crazy necromancer again?" Ed asked, skepticism written on every line of his face.

"No, this spell came from Veris himself. It's not some crazy, half-cocked scheme, Ed. This is real. We can do this; we can bring Johnny back. But we've only got one shot and Veris seemed to think your blood would be better than mine since you're Cidos' twin."

The mention of Cidos had Edis' eyes darkening. Bringing him up at all was probably a mistake, but Jask didn't have time to feel bad about it. Ed nodded once and clenched his jaw as he rolled his sleeve up. "Thanks for not doing this in front of Arro. Just hurry up, and don't take too much."

"I won't," Jask assured him. He wasted little time after that, and in the absence of a needle, he used a kitchen knife to drain what he needed from his brother. The whole thing was uncomfortable at best and horrible at worst, but when the jug was sufficiently full, Jask placed a broad hand over the cut and healed his brother with an apologetic smile. "There's food in the fridge, eat some and drink something too before you go home, okay? Promise me."

"Yeah," Ed said, exhaustion lacing the word. "But this is the last time I bleed for anyone, Jaskian. Make it count."

He kissed the top of his brother's head and once more braced himself to teleport. The continued action was wearing on him a little but sheer determination to see it through had him pushing forward until he was standing yet again in front of Vince and Drazan.

"I got the blood," he said as if they couldn't see the dark red jug in his hand. "Did you have any luck?"

"We didn't read it a bedtime story if that's what you're asking," Vince replied dryly. "But yeah, I think we managed to get it figured out. Don't ask too many questions because I honestly don't have a fucking clue what just happened, but look." He held up the container and Jask could see the difference — now, instead of slamming against the side and glowing an unearthly purple, the essence was solid black and swirling slowly.

Drazan coughed. "You don't actually wanna know, anyway."

"You're right. Okay, let's do this." Jask stepped forward as Drazan pulled the sheet back on Johnny's coffin, and the sight made Jask's stomach roll. While his body was perfectly preserved by Drazan's spell work, seeing him lifeless like that was nauseating.

Something wild and untamed lit in Drazan's eyes as he removed the lid and gathered what he needed. "Spell?" he asked without looking.

And here it was — the make-or-break moment that would either end with Johnny alive or Drazan dead, because the one thing Jask knew for sure was that this couldn't go on. If they failed, Drazan wouldn't stop, and Jask would do whatever he had to in order to protect his family.

He took a deep breath and recited the words that Veris told him: "Sacrificium et sanguinem, sit duobus fieri unum."

The room erupted in white light so intense that Jask had to shield his face, but when it faded, he couldn't believe what he was seeing.

Slowly, Johnny blinked and sat up, looking around at the

breathless, speechless men around him. "What just happened?"

XI

Drazan's arms enveloped Johnny before the question finished. Vince watched as Draz tried to explain exactly what they'd done between kisses and what sounded like quiet sobs. He couldn't seem to make himself tear his gaze away from Johnny and he remained rooted to the spot. His best friend was brought back to life not six feet away from him and Vince *couldn't move.* His fists were clenched, his feet set the way he used to stand before a fight — and he suddenly realized that's why he hadn't stepped forward. He was waiting for the fight.

Vince watched Johnny interact with Drazan and he waited. Waited for the other shoe to drop, for Damian's essence to take over. For Veris or Riskel to show up and tell them that their spell caused natural disasters all over the world. For the building to collapse. When none of that happened, Vince blinked back tears of his own and he felt his body go limp with relief. His legs wouldn't hold him up anymore and he sank down to the ground. Somehow — by some miracle — they'd pulled it off.

"Draz, you dick. Budge up, let us have some too," Jask said, but Drazan didn't move an inch when Jask tried to pull him back.

The angel's face turned almost feral as he blocked Johnny from view. "Back off," he hissed. "You didn't lift a finger to help me until it was too late to back out."

"That's not true." Jask shook his head and held out a hand, taking a slow step forward. "Draz, we're friends. We helped, we're not gonna hurt him."

"Hurt me?" Johnny laid a hand on Drazan's arm, leaning around him. "Why would they hurt me?"

"We wouldn't. Draz, we killed someone for this. You can't think we aren't just as invested." Vince stood as soon as he thought his legs would hold him. "Listen to Jask. Step back so we can get him out of the damn coffin."

Drazan's eyes were wild, and for a horrifying second, it looked like he was about to fight them both. But with an unsure, shaky nod, he released his hold just enough that Jask was able to grab Johnny and haul him out of the glass coffin he'd been in for way too long.

"Good to see you, Pavo," Jask joked with a grin. "You look good, all things considered."

"Thank you?" Johnny looked around the room in confusion. "Where the hell are we? Did you just say you *killed* someone?" He rubbed his face and leaned back against the coffin. "Why do I feel like I've been asleep for ten years? Last thing I remember, Athar had Vince."

"Oh, then we actually killed two people. Wait, three. Four?" Jask squinted, his brows furrowed as he tried to remember. "No, just three. You might want to sit down."

Drazan held out an arm to stop Johnny from moving forward. "No. I want you two—" he pointed to Vince and Jask —"out of my house. I'll tell him everything he needs to know. I'll take care of him. We don't need you."

Ah, here it is, Vince thought as he straightened his shoulders. Here was the fight he'd been waiting for. "You're insane if you think I'm leaving Johnny when we just got him back."

"Wait," Johnny said, but it fell on deaf ears. Drazan took a menacing step toward Vince but was body slammed out of the way before Vince could even react, and in a flash, Jask had Drazan pinned to the ground.

"Don't... *touch...* him," Jask growled, his forearm digging into Drazan's throat. Giant wings sprung from his back as Johnny stumbled over to Vince, whispering a quick warning that they needed to leave.

"I'm not—" Vince immediately began to argue but a sudden charge in the air caused him to turn back to Jask and Drazan. He could feel the electricity crackle around them as Drazan retaliated and he obviously held nothing back. They'd gone through all that work to get Johnny back and now he wasn't even safe. Vince took his best friend's arm, and they ran out the door of the lab. He tried to remember which direction the exit was in while the sounds of a fight erupted behind them. His every instinct screamed at him to go back in and help Jask, but he tugged Johnny further and further away from their battling angels. Only once they made it outside did Vince relax again.

"What the *fuck* is going on, Vince?" Johnny demanded; arms thrown wide. Vince leaned against the wall – which shook beneath him accompanied with the sound of a minor explosion – and just looked at Johnny. Johnny standing here, alive and in front of him after a year and a half of grief and guilt.

"We got you back." Vince answered quietly before stepping away from the house. He wrapped his arms around Johnny and hugged him tightly, the embrace going on a few moments longer than he'd normally allow it. "You were dead, Johnny... but we got you back." He released his friend and ran his hand over his eyes before patting him on the shoulder.

"Dead... I was..." It was Johnny's turn to lean against the wall as he absorbed that little piece of information. "And Draz and Jask? What's that about?"

"There's been a lot going on. You got a year and a half to catch up on, but I'll try to give you the summary." And he did try, starting with what happened to Athar and Cidos. He explained Drazan leaving and kidnapping Jask the night before the wedding. He talked about Arro and Lee and stumbled over what happened to Damian. "So, there you have it."

"You shouldn't have done that. Not for me." Johnny shook his head.

"Out of all of us, you deserved what happened the least. How could I not want to bring you back if I had the means?"

Instead of answering, Johnny sighed and began to walk back toward the door. "We need to find out if they've killed each other and then I'd really like a burger. Could eat an entire cow, honestly."

"Yeah, Jay. Whatever you need." Vince followed him back into the house, hoping Jask and Draz were done with their argument.

Hushed, angry voices grew louder the closer they got, and when Johnny and Vince entered the room, it was barely recognizable. Glass covered the ground and pieces of the ceiling had collapsed, but both angels looked unharmed other than a few random patches of bloody or bruised skin.

Jask turned to them and kept one broad hand on Drazan's chest, effectively pinning him to what was left of the desk. "You two good?"

"*We* are, but what the hell happened here?" Vince hesitated a few steps away from the door. "Do we need to wait outside a little longer?"

"No," Draz grunted. "Get him off of me."

A devious smirk crossed Jask's face. "Told you, babe. If he can't drug me, he can't beat me. We were just doing a little exercise, that's all."

"Right. Johnny's hungry so if you'll let the asshole up, we can all go home and I'll make dinner." He winced when Johnny flicked him in the ear.

"He's not an asshole," Johnny explained. He walked over to the angels and Vince followed with a sigh.

Jask finally let Drazan up and pulled Vince close to him. "I don't know, J. He's become kind of a dick recently, but maybe he'll lighten up now that he's finally succeeded." He kisses Vince quickly. "Take them back, I gotta to deal with Zaepris."

Vince dropped his head onto Jask's shoulder and held him a moment longer. Exhaustion from the day started to creep into his body but his mind stayed wide awake. Now that Johnny knew most of the things he needed to and they were safe, Vince couldn't stop himself from thinking about the way Jask protected him. There hadn't been a second of hesitation before that tackle. He would never admit it to anyone – especially out the men in this room – but Jask's friendship with

Draz always made him feel inferior. Now he knew without a doubt that Jask really picked him and that feeling made him deliriously happy. He felt the jealousy over their friendship break apart inside his chest and crumble to dust. In its place there remained a new warmth – one that reminded him of Jask's healing touch. He grabbed onto that feeling and pulled tighter, wanting more.

"Vin..." Jask sounded shocked but Vince didn't get a second to ask why. Drazan's voice broke into his happy little world as he insisted he and Johnny could handle dinner on their own.

"Son of a bitch, Draz," Vince groaned without moving his head from Jask's shoulder. "I just want to go home where we can all have a nice dinner. Why is that so difficult for you? Why can't we just go *home*?" He held onto that warm feeling in his chest as the temperature rose, keeping his arms around Jask. No one answered and the silence made him antsy. Vince wearily lifted his head and then blinked. They were all standing in his kitchen.

"Did you do that?" he whispered. Jask shook his head slowly, his eyes on Vince's face. Vince looked around the kitchen again and huffed out a tired laugh. "Well, fuck me."

Jask rubbed the spot on his chest that used to ache when they were apart. "Oh good, now I've got two of you that can use my powers however you please," he teased. "I can't imagine that *ever* backfiring on me."

For once, Drazan looked like the jealous one — but it was gone before Vince could fully enjoy it.

"It'll be fun. You go take care of the zombie lady and I'll get dinner ready. Then we can all sit and talk like civilized adults.

You two can make yourselves at home." He pointed toward the living room and then kissed Jask quickly. He began taking things out of the fridge, humming to himself as he got started on dinner.

JOHNNY

Johnny had mistakenly thought that being alive again would be something to be celebrated. However, there was this *thing* in his chest that wasn't quite him — some small, swirling darkness in his chest that made him want things he didn't understand... like revenge on Vince. But for what? From everything Johnny had been told, Vince helped save him. They'd all gone willingly to the fight with Athar, and he knew it wasn't anyone's fault but Cidos' that Johnny died in the first place, but still. It was there, it was evil, and it was making him sick.

"Tell me you're okay," Drazan demanded for the hundredth time. "I need to know you're okay."

The attention had long ceased to be cute. "Yeah, I'm great," Johnny lied, plastering on a fake smile and trying to nonchalantly escape from Drazan's rough grip. "It's just a lot to adjust to, ya know? I feel like I lost a lot of time."

"You did. I'm sorry it took me so long."

The apology felt as off as everything else did, but Johnny truly didn't remember being dead. For him, it felt like no time had passed at all, so hearing the others talk about all the things that happened made him feel off-kilter. Especially the things Vince had told him about Drazan. The Drazan he knew and loved before he died would never have hurt Jask — Vince, maybe... if the situation called for it, but never Jask. Their friendship had lasted through thick and thin, and Johnny knew that Jask was the one person he'd never really be able to compete with. So why, then, did everything seem so upside down?

He'd hoped that a few days away from Jask and Vince would allow Drazan to breathe and relax, but it seemed the opposite was happening. Each day, Drazan left the house less and less, and Johnny began to wonder if he had a job at all anymore. Any time he would ask, Drazan blew him off. "You're more important," he'd say. "They understand what we're dealing with." But how could "they" understand when Johnny himself didn't?

On the fifth day, Jask called. The look of suspicion on Drazan's face as Johnny answered and left the room made the hair on the back of his neck stand up, so he kept his voice down as he said, "Hello?"

"Hey, J. Just checkin' in, do you need anything?"

Define "anything," he thought. "Nah, we're just taking it easy for a while. It's good to be back... I think."

"You think? Johnny, if something is wrong—"

"No," Johnny said quickly. "Drazan's just a little overprotective right now. It's like he thinks I'll drop dead again if I leave his sight."

Jask paused, but Johnny got the sense that he relaxed. "I don't blame him. If something happened to Vince, I'd find a way to permanently handcuff him to me."

"I'm sure he'd like that," Johnny joked. "Maybe you could make that part of your honeymoon."

Drazan's voice echoed down the hall and drowned out Jask's response: "Johnny!"

"Shit," he whispered quickly. "Sorry, Jask, I gotta go. Maybe we'll see you guys soon." He hung up and shoved the phone in his pocket before heading back out to Drazan with a soft smile. "Sorry. He was just checking in."

"It's none of his business," Drazan snapped, but Johnny noticed there was a weird tint in his eyes as he looked directly at him.

He took a step back, holding up his hands in defense. "He was just worried, Draz. It's okay. I'm off the phone, it's just you and me."

Drazan's shoulders slumped a little, but his breathing was still heavy, and that weird color faded from his irises after several blinks. "Yeah, okay. You're right, I'm sorry. I just... tried for—"

"So long to get me back, I know," Johnny finished for him. As strange as it all seemed, he knew the lengths they *all* went to in order to get him back, and it had him softening as he walked over to climb in Drazan's lap. His usually cool skin was warm to the touch and concerned replaced anything else on Johnny's face. "Are you okay?"

"Yeah. Just a little worked up I think, I'll be alright." Their lips met briefly as Drazan wrapped his arms around his waist. "I'm sorry I've been so high strung lately. It just makes me crazy to think about losing you again."

The words had been said so many times over the last few days that they seemed to have lost all meaning to Johnny.

He knew what they meant, knew what they implied — and yet, they hardly seemed to be real words at all anymore. "I know. Let's just go get some breakfast and maybe watch some movies today?" he asked hopefully.

"How about we order in?" Drazan countered. "There's a diner not too far from here that delivers, and they have amazing pancakes."

Why they needed delivery when they had two cars and the diner was truthfully close enough to walk to, Johnny didn't know, but he nodded all the same. It was just easier than arguing. "Sounds good to me. Why don't you order, and I'll go take a shower?"

"Or I'll order really quick, and we'll shower together."

This time, it wasn't a question or a suggestion, it was a correction. Not one part of Johnny minded showering with Drazan, particularly because they hadn't had sex once since Johnny had been back — but it was becoming increasingly clear that things were going to go the way Drazan wanted them to, or they weren't going to go at all. It wasn't something that he remembered from before he died, he'd always known Drazan to be easygoing and good-natured. Whatever this was, whatever he is now, on this side of all the trauma he'd endured... he wasn't the Drazan Johnny knew.

He may be alive again, but one thing was clear: the recovery process was just beginning... for all of them.

JASKIAN

Two weeks after Johnny's resurrection, tensions were high — particularly with Vince. He hadn't seen his best friend at all since that first day and it was showing, and Jask was running out of ways to defend Drazan and Johnny. Sure, some alone time between the two was to be expected, but this? No visits and barely a word in weeks? It was fishy and Jask knew it.

"Okay, okay. I'll call D and see if they'll come to dinner or something," Jask said, finally convinced from all of Vince's nagging. "Give me a few."

He left the room for no particular reason and dialed Drazan, but he had to try three times before the call was answered.

"What?" Drazan snapped. "I'm busy."

"Doing what, exactly? Ignoring us?" Jask couldn't keep the irritation from his voice but he also didn't try very hard. "We wanna see you guys. Both of you."

"Get in line."

Jask's eyebrows shot up at the tone. "Pardon? I've been in line for two damn weeks. Get your asses over here for dinner tonight or I'm gonna send my mom over there to get you. *And* I'll make sure to tell her you aren't letting Johnny eat enough food."

"Ahh hell, Jask. That's just low." Surprise overtook the previous edge in Drazan's voice. "Fine, we'll be over tonight, but we're only staying long enough to eat. I don't like being out after dark."

It was such a strange thing for Drazan to say that Jask was

rendered speechless. The line disconnected as Drazan took advantage of his temporary stupor, and as Jask walked back to Vince, his mind was whirling.

"Well?" Vince prompted. "What did he say?"

"They're coming tonight," he said slowly. "But have you ever known Drazan to be afraid of the dark? That's weird, right? I mean, all the bars we used to go to, the fights, and hell, half the time we'd investigate at night too. It was easier to sneak around the Dreadlands when it was dark. He was never scared before."

Vince squinted. "Everything about Drazan is fucking weird."

"Yeah, fine, but... Cidos is *dead*. He knows this. Athar's dead, now Damian too. Everyone that could conceivably pose a threat to Johnny is gone, so what's he so afraid of? Us? Like after everything we're somehow going to turn around and put him back in that grave? It just doesn't make sense."

"I'm the last person to ask about Drazan's odd behavior." Vince shrugged. "And are you sure tonight works? Lee and Ed are coming, I thought. Already got the lasagna ready to go."

Jask considered that for a moment. "We'll make it work. I'd rather have Edis around for backup anyway, and I'm afraid if we schedule out, they'll just bail. Did you make enough?"

"Of course I did. I always do." The look on Vince's face made it clear he wanted to say more but he went into the kitchen to put dinner in the oven.

Sighing, Jask ran upstairs to shower and contemplated the implications to having a house full of people. He still wasn't feeling like his old self, but things had gotten markedly better since Johnny had been brought back... so why did he still feel so uneasy?

The feeling didn't dissipate as he got dressed and greeted his brother, and when Johnny and Drazan finally pulled in, Jask snapped his fingers to get Edis' attention. "Hey, I've just got a bad feeling about this I can't shake. You should have Lee take Arro home."

"What?" Edis asked. "She's gonna be pissed, she was looking forward to Vince's lasagna."

"Tell her I'll have him make her a batch just for herself, and she can take some with her now. I just don't trust Drazan at the moment. Something's off, and I'd prefer my nephew not be around if shit hits the fan."

Ed looked like he was going to argue, but concern for his son won out. "Right. Stall them, I'll take them out the side door."

"Got it. Just hurry up, okay? Drazan's suspicious as all hell these days." Jask stepped out onto the porch to greet Drazan and Johnny and made small talk until he heard the side door shut. "Come on in."

The kitchen smelled amazing as they all filed in, but when Jask reached out to take Johnny's jacket, Drazan swatted his hand away. "I'll do it."

"For fuck's sake, Drazan. It's a coat, not his v-card." Jask laughed it off but shot Vince a "what the hell" glance as he busied himself setting the table.

Vince caught the look and frowned back, shaking his head in confusion. He turned to Johnny with a smile. "Hey, come help me get the beers and food?"

"Of course," Johnny replied, but Drazan grabbed his arm

and tried to stop him from moving. They shared a hushed conversation that Jask couldn't quite hear before Draz finally let him go, and Johnny smiled apologetically as he made his way over to help. "What can I do?"

"Come on, I'll show you while these two catch up." Johnny followed Vince further into the kitchen and Jask could hear the sounds of the fridge and oven opening but his eyes were on Drazan. The other angel watched the entrance to the kitchen like a hawk and Jask could tell he was barely restraining himself from following.

Jask kept a respectable distance on the other side of the dining room table and said quietly, "He's not going anywhere, D. I promise. He loves you; we love you. No one's gonna take him from you again."

"You don't know that, Jask. You can't know that. If I'm not there *anything* can happen." He stepped forward, his intent clear.

"Look, it's just a kitchen. He's a demon. Nothing in that kitchen can kill him unless the microwave comes alive and strangles him, and that's not gonna happen. You know it's not." Jask braced himself for a fight but kept pushing. "Relax. If there's one place in the entire world that Johnny's safe, it's right here. Ed will be back in a second and that'll be four powerful people in this house hellbent on protecting Johnny. You can relax."

A whirlwind of emotions crossed Drazan's face but slowly — slowly Jask thought he might be imagining it — Drazan's body relaxed. "I hope you're right."

Vince and Johnny came back into the dining room with

Ed following, carrying food and beverages. Vince raised an eyebrow at Jask. "Everything good?"

"Yep." Jask moved and clapped a hand on Drazan's shoulder. "We're good. Right, D?"

"Yeah." Drazan sat down and pulled his chair in, but there was something... twitchy about him. Jask was ready to burst out of his skin with the urge to hurl questions at Drazan until he figured out what was going on, but he was honestly so happy that Drazan seemed to be backing down that he didn't want to ruin it.

Vince sat the lasagna and bread on the table as Johnny handed out the beers. When he finished, Draz immediately pulled him down into the chair next to him. He maneuvered until they were as close as physically possible, relaxing a little further.

"So," Edis tapped the table as he sat down, "How have you two... been? Haven't seen you in a while."

Drazan stared blankly at him like he was daring him to comment further on that particular fact, but Johnny steered the conversation to safe waters. "It's been really good. I can't say I really missed anyone while I was dead, since I was... dead, but I won't complain about getting to spend so much extra time with Draz."

He smiled softly and squeezed Drazan's leg under the table, just in Jask's view. Jask grabbed some food and decided enough was enough — the repetition was starting to kill him. "Okay. Can we talk about something... anything else? No offense, J... but we know all that. I feel like I get stuck in a loop talking to you guys these days. What have you done for fun?

Movie theater, hiking... what's it like having someone else's essence inside of you?"

Johnny shook his head, "We haven't really done any of that. Mostly just stay at home. As for the essence, it's... well, I'm adjusting."

"Adjusting?" Vince frowned, leaning forward a little. "Is something wrong?"

"No no," Johnny said quickly, glancing at Drazan as he stiffened next to him. "Nothing's wrong. It's just weird, ya know? I can feel it's not really me, but it's already a ton better than it was the first couple of days."

Ed took a sip of his beer and tipped the bottom of the bottle toward him. "I can talk to my mom and Amaranth. There might be a spell or something we can look at to help you adjust. I'm not hopeful since this isn't something that's probably ever happened before, but still. Worth a look if it's bugging you."

Johnny spared another glance at Drazan before nodding. "Yeah, every little bit would help."

"Getting out of your house may help too," Vince suggested, smiling a little. "I could probably get you hired on the crew. It'll be like old times."

Drazan's palm slammed down on the table hard enough to knock two of the beer bottles over. "Enough!" he yelled, standing up and hauling Johnny to his feet. "No one is taking him out of my house, and no one is coming *near* him with magic. I knew it was a mistake to come here."

"Wait—" Jask stood to try and stop them, but Johnny shook his head quickly as Drazan dragged him toward the door. "Drazan! It's not —"

Slam.

The silence that filled the room after the sound of that door shutting dissipated made Jask shiver. He wasn't exactly sure what he expected to happen here, but that wasn't it.

That *definitely* wasn't it.

XII

VINCE

Vince tossed his phone on the bedside table after confirming with his boss that the monsoon outside meant no work for him. He rolled closer to Jask and wrapped his arms around him, and the angel let out a sleepy grumble but settled into the embrace with no further complaints. If he remembered Jask's schedule correctly, neither of them would be working today. They could get some finishing touches done on the wedding and check on Johnny and Draz. After the dinner incident a few days ago, things still felt tense.

He sank back into the mattress, fully intending to sleep in. He'd just drifted off again when a banging on the door caused him to jerk awake. Lee's shrill screaming of his name forced his body into motion before his mind caught up, and seconds later he opened the door. The hinges ripped from the frame, but his focus remained entirely on his sister. Leota stood on his porch, drenched from the short trip across the cul-de-sac but the thing that froze his heart was the sight of the one-year-old in his sister's arms: Arro's clothes were saturated in blood. Vince took him from Lee immediately and checked for injuries. He didn't wait for his sister to follow as he took the stairs three at a time, yelling for Jask.

"Vince, he's not hurt! I checked!" Lee burst into the bedroom behind him, watching as Vince handed the baby to a now wide-awake Jask.

"What do you mean he's not hurt? Where the hell is the blood from?" Vince turned to face her.

"I don't know what happened! Edis left for work like usual and I made breakfast for Arro. I went upstairs to wake him and there was a *heart*, Vince. A still beating, warm heart in the crib with my baby!" Tears welled in her eyes and Vince hugged her, looking over to Jask and Arro. He needed to know his nephew really wasn't hurt.

Jask's hands were glowing with the evidence of his grace as he siphoned the blood from Arro's clothes, and after another tense moment, Jask shook his head. "He's unharmed. The blood is from a pig, near as I can tell... but that particular sense hasn't been exercised in a long time." He cooed and made a funny face at Arro to get him to laugh but held him close. "Obviously, someone was in his nursery, which means your house isn't safe. You guys should stay with us until we figure things out."

"Did they leave a note? Anything at all that you can think of?" Vince led Lee to his side of the bed and made her sit. She shook her head and reached out to touch Arro with a trembling hand. Vince glanced over to Jask. "I'm going to go look. You'll stay with them?"

"Of course." Jask let his wings out and wrapped the edge of one around Lee to comfort her, then curled the other in front of him to shield Arro. "Go, Vin. Let me know if you find any-thing."

Without a moment's hesitation, Vince tugged on Jask's power and teleported himself into Lee's home. He stumbled a little on the landing — he wasn't an expert, yet — but stead-ied himself quickly and ran upstairs to the nursery. The heart lay exactly where Leota said it would be. Vince reached in and touched it with a finger, confirming the warmth of a recently living creature. At least the beating stopped.

He left the room and searched the house from top to bot-tom with no sign of an intruder. After stripping the crib and tossing the bloodied blankets to be dealt with later, he grabbed Lee's phone from the kitchen. One last search and he ran back home through the rain.

Vince checked all the locks downstairs before rejoining everyone. "You should probably call Edis." He held Lee's phone out to her. She accepted and stepped into the hall, leav-ing Vince with Jask and Arro.

"Nothing. No trace of anything." Vince sat by Jask on the bed.

"That's not possible, Vin. Everything and everyone leaves a trace, you just have to find it." He leaned forward, bracing his elbows on his knees. "Did Damian have a right hand?"

"Yeah, but Alnaess murdered him. Damian told me that right before—" he waved a hand. Jask knew what happened after.

Jask just blinked. "Who the hell is Alnaess?"

"What do you mean, who is she? I told you-" Vince stopped and thought really hard back over the last few months. The occasion to tell Jask about the witch he'd essentially used and betrayed never seemed to present itself. "Oh."

"Oh?" Jask stood, suddenly looking a little mad and a lot concerned. "Speak, Vin."

Vince scooped Arro up off the bed and held him close. Jask would never do anything to hurt their nephew and Vince wasn't above using that to his advantage. "You were missing! No one would listen to me when I said it wasn't intentional. I needed help and Damian knew a witch." He shrugged like that ended the story, knowing full well Jask wouldn't buy it.

"He knew a witch that turned around and killed his second in command?" Jask asked skeptically. "I figured you'd know better than to mess with magic, Vin."

"I didn't have a choice, Jask! I didn't know where you were and when I left her everything was fine."

Lee chose that moment to come and take his baby shield from him. "Ed's coming home. I'm going to wait downstairs so you two can... talk." She closed the door behind her as Vince turned back to Jask.

"Alnaess found you and then went to live her life. I thought that would be the end of it."

Jask ran a hand over his face and huffed a bitter laugh. "It's never the end of it with witches, Vin. But we gotta look at the possibility that this was Zaepris."

"Oh, good. Another witchy psycho bitch." Vince laid back on the bed to stare at the ceiling. "If it *is* her, we should warn Draz. Although I shudder to think what will happen. Johnny might end up in a fortified tower."

Power sparked at Jask's fingertips. "No," he said firmly. "I — *we* — have gone through too much to let anyone screw it up for us. If Zaepris is crossing the line, I'll deal with her. Can you think of any reason Alnaess would wanna put a beating heart in your nephew's crib? Does *Lee* have any old enemies I don't know about?"

Vince refused to look at Jask as he answered the first part of his question. "Can I think of a reason she may be upset? Absolutely." He rushed forward with the second answer, "And no, I doubt Lee has enemies. Edis might."

"I mean, maybe." Jask pinched his brows together. "He and Cidos did some messed up things at the firm, so it's possible one of them wants revenge."

"Okay, so maybe it's one of them?" Vince stopped as he heard voices. "Sounds like he's here now. Should we ask?"

Nodding, Jask started heading that way. "We're gonna have to split up and check out every possibility. Lee and Arro will just have to stay with our moms or something... or maybe I can have Barlo come stay with them."

Vince sat up and frowned. "Yeah, Barlo would work but why split up? We can check it all out together."

"Do you really want to waste that much time? Apparently, we need to look into Alnaess, Zaepris, and virtually every case Edis has ever taken," Jask argued. "It could take weeks... months, even. We don't have that kinda time if someone is dropping pig hearts in Arro's crib. Barlo's a good guy, we might not have worked together very long but I'm a Veris. He can't lie to me."

"Yeah, fine. But this fucking sucks." Vince followed Jask out of the room and downstairs. Ed held both Lee and Arro, talking to them quietly.

Jask cleared his throat quietly and stepped in to take Arro

from Lee. His body visibly relaxed like part of him believed he was the only person on the planet that could actually protect the little guy. "Ed, I need you to make a list of all the cases you've taken that involve magic or particularly spiteful demons or witches. We both know you never prosecuted a single angel, so they're out anyway."

"You think this is my fault?"

"No," he countered. "This isn't anyone's fault but the person that did it. We just have to figure out who it is and what they want."

"What do we do in the meantime?" Lee asked, stepping into Edis' arms.

"Jask is going to have a friend come stay with you. We were thinking it'd be best if you, Ma, and Astarte stayed together while we looked into this," Vince answered.

For once, Leota didn't argue or try to pretend she had a better idea, which was a mark of how nervous she was for Arro — but also of how much she'd grown in the last couple of years. Jask handed Arro back over and excused himself before disappearing entirely to go get Barlo, and Ed took a deep breath. "Okay, I'll start making the list. It's going to take a while."

"I'm probably going to get eaten by a vindictive crocodile, so we all have our burdens to bear, Eddie." Vince clapped him on the shoulder.

"I'm sorry, what?" Lee demanded.

"Long story short, there's a witch with a giant pet crocodile. I promised the witch I'd do a thing for her and then didn't actually do the thing so now I have to go find out if this is all my fault. Let's not tell Jask any of that, he knows enough of the story." Vince turned to go change into something better than pajamas to find Jask standing behind him, Barlo by his side. "Hey. You got back *really* quickly."

Jask's eyebrows shot up. "Were you expecting me to go slow? We have work to do, Vin." He introduced Barlo to the group and pulled Vince to the side, lowering his voice. "I can't believe I'm about to say this... but we should probably make sure it wasn't Drazan."

"As much as it pains me to defend him, I don't think Draz would do this. Not to Arro." Vince looked over at their little family. Chasing all the leads is what would keep them safe. "We can still check with him though. Just to make sure."

"I'm just saying I'm not going to blindly cross off any option." Jask rubbed his jaw and nodded to Barlo as he led Leota and Arro to the living room and waited for Ed to join him and Vince before continuing. "Let's split up. I'll check with Zaepris and Drazan, Ed... you deal with the top two most likely suspects on your list, and Vin... don't get eaten by any crocodiles, okay? It's good to know I can bring you back to life if you do, but I promise you... that lizard will be the least of your concerns if that happens. Do you understand?"

Vince did not miss the very real threat in Jask's voice. He swallowed once before answering with a nod, "Yes, Sir. Reading you loud and clear."

"Good boy." Jask lightly tapped Vince's jaw and leaned in to kiss him, cupping his chin to hold him in place until he had his fill.

Vince wouldn't be the one to ever break the kiss. He leaned into Jask's hold until Edis cleared his throat. "I thought we were in a hurry?"

"We are," Jask growled, his lips barely leaving Vince's. He flicked his eyes toward his brother. "You have more work to do than any of us, why are you still standing here?" Ed threw his hands up and left the room, and Jask kissed Vince one more time. "He's not wrong."

Vince stepped away before the temptation to kiss Jask again took over his senses. "Go check your leads and I'll do mine. We'll be back home in time for dinner." He flashed a charming smile and ran out into the rain to his truck. Seconds later he drove toward the closest swamp in the area — praying with everything in him that Alnaess wouldn't be there.

JASKIAN

Jask took a deep breath as he knocked on Zaepris' door. He didn't want to be back there — didn't want to see her, didn't want to talk to her — and definitely didn't want to deal with the smell of death that smacked him in the face when she opened the door. "Grief, Zae... haven't you heard of incense? What the hell do you have in there?"

"That's none of your concern, half-wit." She stood her ground and crossed her arms over her chest, seemingly having no intention of letting him in.

"It's my business if the dead thing happens to be a pig," Jask explained. "Particularly if said dead pig is missing a red, beating organ."

She scoffed and stepped aside. "It's not a pig, though don't think I don't know about your little issue."

"And how on earth would you know about it if you're not the one that did it?" He stepped in, pushing past her to go see for himself. "Seems fishy at best."

"It *is* fishy. It's a dolphin, actually. The poor thing got tangled in some fishing gear and dragged just far enough out of the water that he died. I was trying to see if I could bring him back."

Sure enough, when Jask entered a back room and saw the source of the smell, he found a very dead dolphin laying on a table with a giant tank next to it. "Okay, stupid question. How you gonna get the dolphin into the tank?"

"I think half-wit might've been generous," she deadpanned. "What are you doing here, Jaskian?"

"Came to make sure you were okay, for starters. I'm sorry about knocking you out."

A sly, knowing smile creeped across her face. "No, you're not. Next?"

"Someone's been messing with... someone I care about. You say you know... do you know who it is?"

"Nope. But the kind of magic it takes to keep a heart beating after it's been cut from a body? That I *do* know about, and only three people have come to me for that sort of a spell in the last few months. A warlock that lives across the world, an angel teenager rebelling against controlling parents, and a certain witch that used to work for your beloved's boss," she adds.

"Alnaess?"

Zaepris nodded. "Yep, and she also asked for a few other items. Would you like to know what they are?"

"What kinda question is that? Yes!" Jask urged, stepping away from the dolphin and back toward the necromancer. "Tell me."

She hummed, tapping her chin with her finger. "I'll do you one better. I'll get you a location and a general idea of what she's going to do with those items... but it'll cost you."

"Cost me? What do you want?"

"I don't know yet. A favor like this doesn't come around too often. Come back and see me tomorrow, I'll have thought of *something* by then." Zaepris waved toward the door to shoo him out, and Jask knew better than to argue. Chances were good he wouldn't need her, anyway — he had what he needed now.

The minute he made it outside again, he teleported straight to Vince. "It's Alnaess with a little splash of help from everyone's favorite necromancer. Zaepris provided the spell to keep the heart beating afterward, but Alnaess is the one that cast it."

It wasn't until he got the words out that he realized Vince was actually, legitimately wrestling with a crocodile right in front of him. The sight was so insane that for an agonizing second, Jask couldn't do anything but stare as his brain, eyes and body tried to get back on the same page. Finally, he reached out with his grace and made the crocodile freeze. "Why didn't you just come the other way, Vin?"

"The other way," Vince gasped as he relaxed into the water, sarcasm fairly evident. "Why didn't I think of that?"

Jask shrugged, toeing some muck out of the way and making a face at it. "I don't know. But I don't think she's here, anyway. I don't feel that.... *crackle*," he explained. "There's no magic here unless she's somehow hidden it."

"So, I tangled with Betty again for nothing. Neat." Vince dragged himself out of the water and held his arms out, the swamp water and mud dripping off of him. "No hug for your beloved?"

He shook his head and pinched the bridge of his nose. "You smell worse than the dolphin."

"Than the what? Never mind, I'm sure I don't want to know. We should search the swamp anyway. Just in case." Vince looked sadly at his hat before ringing the water out of it and leading the way further into the swamp.

Jask kept staring back at where the crocodile was floating uselessly. "Did you say that thing's name was Betty?"

"Yep. She's never really liked me. Thought I could sweet talk her this time but it didn't work," Vince answered easily.

The thought was hilarious. "No, seriously, *please* tell me how you attempted to sweet talk the giant, feral crocodile."

"First of all, she's not feral. Just moody." Vince pointed out. "And second, I brought her a rabbit. Turns out she just wanted demon for lunch instead. Who could blame her, though? I'm delicious."

Jask laughed and then quieted down as they neared the center. "You are delicious," he whispers. "But she's not allowed to have you, so... I'll have a little chat with her on the way out."

"Don't hurt her," Vince pleaded. "Not her fault she was raised by a witch." Vince's voice matched Jask's in volume as he inspected their surroundings.

"I didn't say I was gonna hurt her," he hissed. "Just set some ground rules." He snuck up a little further and rounded the side of the single cottage, then took a deep breath and peeked in the window. "Looks dark."

"I could light it up?" Vince held up a hand, a little flame dancing happily in his palm.

"Are you trying to set it on fire? Cause I don't think that's smart, though it might send the message that she needs to leave us alone."

"I'm confused. Does that mean yes or no?" Vince extinguished the flame either way. He stepped to the front of the house and gently pushed the door open, and Jask followed with a shake of his head.

It was clear instantly that there was no one around, nor had there been for a while. Jask squinted and lifted up one of the dusty sheets covering a couch and let it go with a sigh. "I don't know why her lizard is here, cause she isn't. Guess we're back to square one."

"Distraction, maybe? Or maybe she thought I'd actually get eaten this time." Vince walked through the house, poking things he probably shouldn't be.

Jask sighed. "Yeah, maybe. Whatever. Let's just go."

~

There wasn't anything to be done about Alnaess at the moment. She'd hidden herself thoroughly and cut off all existing contacts, but Jask didn't do well with inaction. Especially when there were still other issues, other things needing his attention. Not seeing any other options, Jask decided the best thing he could do for Drazan was get him out of his own head.

He showed up on Drazan's doorstep and wouldn't take no for an answer until he finally agreed to come out for a drink — which, Jask promised it would only be one, but he had no intentions of returning Drazan until he was good and drunk and Jask had a chance to see what was really going on with him.

They ended up at a bar just outside of town that was small enough they wouldn't be bothered but also nice enough that it stocked Drazan's preferred brand of scotch. Jask took that as a winning combo and sat down at the small bar, tugging a reluctant Draz down by the sleeve of his shirt. "Sit, damnit."

"I shouldn't be here, Jaskian. I don't *want* to be here, I want to be at home with Johnny," Drazan snapped, wrenching out of Jask's grip but sitting down all the same. It helped that Jask threatened to send Johnny to a deserted island somewhere if Drazan didn't give him one night. "This is ridiculous."

"A lot of things are ridiculous, Draz. Vince's purple velvet suit. My hair in the mornings. The price some places charge for coffee." He waved the bartender down and ordered a round. "Vince wrestling a crocodile and almost *not* winning. The face Arro makes when he drops a diaper bomb. Those things are ridiculous," he explained. "Wanting to spend time with my best friend — who owes me fucking *big* time, by the way — isn't ridiculous."

Drazan's eyes softened. "Johnny's eyes are ridiculous. Have you seen them? Like swirling, dark pits of—"

"Excuse me?" Jask laughed, shoving a drink in Drazan's hand and helping him raise it to his lips. "You realize that didn't sound like a compliment, right?"

"It is," he argued. "Your eyes are freaky-looking. At least Johnny's have a little bit of depth."

Jask laid a hand over his own heart with a look of mock offense. "How dare you. Does this mean you don't love me anymore?"

"That would require I ever loved you in the first place," Drazan said defensively, but the lie bled through and Jask laughed it off.

"Just drink. You're irritating when you're sober."

Drazan rolled his eyes but drank anyway, and the taste of the scotch left him visibly satisfied. Jask instantly called for another round and glanced over at the jukebox, manipulating it from afar to put on something a little more upbeat. When he found his mark, he clapped Drazan's shoulder. "Get up, let's dance! Like old times. Come on."

"No," Drazan said quickly. "I don't want to. *You* do it."

Though that response wasn't out of the norm, Jask wasn't about to give up that easily. He yanked Drazan off the barstool and spun him around, nearly knocking over the table closest to them and sending Drazan off balance. Draz stumbled, standing up with anger flashing in his eyes — but Jask simply grinned widely and did it again, spinning him until they were both dizzy and tripping over their own feet.

"Fucking *stop*, Jask!" Drazan yelled, but there was a hint of laughter this time. Just a pinch of the Drazan he knew before all this... but a pinch was enough.

He climbed up on the nearest upright table and waved a hand toward the jukebox to turn the music up, then rolled his hips and slapped his thigh, trying to make Drazan laugh a little harder. All he really did was draw the attention of the other patrons, but he didn't pay them any mind. He had his sights set firmly on the best friend he was desperate to get back.

"Come on." Jask held out a hand with a smile and *whooped* triumphantly as Drazan took it, then pulled him up to join him. "See, I knew you could still have fun."

"I'm only doing this because Johnny likes to dance," he said firmly, and not a trace of a lie tingled Jask's bones. This wasn't about him, or their friendship, or anything at all other than Johnny... just like everything else.

Disappointed flooded Jask's system but he refused to quit. He danced with Draz on that table until the wood was threatening to split, and the bartender was yelling at them to get down, but the shift effectively killed whatever progress they made, and Drazan wouldn't budge after that.

The fun was over. It was time to go home.

XIII

Johnny gently grabbed Drazan's arm and stepped in front of him to get his attention. "It's not that I don't like this house, Draz. But it's so far away from everyone else, and it's... dark. There are hardly any windows at all, I feel like I'm back in that coffin."

Regret immediately flooded Johnny as Drazan jerked like he'd been slapped. "John... I'm sorry. I didn't mean... didn't want it to feel like that," he said quietly.

"I know." He leaned in, placing a gentle kiss to Drazan's pouty lips. "I didn't get a chance to say thank you for bringing me back, but I really am grateful. For that, and for you keeping me safe since then. But we can't stay locked in here forever. We both need to go back to work, and I need light. I'm sorry."

Drazan nodded dumbly and refused to make eye contact as he skirted around Johnny. "If that's how you really feel, why don't you just leave and go live with Vince?"

"Really? You know that's not what I want," Johnny argued, a little more forcefully this time. "I want to be with you, but just... not here. We can sell this place and buy something closer, something with more windows. Maybe with a kitchen that faces east so I can watch the sunrise as I make —" He stopped, realizing exactly how cheesy and ridiculous that was starting to sound. "I don't want anyone but you, Draz. I'm sorry if I've made you feel differently."

He knew that continuing the fight would be foolish, so instead of lingering, he left Drazan in the living room and went upstairs to the spare bedroom. It was the only room of the whole house with a large window, and he'd sat in front of it on more than one occasion wondering if he'd get away with sneaking out.

Johnny hadn't been lying when he'd told Drazan he didn't want anyone else. But if he were telling the *whole* truth, he'd also have admitted that right now, like this? He didn't particularly want Drazan, either. This wasn't healthy and he knew it — which, by demon standards, was saying something. They were notorious for questionable morals and broken personal relationships, but something about seeing Leota with Edis reminded him that it *was* possible... especially since he'd had it once with Drazan, too. He just had to find a way to get it back.

A couple of hours passed in silence as Johnny stared out that window. The essence they'd stolen from Damian was finally integrating and becoming less foreign to him, but occasionally, he'd still get flashes of anger or the sudden urge to go find Vince and kill him. Obviously, Johnny himself didn't want to do that, and up until now he's been able to fight it off. But his own experience was raising red flags in his mind about Drazan. He wasn't acting the way Johnny remembered, the way Johnny loved. But why? What happened to change him so drastically?

The problem was that Johnny didn't know. Sure, Vince and the others had filled him in on what happened after he'd died, but he knew there were details missing. Either things they didn't want to talk about or simply didn't remember themselves, but either way, it left him with an incomplete picture. He assumed that if it was just the trauma of losing him that caused Drazan to change, he'd be better now. But the opposite seems to be occurring and there doesn't seem to be anything Johnny can do to get through to Drazan when he gets in these moods, which is nearly every day now.

Eventually, hunger overtook Johnny's desire for peace, and he made his way back downstairs. Drazan was still in the exact same spot he'd been when Johnny had walked away — a pained, concerned look on his face that barely dissipated when Johnny came into full view. "Draz?" Johnny asked slowly, starting to wonder if Drazan was possessed.

"You... you went upstairs."

Johnny blinked and nodded as he moved into the kitchen to make food for them both. "Yes, because this house has an upstairs. Why does that matter?"

"Why does that — Johnny, you could've gotten hurt! Fallen out of the window, been taken from me, gotten electrocuted. The wiring up there might be faulty," Drazan insisted.

That was enough to make Johnny back up a step. "Why are you so paranoid? Draz, I'm okay. I'm here. But unless you loosen up a little, I won't be anymore."

"What does that mean?" Drazan asked sharply, that weird glint in his eyes again. "Are you threatening to leave me?"

Every survival instinct Johnny had left told him to say no, to placate Drazan until his mood shifted again, or in the absence of that, until he could get away safely. But this was Drazan, and the very idea that he'd hurt Johnny was laughable — or should've been, anyway. "Yes, I am," he said firmly. "I love you, but this —" he gestured to the room around them — "this isn't love, and you have to know that."

"Yo-" Drazan clamped his jaw shut and clenched his fists at his sides, and for once, the house around them shook just as violently as it would for Jaskian. But just as abruptly as it began, it ceased completely, and Drazan fell to his knees with a deflated, muffled sob. "I'm sorry."

Confusion whirled in Johnny's mind as he took the olive branch and kneeled in front of him. "I know you've been through a lot, Draz. I know you have, and I know all of this is scary. But you have to trust me, okay? We can be happy and not be so... paranoid."

The word once again caused something strange to happen in Drazan's expression, but no anger followed. He nodded, reaching out to take one of Johnny's hands. "You're right. I'll try to be better. We'll get a new house and start going to see the others more often. I still don't want you to have a job yet, but... I'll try. Just please don't leave, I worked too hard to get you back."

It seemed strange to hear that be the reason Drazan didn't want him to leave, but nothing about this seemed right. Nothing about *Drazan* seemed right, and Johnny knew he couldn't be the only one that recognized that. He decided to talk to Jask the next time he was allowed to see him, and for now, he opted to take what he could get while he could get it. "Thank you. I actually have a house in mind already... we passed it the last time we went to Vince's. Can we go look at it?"

A violent shudder ran through Drazan like he was fighting some internal battle with himself and losing, but he dipped his head. "Yes. Come on."

Johnny smiled softly as he helped Drazan to his feet and grabbed his keys. He had a sneaking suspicion that he didn't have a lot of time before Drazan flipped out again, but he had every intention of making the most of the time he did have — and maybe, just maybe... he could help Drazan get back to normal.

VINCE

All around them, nothing seemed to be going right. They'd brought Johnny back only to hardly see him. They couldn't find the witch and her little stunts were worse every day. Jask couldn't get through to Draz and Vince couldn't stop worrying about his family. The stress weighed heavily on them all and Vince didn't know what to do to fix it.

He decided to double his efforts on the things he could control, mainly work and the wedding. Late nights getting the decorations and catering set up again. He decided against any type of cake after a snide remark made by Drazan the last time he'd deigned to allow them over. They still possessed a lot of the materials from the first failed attempt, that helped.

The venue would be the same to save on cost and space. They owned it, might as well use it.

Vince rubbed his eyes and leaned back against the couch with a yawn. The clock on the mantel showed a later time than he realized, and he knew he needed to go to sleep. He closed the notebook he used and stood with a stretch. The relief as his bones popped and settled made him feel a little better. At least he accomplished something today. He quietly checked the doors and windows and climbed up the stairs. Jask retired to bed hours ago and for a moment Vince stood in the doorway and watched his fiancé sleep. If any one of them deserved peace, it was Jask.

He, Edis, and Vince kept watch in shifts over the family but Jask pushed harder than any of them. Always alert, always on his guard, always looking out for every single one of them. Jask continued to be the strongest, most admirable person Vince knew and he fell for him a little more every day.

A sound behind him caused him to turn, ready for a fight. Edis raised his hands sheepishly. "Only me. I'm here to wake Jask for his turn."

"Nah. Let him sleep. I'm already awake, I'll keep watch." Vince looked over his shoulder at the soundly sleeping angel.

"Are you sure? He might not be okay with that," Edis answered with uncertainty as Vince closed the door.

"Good thing you can blame it on me, then. Go back home, Ed. I got it." Vince shoved him gently away with a smile. He didn't miss the soft look in Ed's eyes as he teleported away. He'd be teased about this later but Jask needed rest and Vince didn't mind not sleeping.

He headed back down the stairs and into the kitchen.

The coffee maker gurgled and hissed as it made the caffeine he would live off of for the next few hours and he sat at the kitchen table, back door open so he could hear anything strange happening outside. The night passed quietly enough, and Vince prepared coffee and breakfast for when Jask woke up before going back to their bedroom to get showered and changed for work.

Jask came in when Vince was almost completely ready to go. "Hey. I take it everything went okay overnight? I'm sorry I overslept."

"Yeah, there weren't any problems. Did you sleep okay?" Vince finished buttoning up his shirt as he waited for an answer.

Nodding, Jask stepped in to kiss him. "I did. Thank you. You gonna be late tonight?"

"Shouldn't be. Need me home for something?" Vince thought over the last couple of weeks. Did he forget another family dinner?

"Nah," Jask said, pulling Vince in by the hips. "Just miss you... especially looking like this." He bit Vince's bottom lip and pulled it out slowly just to tease him, then moved away with a smile. "Hurry home."

"Now I don't want to go at all." Vince followed Jask, kissing him deeply before releasing him with a sigh. "Guess I should do the responsible thing, though."

Jask rolled his eyes dramatically but handed Vince his coffee mug and stepped aside. "Doesn't mean we have to be happy about it. I'll see you later."

"I'll be home right on time." He accepted the mug gratefully and drove to work with a smile.

Four hours into the workday and Vince almost regretted not getting at least a couple of hours of sleep. The sun beat down on them, making the day unusually hot for that time of year.

He finally finished breaking the rock that caused the dig to stop and he pulled himself out of the hole with a grunt. A quick hand signal to the backhoe operator meant business resumed as usual, so Vince made his way over to the cooler holding water for the crew and drank it in one long, satisfying swallow. He rested against the metal frame of the building they were currently working on and took a breath.

In a few hours, he would be back home and have Jask's cool hands on him. Based on Jask's words from this morning, he might be able to convince the angel to fuck him into their mattress. A new pair of panties were hidden in his drawer and waited to be modeled anyway, and they could both use a little stress relief.

A shout reminded him that he wasn't exactly alone enough to be entertaining those types of thoughts. A trickle of sweat ran down his lower back and Vince grabbed another bottle of water to dump over his head. He unbuttoned his now soaked shirt and dropped it by the cooler. Might as well be comfortable while getting through the rest of the day. Cat calls and whistles met him as he returned to the main work site, and he flicked every one of them off with a grin. "Yeah, yeah. Fucking animals."

For the next two hours, Vince focused on the physical aspect of his job, losing himself in the repetitive, familiar motions. The sounds and tasks blurred together as his sleep deprived mind ran on autopilot. During a lull in activity, he snuck away to one of the supply dumps and looked around for a good spot. Sitting against a pile of bricks, Vince got as comfortable as he could. One quick cat nap and he could go back to work. He allowed his eyes to slide closed and let the exhaustion take him.

"Vince! Look out!" someone yelled from across the way. He stood up quickly to twist around and look for the danger. A flash of green hair and a wicked smirk caught his attention before a concerning noise took all of his focus. The tower of bricks in front of him started to shake, and as Vince watched in horror, it began to cascade down right on top of him. His limbs were still slow from sleep, so Vince didn't make it far enough before the entire mountain of material buried him underneath it. His world faded to black — his last thoughts going to Jask and how disappointed he'd be if Vince didn't make it to dinner.

~

"Where is he?" Vince heard the muffled yell as he blinked open his eyes. Why couldn't he see anything? His brain worked on figuring out his predicament as he began to recognize the voices. Why was Jask asking where he was? Why didn't Vince know the answer to that question? Memories began to trickle back to him as he pushed against the heavy material covering him with a groan. Everything hurt, but he knew he needed to get out before he suffocated. He coughed as dust began to fall from his efforts. The yelling stopped abruptly and sunlight blinded Vince. He squinted against the sudden light and smiled when he saw Jask, looking like the avenging angel he absolutely loved. "Hey, you found me."

"Fucking hell, Vin." The bricks disappeared quickly as Jask fought to get him free, and with a pained grunt, Vince ended up in Jask's arms. "How the hell did this happen?"

"Alnaess." Vince leaned against Jask's body gratefully. "Fucking bitch tried to kill me."

Darkness shrouded Jask's normally bright eyes. "Then she just signed her own death warrant. Good for her."

"Good news, they'll probably let me go home early so I'll be home in time for dinner." Vince tried to give a thumbs up but realized most of his fingers seemed to be bent at an odd angle. "Ow."

Grimacing, Jask folded his hand over Vince's and healed them, then started meticulously checking him for injuries in front of the growing crowd of his coworkers. "Good, you in the mood for witch's stew?"

"That sounds like you're planning to cook Alnaess. I'll pass on that. Who knows where she's been?" Vince relaxed as he felt the wave of Jask's power go through him. "How'd you know what happened, anyway?"

"Your foreman called me, and I'm absolutely going to cook Alnaess, but we don't need to eat her. Cannibalism isn't my thing."

More of Jask's warm grace worked through his system until he was standing straight again, and Jask did such a thorough job that he wasn't even tired anymore. "You're a fucking miracle worker, sweetheart." Vince stretched his muscles and waved to his coworkers. "Let me get my shirt and talk to Kagan and I'll drive us home?"

Jask smirked slightly as he took in Vince's appearance. "Go talk to Kagan... but skip the shirt."

Vince saluted and found his boss in the crowd. After a quick, slightly dishonest discussion of Vince's emotional status — "I'm very shaken up, boss" — Vince returned to Jask with his shirt hanging from his front pocket. "Ready to go?"

"Yep. But can you drive back alone? I wanna go ahead and set some things up." Jask's eyes raked over Vince's frame, and the promise in them had Vince almost vibrating with need and anticipation.

"Yes. *Hell* yes. Go now." Vince didn't wait for an answer as he ran for his truck, keys already in hand.

JASKIAN

Once he had everything ready, Jask looked around and smiled at the spread he'd set up: sushi, a special bottle of bourbon he'd been saving for their honeymoon, and candles lining the counters and table. It was all set when he heard the roar of the truck engine getting closer, so Jask stripped down until he had on nothing at all but an apron and waited at the front door with a smile.

Vince jumped out of the truck almost before it stopped moving, still shirtless and grinning. He stopped halfway up the walk to take in the sight of Jask in only the apron. "Are you... is that all you're wearing?"

"I don't know. Come find out," he teased, ducking back inside and heading for the kitchen ahead of Vince. Instead of offering himself up like a prize pig, he hid — knowing Vince enjoyed the hunt almost as much as he did.

The door slammed closed a few seconds later and Jask could hear Vince's slow steps as he searched. "What's my prize when I find you, Jask?"

"What do you want?" Jask asked, but instantly teleported himself to another hiding spot so Vince wouldn't be able to find him by his voice.

"Earlier I wanted you to fuck me so hard I wouldn't be able to walk for a few days. Now? Kinda thinking the opposite," Vince admitted easily.

Jask grinned, knowing exactly what he meant but wanting to distract him. "You want me to take you so slow you barely feel it?"

"Cute. You act like I wouldn't like that just as much." The sound of doors opening and closing accompanied Vince's search. "No. This time I want you writhing under me and screaming my name."

It made him shudder, and he realized quickly that the apron wouldn't do a whole lot to hide an erection long enough for them to eat dinner. He jumped down from where he'd been perched on top of the china cabinet and landed softly behind Vince, then dusted himself off as he straightened up. "Then I suggest we eat. I also have an actual surprise for you that's related to but *isn't* actually my ass."

Vince turned and pulled Jask into his arms. He sneakily began to pull the ties of the apron loose. "You think I can focus on food right now?"

"No," he admitted. "But I can guarantee you the sex we're

about to have will be even better if we stop long enough to at least have a drink." He backpedaled slowly, then reached for the bottle of bourbon. "I had this bottled for our honeymoon, but... I think we deserve it now. It'll amplify... well, pretty much everything."

"Isn't that what alcohol normally does?" Vince looked over the bottle curiously.

"Yeah, but this is... different. You'll see. Try it," he urged, stepping in to take the bottle from him and open it up. He took a swig himself then held the bottle to Vince's lips. "Open, baby."

Vince obeyed immediately and a shiver worked its way down his body as he swallowed. "What is that?"

"Bourbon. Magic bourbon." Jask stole the bottle for another sip, then gently pulled Vince's chin down to feed him some more.

Vince accepted the offered amount and his eyes closed as his breathing picked up. Seconds later, he backed Jask up against the kitchen wall as a growl worked its way up from his chest. His hands and lips were everywhere they could reach, and even that felt so good that Jask tipped his head back and pulled their bodies flush for more.

"See? Not just regular alcohol," he rushed out, using his grace to disrobe them both. The heat from Vince's skin seeped into Jask's bones, and he spun them quickly as he caught Vince in a messy kiss.

Vince's hand gripped Jask's hair to deepen the kiss as his other slid between them. He wrapped his fingers around them both and stroked slowly, and Jask gasped quietly when it sent a wave of pleasure throughout his whole body.

"Vin..." Jask tugged against his grip and added his own hand to speed up, then pulled them both toward the dining room table. One distracted blink later and it was completely clear, so Jask sturdied it up and climbed on.

"Fuck, look at you," Vince breathed out. His eyes were glued to Jask as he settled and then Vince sank to his knees, swallowing Jask's cock down.

Nothing in Jask's memory had ever felt this incredible, and he slid forward, barely balancing on the edge of the table and driving himself deeper into Vince's mouth. "Vin... babe, I — if you're gonna fuck me, fuck me," he mumbles. "Not gonna last long."

Vince hummed around him and then pulled off with a pop. "Sorry. Got distracted, needed a taste..." He licked up Jask's length one more time before standing and positioning himself against Jask's waiting body. Jask knew the exact moment Vince felt his grace encompass them both by the filthy moan that came out of his mouth. Vince shifted his hips forward and slid into Jask, pulling Jask's legs over his arms and tugged him the rest of the way until no space remained between them.

Instantly, Jask knew he was wrong earlier — *this* was the best thing he'd ever felt. He reached down to stroke himself quickly as he rolled his hips, desperately moaning and trying to get Vince to move faster.

"Just... *fuck*..." the next sound out of Vince's mouth resembled nothing more than *nngh* and he tilted his upper body forward to pin Jask down. He placed his hands on either side of Jask and began to thrust hard and fast until the table was shaking more than Jask.

Sure enough, Jask felt his orgasm building twice as fast as normal, and he knew exactly what he wanted. "Vin... do it, now..."

Vince lifted up and placed a hand on Jask's chest, a lust pulse stronger than any before hit Jask right above his heart and he felt Vince fill him up seconds after.

It sent Jask over so powerfully that the windows shattered and every single one of those candles went out. He covered his bare stomach and wrapped his legs around Vince to hold him in place. "Don't move, we're not done."

"Yes, Sir," Vince answered and for once in his life, he obeyed completely. His eyes were the only part of him that moved as he surveyed the mess Jask made and waited for further instructions.

Jask smirked faintly as he scratched down Vince's chest. So many things ran through his mind in that moment, but one thing was clear: they wouldn't be getting to that sushi anytime soon.

XIV

VINCE

Vince hummed to himself as he cleaned up their dinner dishes and wiped down the table. He picked up the bottle of bourbon and placed it on the top shelf in the liquor cabinet, deciding that first thing tomorrow morning, he was going to go buy six more. He could hear the shower still running, which meant Jask wouldn't be down for a bit, so he took the time to get some extra blankets for the couch.

He was looking for a movie to watch when a knock sounded at the door. He dropped the remote on the table and opened it with a smile. "Yeah, we know the power — oh, hey Johnny. Thought you were Edis." He looked over his friend's shoulder. "Drazan isn't with you? Thought you two were glued permanently at the hip now."

"Yeah, about that." Johnny took his hat off and stepped inside, giving the driveway one more look before ducking out of view. "He let me come here, but it took forever to convince him."

Vince refrained from making his usual comments about something obviously being wrong with Draz. Johnny legitimately seemed upset, and Vince wanted to be supportive. "Alright, tell me what's been going on."

Johnny looked like he was about to launch into a story that would take the next six years to tell, but instead, he shook his head. "I would like to have two hours of my life that aren't revolving around Drazan, actually. Can I have a beer?"

"Absolutely." Vince stepped into the kitchen and grabbed one for them each and then pointed at the liquor cabinet he'd just closed. "If you're in the mood for something stronger, we also have whiskey and vodka. Hands off the bourbon, though."

"Why, is it old?" He opted for vodka and poured himself a glass just as Jask came down.

"No, it's magic."

"Kinky magic." Vince grinned as he made himself comfortable on the couch, leaving room for Jask. He motioned to the chair for Johnny. "Have a seat, relax."

Johnny looked like he got a few ideas from that bourbon but sat down and seemed to refocus. "So, how are you two? I feel like I haven't gotten to see you at all."

"You haven't," Jask said. "Is he at least gonna let you guys come to the wedding?"

Vince sat up a little straighter. "Of course, they're coming to the wedding." He looked over at Johnny and couldn't help but notice the look on his face. "Right?"

"We haven't actually talked much about it," Johnny answered with an apologetic smile.

"Well, fuck." Jask reached over to take Vince's hand. "No way we do this without you, Johnny."

"Yeah, actually, since you and Drazan are back I kind of hoped you'd both stand with us," Vince admitted. He'd kept that hope secret since the day Johnny came back, and now that he'd said it, he was worried it wouldn't get to happen at all.

Jask chuckled. "Edis will kill me if I revoke his best man status now, especially with the way Drazan's been acting. But yeah, it would be great if you could be up there with us."

Johnny looks genuinely pleased for the first time since his resurrection. "Not even getting killed by your almost-future brother-in-law could stop me from being there."

"Great." Vince relaxed back into Jask and pulled the blanket over them both. "Hey, Edis can stay the best man. We can make Draz the ring bearer." Vince waited for everyone to find him as hilarious as he found himself.

When no one did, Johnny cleared his throat. "I probably don't have much time. He's waiting for me, and I don't want to piss him off."

"You're not out screwing around, Johnny. You're with fr—"

The sound of shattering glass interrupted him and all three of them got quickly to their feet. The living room window was in pieces all over the floor for a second time that night, and in the middle of those pieces lay a bloody, black, feathered mass.

Jask held up a hand to keep Vince and Johnny from moving closer and used his grace instead to lift it off the ground. He squinted at it for a moment then grimaced. "Anyone order a headless crow?"

"Think that's a sign Alnaess is pissed her bricks didn't finish me off?" Vince guessed.

"Sounds like you've had an interesting few days." Johnny made a face at the carcass.

Jask matched his expression as he sent the crow somewhere else and started to mend the window. "I guess I better go back and see Zaepris. She said she can find her, and at this point, I don't see what choice we have."

"But not right now, yeah?" Vince pointed to the couch and the mountain of blankets that were perfect for cuddling.

Johnny shifted. "I actually agree with Vince. I don't get many opportunities to—"

"Yeah, yeah. I know." Jask rubbed the stubble on his chin and took his hair out of the tie just to put it right back up again, looking lost in thought. "That's a problem too, though. We just have... too many problems and not enough time or energy to deal with all of them."

"Well, they'll still be problems tomorrow. Come sit back down. Tonight, we're just going to focus on this." Vince got comfortable on the couch again and waited for Jask to join him.

It looked like Jask didn't want to — his muscles were tense, shoulders hunched slightly, face pained — but one more glance at Johnny had Jask settling down next to Vince and trying to relax. He took his hand and brought it to his lips to kiss his knuckles. "Okay. I'll go back to see her first thing tomorrow morning, then."

"Fantastic." Vince shifted until Jask leaned slightly in front of him and began to rub his shoulders. He cheated a little and sent just enough pleasure through his hands to relax Jask's muscles. "Now what were we talking about before we were interrupted?"

"The wedding," Johnny grinned. "I think you were offering me the spot of your best man. Can I wear my hat?"

Jask nodded quickly, reaching to clamp a hand over Vince's mouth. "Yes, and I'll pay you if your hat is bigger than Vince's," he whispered.

Vince pushed Jask's hand down. "Ha-ha. Very funny." He turned to Johnny and narrowed his eyes. "I don't care how much he pays you; I'll burn your hat if it's bigger."

"It won't be," Johnny assured him. "But maybe I'll hide something in the brim to throw at you every time you say something cheesy in your vows."

"Glitter works," Jask offered. "Just keep it to his side of the aisle."

"Glitter is worse than herpes. You can guarantee if there's glitter on me it'll only be a matter of time before it's on you," Vince warned Jask.

"That's hilarious. I'm definitely using glitter." Johnny nodded as he got up to refill his drink.

Jask leaned in, nipping Vince's ear. "If you strip for me, I'll get over the glitter. Maybe we need to get a seedy little motel with a stripper pole in front of the bed. Screw a beach."

"I would look amazing on a stripper pole," Vince mused.

Johnny hesitated before he took his seat again. "Do I need to leave you two alone?"

"Nah. Are you hungry or anything? There's food left over I think, or we can make you something else if you're not a fan of sushi. We're not used to having guests outside of the immediate family these days so we're kinda rusty," Jask said apologetically.

He was hungry, so they reluctantly got up from the couch to feed him. The change in scenery didn't last very long though — just as Johnny was clearing off his plate, someone started knocking incessantly on the door. "Who the hell..." Jask stood, his wings curling behind him in a way that screamed defensiveness. "Stay here."

Vince nodded and stood himself. He took a stance in front of Johnny that gave him a clear view to the front door and waited for Jask to welcome their third surprise visitor of the night.

DRAZAN

He barely noticed the way the cool night air was making him shiver as he stood outside of Jask's door. He'd forgotten a coat, forgotten just about everything but his keys — and honestly, they should be grateful he bothered to drive at all instead of simply coming through their bathroom mirror. There was a line... he just forgot where it was most of the time.

Jask opened the door shirtless and eyes flashing, but he quickly relaxed when he saw who it was. "D? Shit, you scared the hell out of me."

"Where is he?" Drazan growled; all pretenses thrown out the window. He pushed his way under Jask's outstretched arm and looked into each room until he finally spotted him. "Johnny, let's *go.*"

"Hold on a second, Draz. Why don't you take a seat and have a drink with us?" Vince suggested and Drazan blinked. He didn't realize Vince occupied the room at all.

"No, I don't think so." Drazan shook his head, but Johnny

didn't stand up, he didn't grab his hat. Instead, he looked between Vince and Drazan and it was clear an internal battle raged.

It was just a shame that Drazan didn't care about Johnny's internal battles. "Now," he hissed.

Jask put a hand between Drazan's shoulder blades and gripped the fabric there. "He's not going anywhere, D. And neither are you. I don't know what the fuck has gotten into you, but I'm not letting you take poor Johnny anywhere until I figure it out. Now, we can either do this the easy way and you grab some food and a beer and sit your ass down... or we can do this the hard way. If you remember, that didn't work out so well for you last time."

"You don't understand! There's nothing wrong with me. Johnny isn't safe here. Catastrophe follows the two of you and has since the day you met. We need to go." Drazan ignored the pained look on Vince's face and tried to shake Jask off.

"I believe Jask gave you a choice, Drazan. So, choose." Vince's voice held an edge to it, almost like he hoped Drazan would choose to fight. For a moment he contemplated doing exactly that, but Johnny could be hurt if he fought. His thoughts were interrupted by Jask forcibly sitting him in the chair closest to him,

"Good choice."

Drazan locked eyes with Johnny and tried to silently communicate he was sorry — an old lie he was getting tired of, but a necessary one, nonetheless. Johnny wouldn't stick around if he didn't think Drazan felt at least a *little* bad about keeping him under lock and key, but the truth was plain. He didn't feel bad, and he'd continue to do it if Jaskian and Vince quit getting in the way.

Food was shoved into his hand by a pissed off Jaskian. "Eat, then we're gonna talk. Understand?"

"What the hell? Sushi?" Drazan made a face and shoved it right back. "No thanks."

"The hell is wrong with sushi?" Vince frowned as he rescued the sushi from tipping off the table.

It didn't seem worth dignifying, so he didn't. He took a sip of the beer Jask offered him and started plotting a way out that involved taking Johnny with him. That began with distracting Vince and Jask, and there was definitely an easy way to do that. "Jask, remember when we traumatized Edis?"

"Which time?" he said through a laugh. "We've been traumatizing him since the day we met, I think."

"The time he came to visit and we wouldn't stop touching each other."

Every single person in the room stilled, and Drazan knew he was on the right path. Johnny would forgive him eventually, and if he could push Jask to say something that pissed Vince off, it would be easy to get away.

"Anyone need a refill?" Vince asked suddenly. Everyone looked pointedly at their mostly full drinks and Vince shrugged. "I'm going anyway. Need to be... anywhere but here." He left the dining room and took the sushi with him.

"Maybe we should talk about something else?" Johnny said quietly.

Drazan smirked — he was halfway there already. "What's the matter, Jaskian? Don't remember what I'm talking about? Or is it that you remember a little *too* well?"

"Neither," Jask said. "It's just not relevant information any-more, and I'm not going to let you be a dick. What the hell is going on with you?"

"He *is* a dick," Vince mumbled on his return, slamming the four beers down a little harder than necessary.

"Just reminiscing. Isn't that what friends do?" Drazan raised an eyebrow.

"No." Jask shook his head and got to his feet, and Drazan was far too eager to join him.

"You don't like it, Jask, let me go. I'll take Johnny back home and you won't have to listen to me anymore. Seems like a simple solution, so what seems to be *your* problem?"

He barely had time to register the look on Jask's face before his airway was cut off and he was ripped through space itself. They landed roughly on the guest bedroom floor and Jask's eyes flashed as he yelled, "Vin! Get the damn cuffs!"

"Get... *off*, Jask," Draz spit out, trying in vain to squirm out of his grip. "Regular cuffs won't hold me anyway."

Jask sneered. "You're not the only one that knows how to etch a spell into some metal, Drazan. And how quickly you forget we used to arrest angels and demons for a living."

Vince entered the room and tossed the cuffs to Jask. "Make them tight."

Drazan screamed, thrashing and kicking to try and get free — but Jask had him flipped over and pinned to the ground again with barely any effort at all. Panic flooded Drazan until he thought his heart would burst, and he could just make out the sound of someone asking what's wrong with his eyes before Jask knocked him out.

~

He came to slowly, the cuffs digging into his skin and back aching from the hardness of the chair he was in. Jask, Vince, Edis and Johnny were all huddled over him like creepy, asshole gargoyles, and Drazan tried to force a smile. "I bet I look good, but damn. Can you guys give me some space?"

Vince leaned close to Jask and whispered loudly, "Does that mean it worked?"

Johnny sighed. "Thirty-five years old and you *still* haven't learned to whisper?"

"Yeah, he won't be able to go anywhere until we can find the cure." He reached forward and ruffled Drazan's hair, and irritation spiked through him until he was once again futilely trying to get free. "Calm yourself, D. You're lucky... Ed here figured out you're not a dick at all, you're just a little compromised at the moment."

"I, for one, think you're still a dick but I'm happy we figured this out for Johnny's sake." Vince grinned. "Now get comfy while we go figure out how to fix you."

Not one part of that made any sense, but Drazan knew he couldn't do anything to help himself — or Johnny, for that matter, and that hurt a lot worse. If he was stuck in here and handcuffed, anything could happen. He didn't trust the others to care for Johnny the way that he would, but they'd all clearly lost their minds.

"Just do whatever you're gonna do to me and let me go," he spit.

The sooner he got out of this chair, the better.

JASKIAN

The last thing Jask wanted to do was leave Drazan and go see Zaepris, but he didn't feel he had a choice. Johnny and Edis had things under control with the cure and they *needed* to deal with the witch — things had gotten bad enough and they'd let her go for far too long. So, he grabbed Vince's hand and teleported them both back to Zaepris's front door. "You ready?"

"As I'll ever be," Vince said as he knocked on the door.

She made them wait entirely too long, but eventually answered the door and stepped aside. "I don't remember inviting the demon," she commented.

"Yeah, I wasn't coming alone. I know you and I'm not agreeing to give you anything without Vince's consent."

"We're a package deal, doll." Vince nodded. "You going to invite us in?"

Zaepris rolled her eyes but gestured for them to come in, and Jask was just happy the smell of rotting dolphin was gone. He opted not to ask the outcome of that little experiment and instead cut right to the point. "How do I find her, Zae?"

"Why would you want to?" She stepped back up to her table.

Vince watched her curiously. "She tried to kill me."

"Pity she failed," Zaepris deadpanned.

Jask held up a hand. This wasn't going to work if the two of them couldn't keep themselves from fighting, but he hadn't been kidding. He didn't want to agree to anything without Vince being there, and this seemed easier than teleporting back and forth. "Enough. Stick to business, Zaepris. We'll be out of your hair faster if you give us what we need quickly."

"I can find her, but as I said... it'll cost you."

"Well, first born isn't an option in this scenario," Vince quipped. "So, what is it you want?"

A sly, evil smile spread across her face. "Oh, just a little of this, a little of that," she singsonged, poking each of them in the chest in turn. "A little grace, a little demon juice, and we'll be on our way."

"No," Jask barked, swatting her manicured hand away from his chest. "You already got my feathers; you don't get anything else like that. Pick again."

"Fine, be that way. The Veris clan has a very old book. I want it." She made the request seem like it was nothing.

"Why?" Vince asked with suspicion.

"None of your business. You asked my price, I named it."

Jask ran through all the books he remembered seeing in Athar's collection, but none particularly stood out to him. "What's it called?"

"It doesn't have a title, or anything on the binding. It's sleek, small, and dark red... almost black. You'll know it's the right one if you pick it up and it makes you bleed," she said lightly.

He only knew of one book like that, and he didn't particularly want to hand it over to Zaepris of all people. "What exactly do you plan to do with it?"

"Ahhh, see, I thought I already said it was none of your business. Hand it over and I'll hand you the witch. Have you figured out what's ailing Drazan yet?"

"Are you saying you knew something was wrong with Draz?" Vince demanded.

Zaepris scoffed. "Like you didn't," she accused. "He reeked of magic and desperation; how do you think I found him in the first place? Magic leaves a trace, a *scent*. And I could smell Drazan from three towns over with my nose plugs in."

"You could've saved us a lot of trouble, lady." Vince huffed and then faced Jask. "So, is this book something we can offer?"

No, he thought to himself. *We'll just be asking for more trouble... but if we don't, we may not survive the current trouble.* He knew that Zaepris knew she had him, it was written all over her smug face. He nodded once, conceding, and took a deep breath. "Do what you need to do to get her location... *and* whatever we need for Draz. I'll be right back."

He vanished, reappearing in the room housing what was left of Athar's collection. It took him roughly ten minutes to find what he was looking for, but sure enough — blood dripped down his palm when he picked up the small, plain book. "I better not regret this," he muttered before teleporting back and landing behind Zaepris. "Well?"

"Place it there." She pointed without looking at him. "I'm almost done with your locator spell."

Vince waited until Jask sat the book down before he pulled off his t-shirt and wrapped Jask's hand. Jask began to argue but Vince kissed him to stop the words. "Yeah, I know you can heal it. It makes me feel better, okay?"

"Any excuse to take off your shirt, Himbo?" Zaepris raised an eyebrow at them.

"Shove it. Did you find her?" Vince kept his hand in Jask's.

A few more moments passed, then Zaepris let out a triumphant hum. "Got the bitch... I mean, witch," she said excitedly, then turned to slam the map down on the table. Her long, purple fingernail pointed at a spot on the map that was glowing like the embers of a fire. "She's here."

"Good, that means we can leave." Vince checked out the spot on the map but Jask held up a hand.

"One more thing. What happened to Drazan? Were we right? Was it Cidos?"

They'd figured out that magic still had some sort of a hold on Drazan from the changes in his eyes, and the only thing they could figure was that the spell he was put under before Cidos died never faded.

"Yes, which means you'll need this." She rifled through a drawer to the left of the table and set down a bag full of *something* right in front of him.

"Do I even want to know what that is?"

"No, but I'll tell you anyway." She grinned when Vince pulled the bag and immediately gagged. "That is a desiccated monkey brain, the tail of a rattlesnake, and the shredded genitalia of a large bull."

Jask groaned, wishing magic wasn't as disgusting as it really was. "That's nasty. Don't... don't touch it, Vin." He turned back to Zaepris and narrowed his eyes slightly. "I don't think I need to tell you what will happen if this doesn't work, do I?"

"Yes, dear, you're very threatening. I promise it'll work. Let's not forget I didn't have to help you with this."

It was true but he didn't care — Zaepris was exactly the type of person to betray them on a dime, and they'd had more than enough of that going around. "Then great. After this, we stay out of each other's way, yeah? Never see each other again?"

"Sounds perfect." She snatched the book up and waved her hand toward the door. "Now get out before I decide to test out page three of this book."

"Wait, what's on page three?" Vince actually sounded curious and Jask teleported them back home before they found out the bad way.

When they landed, Jask clenched his jaw and glanced up to where Johnny and Ed were watching over Drazan. "If this doesn't work, I don't know what we're gonna do, Vin. I can't lose him again."

"It'll work, Jask. And if it doesn't, we'll find something that does. Whatever it takes, I'll do it." Vince lifted their joined hands and placed a chaste kiss on Jask's. "But I have a good feeling about this."

"I hope you're right." With a deep breath, he transported them both up to the room, then apologized to Drazan before punching him square in the nose. By all rights, he knew none of this was his fault — but that just meant that once he was back to normal, Jask wouldn't have an excuse to do what he just did. "Sorry, D. But not really."

Drazan tilted his head and stretched his jaw. "It's okay. I guess I deserved that, but that's the only one you get."

"Is it inappropriate for me to point out how insanely hot that was?" Vince asked from behind them.

"Yes. What's in the bag?" Johnny changed the subject.

Jask just shook his head and smiled at Vince. He'd half expected Vince to hit him too and was actually pleased that he didn't.

With any luck, all of this was about to be over, and he'd get his best friend back, and if not... it was like Vince said. They'd just keep trying.

XV

DRAZAN

The difference was shocking, even to him. Jask, Vince, Ed and Johnny had found a cure to a problem Drazan hadn't even realized he'd had, and he finally felt like he could breathe again. Gone was that pull in his chest that made it impossible to be away from Johnny, to let go of the reins for even a moment. But now, he had a lot of making up to do.

"Johnny, do you want to go look at that house again? I know I was kind of a dick last time..."

"Understatement," Johnny said with a small, almost forced smile. "Yeah, though... I'd like to buy it. I don't like being this far away."

He nodded, and truth be told, he didn't like it either anymore. Once, the distance meant safety, privacy, and keeping Johnny all to himself, but now it just meant that they were both far away from the people they cared about after being separated for long enough.

"I agree," he conceded. "Get dressed. We'll go swing by and see if the happy couple wants to come check it out with us?"

"Yeah, that sounds great." Johnny's smile grew, looking more genuine before he left to change. It wasn't even ten minutes later that he emerged completely dressed and looking eager to go.

Drazan felt a little like he was walking on eggshells — not necessarily around Johnny, but around himself. He was still having a hard time reconciling how he'd felt for the last year and a half and how he feels now. "Do you want to drive?" he offered, tossing Johnny the keys and grabbing his hoodie off the back of the couch. "Think you can still manage it?"

"Yes, I can manage." Johnny opened the front door. "I got plenty of practice trying to run Vince over in a field."

He barked a laugh. It had started as a joke about Johnny being dead, but that... "I genuinely wish I'd have been there to see it."

The drive to Jask's was filled with music, the wind whipping through the windows, and Johnny's easygoing grin. Without a doubt, it was the best Drazan had felt in a very long time. He took Johnny's hand and sang along to the radio until they were pulling up in the cul-de-sac.

"Maybe you should go get them," Drazan said quietly. "I don't know if Vince would even open the door if he saw me right now."

Johnny looked like he wanted to argue but they both knew Draz wasn't wrong. "I'll be quick." He kissed Drazan's cheek and exited the car. His suspicions were confirmed when he got a good look at Vince's face as Johnny explained what they wanted to do. He shifted in his seat while he waited and he only relaxed when he heard Vince ask Jask if he wanted to go.

Jask bowled past Vince and Johnny and ran to the car, hopping in the backseat. "It's about damn time. It's been, what, three days? I was starting to think I was gonna have to come track you down again."

"It was an adjustment," Drazan said slowly, but he had to admit it was good to see Jask and not have an underlying urge to murder him. "I didn't realize you missed me that much."

He received a sharp smack to the back of the head for that, but Jask was saved from having to answer as Vince and Johnny got back in.

Johnny immediately backed out of the driveway, obviously excited to get this done.

"So, how's the honeymoon period been?" Vince leaned against the back of Johnny's seat.

"Not much of a honeymoon yet," Drazan said lightly. "I think we're both just trying to adjust. In a way, we've *both* been dead for a year."

Johnny nodded. "Just doesn't seem real yet, y'know? Just waiting for the other shoe to drop."

Jask regarded him sadly for a moment but the empathy was clear. "I know how you feel. I really do. And it takes time, but you guys will get there. I did."

"And hey, we're here to help. We have a guest bedroom, so anytime Johnny gets tired of you, he can come over for a slumber party." Vince grinned at Draz.

Drazan agreed instantly. "That would actually be great. I'm sure he missed you guys, and after everything, I'd want some time away from me, too."

"It's not like that," Johnny said. "But we're here, so can we all just try to get along? I really like this house." He parked the car and slid out without waiting for confirmation. The house itself wasn't exactly Drazan's style, but at this point, he'd do anything at all if he thought it would make Johnny happy.

It was basically an oversized log cabin set in the middle of a street of modern homes, so it stuck out like a sore thumb. But the front and back yard were both big enough that the houses next door probably wouldn't even seem like neighbors, and Drazan *did* like that.

"You need a gazebo." Vince shared a look with Jask, and Drazan didn't want to know what that meant. He left the others to talk about changes and upgrades that could be done and stepped into the main bedroom. He let himself imagine having a home — a life — with Johnny here. Did he even deserve that?

"Well?" Johnny asked softly from the doorway. "Be honest. I want you to be happy here too, so if you don't like it..."

"I do. I like it. More than that, I can see a future here," Draz answered quietly. He turned fully to face Johnny. "So, I say we get it."

The instant happiness on Johnny's face made it all worth it. Every bit of it — the year of anger and fog, the beatings he'd taken from Jask. Without the spell that Cidos put him under, Johnny wouldn't be here. He'd never have taken the time or put in the effort to bring him back, he simply would've grieved and moved on.

With that in mind, Drazan stepped forward until he was pulling Johnny in. He kissed him softly and planted his lips to Johnny's forehead after as he let out a steady breath. "We'll definitely take it, and whatever else you want. I'm really, really happy you're back."

"Me too, Draz. More and more every day." Johnny tightened his hold on Drazan. "Think we should go share the good news?"

Something crashed below them, and Drazan rolled his eyes. "We can share the good news, sure... but I'm pretty sure they just broke something in our new home. Care to do the honors?"

Johnny stepped back but entwined their fingers so that Draz followed. "I'll bet you a full body massage Vince is to blame." It didn't take them long to confirm Johnny's suspicion. The view that greeted them caused Drazan to tilt his head in confusion. Vince stood on the island in the middle of their kitchen, holding up the light that seemed to be hanging by only one chain instead of the four Draz knew had been there earlier. Jask seemed consumed by laughter over by the sink and Johnny appeared just as speechless as Draz.

"Would you believe it looked like this when we got here?" Vince asked sheepishly.

Drazan finally found his voice. "How? That's all I want to know."

"Trust me," Jask said through laughter. "You don't actually want to know at all." He waved a hand and fixed the light while Vince guided it back to the spot, then helped Vince down off the island. "Better we take this one to the grave."

"Just like the pumpkin." Vince leaned into Jask.

"The—" Johnny started.

"Nope. Don't want to hear about that, either." Draz shook his head. "We're here to share good news."

Jask's face lit up as he realized what he meant, and he instantly jumped on Drazan and ruffled his hair. "Hell *yes*, we're going to be neighbors! Sort of, anyway. Close enough." He stepped back with a cheesy expression as Drazan tried in vain to fix his hair.

"Yes... neighbors. I'm sure that won't be annoying at *all*."

VINCE

Vince couldn't remember another time in his life that he'd felt this happy. His best friend would stand with him at his wedding – something Vince could only dream of a year ago – and Drazan had returned to tolerable levels of assholery. His family remained close and happy. Arro took his first steps at the family dinner the night before and would soon be a menace to his sister and brother-in-law.

That thought made him chuckle as he finished getting the ingredients ready for dinner. Draz and Johnny were on their way and Jask should be due home soon. All in all, Vince's day had been fantastic. The absolutely stellar blow jobs he'd traded with Jask this morning probably contributed greatly to his mood.

He triple-checked everything again before running upstairs to stash the bottle of bourbon by the bed. Better to plan ahead to get the most out of the evening. As far as he was concerned, nothing could ruin his happiness.

And so, when he ran back downstairs, he wasn't prepared for the blast of fear at what waited on his kitchen table — a photo of everyone at dinner from the night before, but each face blotted out with a bloody mark. The ice in Vince's blood immediately became replaced with white hot rage. His hand shook as he picked up the frame and felt moisture on the back. He flipped it and read the note Alnaess left for him: *"One by one, I'll take them from you."*

He couldn't stand it anymore. Everything finally seemed to be going right apart from this one dark stain on their existence. The back door was still open thanks to the intruder and he stepped into his yard, hurling the frame and watching as it shattered against the gazebo.

"Alnaess! I know you're here. I know you're watching. You want me? Come and get me, bitch." His hands lit with flame he couldn't control, and it only grew as she sauntered out of the woods behind their home.

"Giving yourself up, demon?" She stopped and lifted the photo from the ground. "Which one should I kill first? I'm having trouble deciding, you see. I know who will be last. Your angel lover, I'll let him watch with you as I destroy everything you've ever loved and then I'll gut him. That's a slow way to die, Vincenzo. Very painful."

"Great. Are you done? We both know this isn't about any of them. You're mad about Damian. He's *dead.* You got what you wanted!" Vince stepped forward with the full intention of ending this now. The problem was that his feet didn't obey his command. Vince looked down at the vines now crawling up his legs towards his torso. He burned them easily but more kept coming. He sent a ball of flame directly toward her face.

"He died after. You think I don't know that?" Alnaess continued conversationally as she dodged the flame.

"You're mad about the timing? Come the fuck on, lady!" Vince growled as he burned more of the rapidly appearing plants. Suddenly a cold, damp hand wrapped around his throat. How did she move so *fast?* He wrapped one hand around her wrist and with the other hit her straight with a burst of flame. The enraged shriek from the witch gave him no small amount of satisfaction as she released her hold on him. The wound smoked as she glared at him.

Before either of them could speak, a voice rang out from the house, "Vince? Where are you?"

"Stay inside, Johnny!" Vince broke free of another vine prison and launched himself at Alnaess. They hit the ground hard, and her hand found its way back to his throat. Vince put his arm against hers, more than willing to choke the life out of the witch that'd been tormenting them for weeks, but something happened that made him stop. He couldn't breathe. His lungs seized as if he were underwater.

"Draz, get Jask!" Johnny yelled and Vince could hear boots running in his direction. Alnaess would not hesitate to kill Johnny and Vince couldn't lose him again. He rolled away from her and jumped to his feet, coughing as he waved Johnny away. He wasn't on his feet for a full moment before a vine tripped him and Alnaess took the opportunity to get to Johnny.

"Ah, yes. Johnny. The miracle best friend. You shouldn't be here. Why don't we remedy that?" Vince looked up in time to see Alnaess pinning Johnny to the outside wall of their home. Even from the distance, Vince could hear Johnny's gasping breaths. He cursed and yanked his foot free to rescue his friend. Vince reached them just as Johnny's lips were turning blue and he gripped her by the waist and tossed her as far as he could in the opposite direction. He turned back to check on a now thankfully breathing Johnny when a vine wrapped around his throat and pulled him back with a force he hadn't been expecting.

Vince landed on his back with a grunt and rolled, wrapping the vine around his arm and pulling. It ripped out of the ground and he unwrapped it from around his body. "Enough, Alnaess! They have nothing to do with this."

"They have *everything* to do with this! Damian kept me locked in a cage for decades. I lost everything. Everyone. And you trivialized that when you lied to me. I took from him and now I will take from you. It is far past time I gained my pound of flesh!" The crazed look in her eyes sent a cold shiver down his spine and he clenched his jaw. He needed to kill her now or spend the rest of his life waiting for her to murder his family. He pulled on every ounce of power he could muster, prepared to take her out or die trying. He didn't even get the chance to release the energy building inside of him before Alnaess coughed out blood. Vince blinked as she looked over her shoulder in shock. Drazan stood behind her and Vince could see the tip of a blade sticking out of her chest. A twist of the angel's arm and she crumpled to the ground, the life draining out of her.

"Could I borrow you for a moment, Vince?" Drazan's words were calm, as if killing a witch was just another Tuesday for him. Vince came forward at Draz' beckoning and after a quick discussion, Drazan stepped back so that Vince could burn the body. He used all that excess energy he'd built to make the fire as hot as possible. He wanted there to be no chance of a return.

He glanced over at the house to see Drazan checking over

Johnny. It pleased him that the insanity that plagued Drazan didn't show at all in the gentle touches he shared with his best friend. Vince lowered the flames once he deemed the body disintegrated enough and he walked back to the house.

He entered just as Jask teleported in and he'd never been so glad to see the angel. Without a word he walked to Jask and wrapped his arms around him. Vince buried his face in Jask's neck and took the comfort he needed.

"Vin? Are you okay? What'd I miss?"

"A barbeque," Drazan joked from the door to their back yard. Vince couldn't help it, he laughed until his sides hurt.

JASKIAN

Just the mention of the word barbecue had Jask sniffing the air, but the stench that greeted him made him retch. "What the—"

"I slave over a hot stove for your dinner and that's the face you make?" Vince placed a hand on his chest in mock out- rage.

"What he *means* is we took care of your witch problem, and maybe we should go out for dinner while the smell dissi- pates," Drazan translated.

Jask's eyebrows shot up. "Alnaess is dead?"

"Wow, you're not exactly quick these days, J. Yeah, you missed all the fun," Drazan teased. "I had to do your dirty work and protect your missus since you weren't around to do it yourself."

"He's right. I was in hysterics, don't know what I would've done if Drazan wasn't here," Vince deadpanned.

Johnny nudges him. "You'd have died, actually." He grinned, ducking out of the way like he was anticipating a hit.

No strike came but only because Vince hit Johnny with a full body tackle. They rolled around on the floor as Drazan joined Jask. "That's what you're marrying."

"I could say the same to you, but you haven't popped the question yet."

Drazan looked at him like he was insane. "Yeah, well, there's a reason for that. And I don't want to scare him now, I mean... I'm pretty sure at one point during all that, I started talking about trying to bond us together like you and Vince used to be."

The scuffle continued and Jask sidestepped to get out of their way. "Is that even possible? Do you remember looking into it at all?"

"Yeah, and as far as I can tell, only Veris and Riskel know how to do it. It's probably best, can you imagine what would happen if people just went around tying their lives to someone else that literally? It would be chaos and we'd die out in like six months."

It hadn't occurred to Jask that if Riskel and Veris could pull it off once, they could do it again. While he was happy with the way things were with him and Vince, going from bonded to not bonded was horrible. To know the depth of emotional connection that they were missing, that they'd never be able to replicate without the bond no matter *how* in love with each other they were? It was enough to have him lost in thought.

A victorious yell from Johnny broke the seriousness of Jask's thoughts and he looked over to see Vince curled up on the ground.

"Not cool!" he groaned. "Family jewels should be off limits."

"Me against you? That's the only fair move I have." Johnny grinned and helped him up.

Jask grimaced but couldn't help it when it turned to something more amused. "I hope you didn't hurt them too bad; I need those later."

"He'll be fine." Johnny dusted Vince off and pushed him toward Jask.

"You could kiss them better if you're concerned," Vince said with a smirk.

"See? He's already back to normal. Dinner?"

Johnny's reminder had Jask's train of thought shifting yet again. He was definitely hungry, but he wasn't sure he was up to having company. If anything, the news of Alnaess' death snapped the last bit of adrenaline Jask was running on. For weeks now, he'd been pushing forward and trying to stay focused to help Drazan and protect his family — but now, in the absence of either of those motivators, he was starting to feel that pull of darkness again. All he *really* wanted to do was crawl into bed and sleep for a month, and it was getting harder to convince himself he didn't deserve it.

Unfortunately, it was clear he wasn't going to have that option anytime soon when Vince once again pulled on his powers and transported them all to their favorite restaurant.

Jask clicked his tongue as Vince swayed on his feet from the effort, but held him up, nonetheless. "You could've just asked."

"And miss the chance to show off how awesome I am now? Nope." They entered the restaurant and were seated quickly. Vince grasped Jask's hand under the table as he perused the menu, and Jask watched him fondly instead of picking something to eat.

More and more, the thought of bonding with him again sounded like a good idea, but he wasn't about to bring it up in front of other people — if he ever got the courage to bring it up at all.

They carried small talk through the shared appetizers and the first two rounds of drinks, and it wasn't until their main courses arrived that Drazan brought up the biggest reason they were all out to dinner together. "So... bachelor parties? Or... party? Is it one or two?"

"One," Jask said quickly. In this respect, he didn't care what Vince's opinion was. The last time Jask had a makeshift bachelor party without him, he was kidnapped by the very man asking the question. "Just one."

"Couldn't agree more." Jask didn't miss the quick glare Vince shot at Draz but it didn't last longer than a few seconds. "Anyone have any ideas on where?"

Crickets. It would seem none of them had any idea where a broken angel and his former mate should go for such a thing, and it wasn't like Jask had any good ideas, either. "Could just go back to Ares. I miss Ares."

"You know what we should do? Set up a fight at Pattie's," Vince suggested with a laugh.

Honestly, it was a better idea than any other they'd come

up with, and Jask found himself intrigued by the possibilities. "You and me?"

"Yeah. We can have him make a big deal out of it, take bets. Show up separately. The whole deal. Can even pretend we don't know each other if you want to get kinky." Vince winked.

"I don't think anyone would believe us, but we could try." Jask shrugged, liking the idea more by the second. "We'll have to do it like two weeks before the wedding though just to make sure any injuries heal."

Drazan wrinkled his nose. "You guys are gonna... hurt each other as a bachelor party?"

"Nah, not hurt each other. Just a little bit of public, rough foreplay," Jask clarified.

"I'll tell Pattie tonight. Might even make some money off of this." Vince pulled his phone out of his pocket and began typing.

Johnny put an arm around Draz. "As long as everyone keeps their pants on, we should be fine."

"No guarantees." Vince continued typing, which only made Jask more amused.

It didn't take long for Pattie to get back to Vince with a resounding negative — after what they'd brought down on him last time, he wasn't eager to repeat it. Vince called him after that and nearly begged him to let us do it just once, and Pattie eventually agreed if for no other reason than to get Vince to shut up.

"Well done," Jask chuckled. "We need to make sure we don't destroy the place now."

"Yeah, he was pretty insistent on that. Might even make us do it outside." Vince shrugged.

"Can't really blame him. Bet it took him forever to get the wall fixed," Johnny pointed out.

"I could've done it instantly if he'd have just asked," Jask muttered, but he was quickly reminded why Pattie *didn't* do such a thing and had to laugh.

Drazan flagged down their waitress and ordered them all one final round of drinks. They reminisced about some of their earlier fights and that fateful day where Vince signed up to fight an angel, and the memory made Jask smile almost sadly. So much had happened since then. Blood, sweat, tears... death, and now life again. He watched Johnny lean in and whisper something in Drazan's ear that made him blush, and Vince snapped his fingers in their faces to get their attention again.

It was so normal, so... natural, that Jask finally started to breathe again. Not the labored, shallow efforts he'd been putting forth since the day Cidos took Vince and this all began, but real, fruitful, lung-filling and life-saving breaths.

The past was behind them — every threat to them vanquished, and for once, they were allowed to just *be*.

Maybe all that had happened was worth it, after all.

XVI

VINCE

Whistling a tune he couldn't remember the words to, Vince let himself into the house their mothers occupied. His sister and Edis seemed to already be in attendance if the baby sounds from the sitting room were any indication. He headed in that direction and waved to Edis, Astarte and Arro before continuing to the kitchen. His mother and Lee talked quietly as they made this week's family dinner and Vince stole a piece of cheese out of a bowl before hugging them both. Lee looked around the room and then out into the hallway with a raised eyebrow. "Where's Jask?"

"Finishing his shower." He reached for a slice of freshly cooked bacon but backed off when his mother slapped his hand with a spatula.

"I thought he said he was getting in the shower when Edis called him an hour ago?" Lee put a covered dish into the oven.

"You are correct, but then Jask made his first mistake of getting naked right in front of me. Then he made his second mistake when he let me into the bathroom with him.

And *then*—" Vince's next words were stopped by Amaranth putting her hand over his mouth.

"We get it, Vincenzo. Jask will be here soon, that's all we needed to know. Go see your nephew." Amaranth shoved him out of the kitchen and Vince went back to the sitting room with a grin on his face.

"Don't expect me to ask you where Jask is. I heard the entire thing and couldn't stomach a repeat." Edis placed Arro in Vince's arms and left the room. Vince sat on the couch, tickling Arro until the kid screeched with laughter.

A quiet noise – the sound of a polite throat-clearing – caught his attention and Vince looked over. Jask's mother sat to his right, sitting primly in a chair and looking incredibly uncomfortable. Vince turned a little to face her and bounced Arro on his knee as he waited for her to speak. Watching her visibly search for words made him wish Jask would show. In the entire time he's known the Veris family, only once could he remember being alone with Astarte. Here lay uncharted territory and Vince did not know how to navigate it.

"Something wrong?" He did his best to sound supportive.

"Yes, actually. I owe you an apology." Astarte sat a little straighter.

"You... what?"

"I owe you an apology. For multiple things I'm sure, but specifically about Drazan. I shouldn't have told him about Jask being here or the wedding. When he asked, I should've told the both of you immediately." If possible, her spine straightened further – as if she were steeling herself for a reprimand. Arro began to squirm, and Vince took the opportunity to think about what he wanted to say as he sat the baby in the playpen in the corner of the room. When he sat back down, he took the corner closest to Astarte. Very slowly and carefully, he reached out and took her hand. He gave her plenty of time and opportunity to pull away and showed only a little surprise when she didn't. It was another rare occurrence for them, and he smiled at her and thought hard about his words.

"Drazan taking Jask could absolutely be considered one of the worst days of my life. That includes the torture." He watched her deflate and rushed on. "I'm telling you that because I want you to know the rest. If you hadn't told him, he would've never taken Jask. We wouldn't have found out what he planned, and we wouldn't have Johnny. I wish with everything in me that Jask didn't need to suffer for it but that's only because I never want Jask to suffer in any capacity. I'd do whatever I could to save him from any type of pain. Even the smallest splinter. So, do I wish things happened differently? Yes. But do I blame you for any of it? No. In fact, I should probably thank you. You raised two amazing sons. Edis and Jask are two of the most amazing men I've ever had the pleasure to meet, and despite the initial rocky beginning, I'm so happy that you three are a part of our lives." Throughout the entire speech, Vince kept his eyes on their hands. For some reason, looking her in the eye still made him nervous. At the last word, he lifted his gaze to meet hers and panicked when he noticed the tears flowing down her face.

"Oh no. No, no. I didn't mean to make you cry! Let me..." He stood and patted his pockets for a handkerchief but then remembered he really wasn't the type to carry one. "I'm sorry,

I'm so sorry. Just... Uh... shit." He pulled off his flannel over-shirt and held it out to her.

She took it with a startled expression, but a hand holding a tissue cut her off. "Here, Ma," Jask said quietly. "I'll just pretend I didn't hear any of that heartwarming and incredible speech and leave you two alone again." He kissed Vince slowly and whispered "thank you" before heading into the kitchen to help Ed and Lee.

Astarte blushed as she dabbed the tears from her cheeks. "I was wrong about you, too. You're a far better man than I gave you credit for. You and your sister make my sons happy, and that's more than most mothers could ever hope for."

"Thank you. That means more to me than you'll ever know." Vince smiled and held out his arms. "Can I hug you?"

Surprisingly, she didn't hesitate before standing and wrapping her arms around him, but she did pull back pretty quickly. "You're... warm," she said like that fact actually shocked her. "Really warm."

"Yeah. I honestly think it's why Jask keeps me around." He laughed and rubbed the back of his neck.

Astarte softened and blotted the tissue on her eyes again before stepping back. "He keeps you around because he loves you. But I'm sure the heat doesn't hurt."

"Guys," Ed said from the doorway. "Dinner's ready, get it before Lee and Jask eat literally all of it."

"Guess we better hurry." Vince lifted Arro up and planted the giggling baby on his shoulder. He offered his free arm to Astarte with a small bow. "May I escort you to dinner, ma'am?"

She took his arm and walked with him into the dining

room, and all five of their companions turned to stare. His own mother was the first to comment: "Why don't you ever walk me into rooms like I'm a queen?"

"Uh... because... well—" he looked around for help and found none — "I don't have a good answer."

Everyone laughed and Astarte kissed his cheek before sitting down, and Jask was giving him a look that suggested he just earned every brownie point in the entire world. With their reunion fight just two nights away, that was probably a good thing.

Dinner remained light-hearted and Vince finally let go of that feeling that something would go wrong. Smiles were plentiful and Arro kept them all laughing. Vince helped Lee clean up after dinner and then sat back with Jask, handing him a piece of pie he'd stolen out of his mother's stash.

"Are you trying to fatten me up before the fight?" he asked with a pleased expression.

"Yes," Vince answered with a very serious nod. He took the fork from Jask and cut off a small bite before holding it up. "So, open up."

His teeth close around the fork and he pulls the bite into his mouth. "You know I won't hurt you."

"Is that what you think I'm worried about? I just want to win. I don't care about getting hurt." He cut another piece of pie and Jask shoved him playfully.

"Yeah? Good luck then, I don't intend on tarnishing the Veris name by losing."

"And I don't intend on breaking my win streak at Pattie's." Vince held up the fork to point at his lover. "The angel fights don't count, both times I was distracted by forces beyond my control. I don't lose fights, not fair ones." He tilted his head a little. "Some not so fair ones, too."

"He's not wrong," Lee spoke up. "Remember that night you got stabbed in the side with that broken beer bottle? I don't think I ever heard Ma yell as loud as she did when she patched you up."

"But I didn't lose. And he looked worse at the end. I made six hundred bucks that night, too." Vince offered another bite to Jask.

He chewed it quickly. "Technically this won't be a fair fight either," he pointed out. "I'm undeniably stronger than you so I'll either kick your ass or have to take it easy on you."

"Undeniably. Rub it in, why don't you? I'll just have to use my wits. Or fight shirtless, you won't have a chance." Vince winked.

Ed snorted. "Yeah, that doesn't sound fair to me. But you guys fought shirtless last time, didn't you? That's probably what started all of this. Jask was too busy trying to figure out what all of Vince's tattoos were."

"Yeah," Jask agreed lightly. "Let's go with that."

"Actually, I can tell you exactly what his thoughts were and it—" he noticed both their mothers watching from the couch — "The tattoos. Definitely the tattoos."

Amaranth threw a pillow at him. "I can't believe you two actually think this is a good idea. What good will *possibly* come from it?"

"I'd like to know that myself, but I gave up trying to understand them a long time ago," Ed joked.

"Who said we want it to be good in the first place? Sometimes it's fun to be bad." Vince wiggled his eyebrows and ducked another pillow missile from his mother.

Jask took both of the pillows and laid down despite the complete lack of space on the couch. "Don't worry, it won't be a very long fight. If it goes on too long, Pattie will shut us down anyway."

"That doesn't make anyone feel better," Astarte said.

Vince wiggled enough to get Jask in his lap, looking at their little family. "You don't actually think we'd hurt each other, do you?"

"Not on purpose," Lee said. "But you're both stupidly competitive and notorious for being idiots, so... it's a definite possibility."

Jask smiled softly. "I left my idiot days behind me."

"Not so sure about that. You're still marrying me, after all." Vince joked as he ran a hand through Jask's hair. "But he's right. We've grown and we promise not to hurt each other. A lot, anyway."

Lee sighed. "I should've known better. Anyway, we should get Arro home. It's almost his bedtime."

"Is it your bedtime too?" Vince looked down at Jask.

"Mmm, maybe. Depends on what's waiting for me in that bed."

Edis groaned so loudly it actually made Jask jerk in surprise. "You guys suck," he lamented. "Were Lee and I ever like this?"

"Yes. You're disgusting, honestly," Vince answered his brother-in-law before standing and pulling Jask to his feet. "Come on, let's get you tucked in."

They said their goodbyes a little quicker than normal and

waited outside until they could be sure Ed, Arro and Lee got inside safely. The night was chilly but not too cold, yet Jask plastered himself against Vince's body as they walked home, anyway. "You really think things will be good now?" he asked.

"Honestly?" Vince wrapped an arm around Jask's shoulders and tugged him closer. "Yeah. I really do. I don't know why, but that negative feeling I've always had at the back of my head? It's gone. All I have there now is hope." Vince opened their front door and as soon as they were in and safe, he pushed Jask back against it. He stepped into Jask's space and placed a gentle kiss on his lips. "Do you?"

The love in Jask's eyes answered for him. "Yeah, Vin. I really do."

Another kiss and one shared smile, Vince interlaced their fingers. Hand in hand they climbed the stairs and for the first time in months, sleep came without trouble for them both.

JASKIAN

The morning of the fight, Pattie called Vince three times to try and get him to cancel. Jask watched with amusement as each time, Vince got a little more excited to actually do it, so in the end they had to agree to go build their own ring out back of Pattie's main warehouse. It wasn't a bad deal — this way, they didn't have to worry about breaking anything. They could be as destructive as they wanted, and Pattie would simply reap the benefits.

It took them all afternoon to set it up right. Jask and Drazan could've done it in about ten minutes but Vince, Johnny, and Pattie himself kept yelling out changes they wanted. A pillar here, and overhang there. A wall of cement blocks that was *supposed* to be to protect the crowd, but Jask knew it was ready just so Vince could knock it down.

They didn't have much in the way of audience seating, but Pattie had sent out a text blast telling people to either stand or bring their own chairs, which Jask found amusing. He'd ask if people were supposed to bring their own alcohol too, but Pattie would never miss out on that kind of revenue. As it was, Jask himself bought almost a full bottle from the demon already and the fight was still an hour away.

He didn't see Vince much during all of that. They were both busy setting up traps and other things to trip the other up — something Drazan found hilarious. "So, what, you're not gonna hurt each other, you're just gonna... embarrass each other?"

"Pretty much," Jask agreed jovially. "Tell me it's not going to be hilarious when Vince charges at me like a bull and slips on a damn banana peel."

"You actually put banana peels out?"

"No, but now that I say it, maybe I should. Can you go grab me like... twenty pounds of bananas from somewhere?"

Drazan smacked him in the side of the head. "No. I'm not going to do that, and I'm not going to let anyone else do it, either. Don't even think about asking Lee."

"She'd do it," Jask pointed out. "She'd probably bring me back fifty."

As true as it was, Jask knew it was ridiculous. He decided

instead to focus on the things Vince wouldn't see coming — trap doors, trip wires, things of that nature. It was becoming less of a fight and more of an obstacle course with an extremely sexy finish line, but even that was giving Jaskian all sorts of ideas for the future. Maybe now that the *real* danger had passed, they could stand to throw a little bit of it in themselves.

"Okay, is it time?" Jask asked, his wings tucked away and shirt off. "It's getting darker out."

"Yep." Drazan rubbed Jask's shoulders like he always used to do before a fight and then slapped his ass. "You hear that crowd? Not one of them is rooting for you. Hell, *I'm* not even rooting for you."

Jask scoffed. "Why? Cause your boyfriend is helping my almost-husband and you think you'll get laid if Vince wins?"

"Uh... yeah, yep... pretty much." Drazan laughed, ducking to avoid the playful right hook Jask threw at him. "Save it for the ring, big guy. C'mon."

With a deep breath and a slowly spreading smirk, Jask tied up his long hair into a bun and cracked his neck. After what felt like decades, he was right back where he started with Vincenzo Riskel, and it was right where he wanted to be.

Two steps out of the room they'd been getting ready in, he got sideswiped by the bumper off a rusty old truck. He absorbed the impact, but it reverberated down to his toes, and he could hear his fiancé's laughter as it falls to the floor. "Come on, babe. Don't hold back on me now."

"Oh, don't worry. I won't." Jask looked up and squinted at the rudimentary light fixtures they'd installed and willed one of them to fall. It missed Vince by a few inches, but it distracted him long enough that Jask rolled to the side and took refuge behind a cinder block the size of a small shed. From there, he gathered white-hot balls of power in his hands hand lobbed them up one after the other, not bothering to aim much.

Someone screamed like he might've hit someone from the crowd, but as expected, it didn't slow Vince in the slightest. He kicked at the blocks and said "knock knock" in a singsong voice, then tossed flames around at Jask.

He froze the flames in midair, but that act alone distracted him. He'd never tried it before and the way the frozen flames shattered on the ground sent crystallized light shooting up above their heads. Jask teleported behind Vince and grabbed him around the middle, lifting him up and tossing him into the one actual boxing ring they'd added, then stalked toward it as he fixed his hair. "Now that we've got a little ambiance..."

Vince rolled to his feet, grinning as he took a stance on the opposite side of the ring. "I'll let you fix your hair, wouldn't want to burn it off." His tone may have been teasing, but Jask knew he truly meant it. Vince loved those long, wavy locks too much to see them damaged.

"You'd have to actually hit me first, Vin." Jask teleported to the other side of the ring and dropped down, sending a pulse through the springy floor that felt a lot like an earthquake.

Leaping from the floor, Vince clung to the makeshift cage as he waited for the aftershocks to end, but thanks to the constant movement of the floor, he didn't feel when the cage began to lean backwards from his weight. The gasp from the crowd is the only thing that made the demon look around and by then it was too late — the cage slammed onto the floor with Vince still on top of it. "Shit!"

"Give up yet?" Jask pounced, pinning Vince to the cage below him. He couldn't help it, the adrenaline pumping through his veins made his eyes shine with power and promise, and having Vince so close was making him want something more. He rutted against him just enough that they could feel it without the crowd seeing. "Pinned ya."

"If I give up, will I get some of that?" Vince grunted out and thrusted up into him. "This show is about to switch lanes if you don't let me up, sweetheart."

Part of Jaskian wouldn't mind that at all, but the chase was half the fun. "So, push me off—" He barely got the words out before heat and power were sending him flying backward, and he hit the far wall so hard it actually made him dizzy for a second. Vince stalked after him and Jask had just enough time to roll under the tripwires he set before Vince got there, and the noise of the crowd drowned out the sound of the oncoming barrels.

Vince spotted the first one and sent a ball of fire at it, but the second hit him from behind and sent him flying forward — Jask grabbed him in midair to stop his progress and let him fall to the ground, then got up and planted his feet as he let his wings out for the first time. "C'mon. Hit me."

"Not fair, you know how distracting those are for me." Vince swung anyway, cackling when his fist connected with Jask and even in the heat of the moment he could tell Vince was holding back. A second later, another ball of flame came flying at Jask's feet and he jumped, but not quite fast enough.

He hissed when his shoe caught fire and put it out quickly,

then growled a little too genuinely as he launched himself at Vince again. This time, they went straight through the wall of cement blocks. They thundered to the ground around them, splintering and sending dust flying everywhere — just enough to shield them both from view.

Jask kissed Vince heatedly as he caged him against the debris-ridden ground, then bit his bottom lip hard as he pulled back. "Timer says we've only got two minutes left. The second we're done with Pattie, we're going home. Understand?" He gripped Vince's crotch between them and sent a wave of grace strong enough to rattle the blocks around them.

Vince groaned and nodded breathlessly as he shoved Jask back and hopped to his feet. "Two minutes, huh? Let's put on a show."

Grinning, Jask flapped his wings hard and shot up into the air, spinning and swirling as Vince hurled fireball after fireball at him. It lit up the whole area with brilliant light, and Jask sent a powerful burst of grace straight down the middle of what had become a tunnel of fire.

The timer buzzed just as grace collided with shadow. All around them, people cheered and begged for more — begged for a clear winner when they had no idea there would never be one. Stronger or not, Jask wouldn't ever hold that over Vince's head beyond a joke here or there. They were equals.

"The fuck was the point of that?" Pattie asked as he limped over to them.

Jask laughed through heavy breaths and gestured around them. "Happy audience, happy fighters, happy owner who just made a shit ton of money. There was no winner so everyone that bet one of us would win... was wrong."

It was exactly the kind of loophole that someone like Pattie loved, and it got them off the hook faster than Jask anticipated. With the promise to come back and clean up the mess the next day, Jask grabbed Vince and teleported them straight to bed — Drazan and Johnny would just have to understand. Some things *weren't* worth waiting on.

~

The night before the wedding went a lot different the second time around. There wasn't a question this time, no matter what anyone said or what stupid superstitions their mothers threw at them, Vince and Jask knew they weren't going to separate. They made a point to agree not to have sex just to get them both a little worked up for their wedding night, but Jask found he didn't mind that nearly as much as he thought it would.

It was nice to just be able to *be* for the first time. They curled up on the couch with pillows and snacks and watched some old movie that Vince knew every word to, but the constant commentary and bad accents were music to Jask's ears. There was no danger. No one to hide from, no reason to rush through their time together. So, when Vince fell asleep laying on top of Jask, he didn't try to get him to move. He didn't have anywhere else to be and was happy that for once, Vince could truly rest.

As bad as things had been for Jask through all of this, things had been equally horrible for Vince — maybe even worse at times, and Jask had never known anyone that deserved some peace more than Vince. If he could give him even a little piece of that here on their couch, that's what he would do.

When the menu screen on the DVD started its song over for the thirteenth time, Vince finally stirred. "What day is it?"

"Mm, it's the day before we get married," Jask whispered.

A happy hum vibrated through Vince's chest and he lifted his head to plant a soft kiss to Jask's lips. "My second favorite day, then."

"What's your favorite day?" he asked with a laugh.

"The day I actually marry you."

"Good answer." He slowly sat up and brought Vince with him, then slid his arms under the demon to lift him up. "We need to sleep for real. I know how much you value your beauty sleep."

Vince huffed but bit Jask's earlobe. "Hey, I don't hear you complaining when I'm the best-looking thing around."

"I'll be sure to start complaining, then," he teased, but the smile on his face told a different story.

They laid in bed together sharing soft kisses and gentle touches, but they were careful not to cross that line. They only had one more day... they could make it.

They had to.

XVII

⧉

VINCE

Step, step, step. Vince turned on his heel and continued pacing. *Step, step, step.* He supposed most people wouldn't return to the place the first wedding failed. Another turn. *Step, step, step.* Most people probably wouldn't have let their fiancé out of their sight after the first mishap. *Turn, step, step.* So perhaps that could account for the anxious pattering in his chest. *Step, step, step.* He spun again and came face to face with Johnny. With no words and a raised eyebrow, Johnny pointed to the couch in the room. Vince smiled and planted himself on the edge of the couch cushion. The nervous energy still thrummed through him and now that the pacing stopped, he had no outlet. His leg began to bounce in a steady rhythm, and he gratefully accepted the drink Johnny brought to him. One sip later and the grateful feeling vanished. "The hell is this?"

"Tea. To calm your nerves." Johnny walked away.

"You've betrayed me, Johnny."

"You're a drama queen, Vince." His best friend peeked out the door and Vince couldn't lie that he felt a bit jealous. Why couldn't he look out the door? As a matter of fact, why shouldn't he? The tea forgotten – and his anxiety skyrocketing – Vince stood again and made it three more steps before Johnny closed the door. He sighed and resumed his trek across the carpeted floor. *Step, step, step.* On the next turn Vince stumbled on the first step when the music started. *The music.* Their song. "Oh fuck, it's starting. Johnny, what if..."

Johnny laughed and straightened the lapels on Vince's coat. "No what-ifs today, Vincenzo. Your man is waiting." Johnny dragged him over to the door and when the time came – when the chorus started – he pulled open the door. Across the way another door opened, and Vince got his first look at Jask since they'd split early that morning. As soon as their eyes met, Vince smiled so big it hurt. He'd never seen anything as gorgeous as Jask in his tux.

A gentle shove from behind reminded him that he needed to be moving. A look at Drazan's face behind Jask let Vince know his angel suffered a similar fate. It warmed his heart to know Jask felt just as overtaken with emotion as Vince.

They met at the altar and Vince allowed himself another moment to look over Jask. Their suits still matched, a lovely royal blue with deep golden accents tailored to fit them both perfectly. Vince pushed down the urge to ruffle Jask's perfectly tied hair. As good as it looked today, he always preferred it looking a little wild. Ice blue eyes locked onto his and Jask held out a hand to him. "You ready for this?"

"More than anything, sweetheart." Vince clasped Jask's hand in his and they turned to Edis, the new officiator. Edis waited for everyone to settle before smiling at them and then speaking to their gathered friends and family. "Are there any here today that object to this union?"

Jask looked over his shoulder and without a hint of humor

addressed the crowd, "He who objects, dies. Remember that." Vince covered his laugh with a cough and nodded his agreement before they put their attention back on Edis.

The smile on Ed's face almost blinded them as he continued. "We're gathered here to celebrate the union of Jaskian Veris and Vincenzo Riskel. Today, they will pledge their love and devotion to each other in front of the gathered witnesses and officially be declared husband and husband. It's my understanding you've written your own vows?"

Vince watched as Jask swallowed and began to speak. "My entire life, I've been trying to be someone I'm not. Trying to fit into one box or another, whether it was society's, my father's, or someone else's. With you, I don't have to worry about any of that because I know I can be exactly who I am around you. I don't have to hide whatever darkness is in me and I'm not afraid to *let go*. Because you've always been able to handle the best and the worst of me. Without judgement, without trying to change me. You accepted me for exactly who I was before you even admitted you wanted me, and you've shown me more devotion than anyone else ever has. You're funny, smart, every single person here knows you're *smoking* hot." Quiet laughs accompanied Jask's own chuckle as he grinned at Vince. "See what I did there?" The angel licked his lips and continued. "No matter what anyone throws at us, we saved the world and our family together. Because we're a team. You're my equal, Vin. And I wouldn't have it any other way." He lifted Vince's hand and kissed it.

For a moment, Vince could barely breathe, much less recite his own vows. He held back tears as he collected himself enough to be able to reciprocate. "You were the first angel I'd ever met. The first fight I ever lost. The first man I ever truly loved. If I have my way, you'll be the last. You are my everything, Jask. You are it for me until the end of time and I am yours for as long as you'll have me. I will never ask anything of you that you aren't willing to give, and I promise to make sure you always have a choice in our lives. To be or do whatever you want." He gazed into Jask's eyes, ignoring the tear falling down his cheek until Jask reached up to wipe it away. "I'd choose you; in a hundred lifetimes, in a hundred worlds, in any version of reality. I'd find you and I'd choose you each time."

"I'd choose you too, Vin." Jask sounded just as choked up as Vince felt and he looked at his brother. "Can I kiss him now? Cause I'm going to anyway."

Edis laughed. "Still gotta do the rings, Jask."

Jask turned to Drazan and held out his hand impatiently. Drazan looked amused as he dropped the ring in Jask's palm and Vince held out his hand for Jask to place the ring. When he finished, Vince took the second ring from Johnny and reverently slid it onto Jask's finger.

Edis spoke up before Jask could ask again, "Now by the power vested in me by... well, me – I pronounce you husband and husband. You may kiss." Edis hadn't finished speaking before Jask yanked Vince to him. Vince felt the kiss to his toes as cheers erupted around them. He wrapped an arm around Jask's waist and deepened the kiss. The world around them ceased to exist as they lost themselves in each other. Vince gave in to his earlier urge and lifted a hand to Jask's hair. He pulled the tie off and buried his hand in the golden strands. He didn't even notice the silence until Johnny started shaking his shoulder. Reluctantly he stopped the kiss but couldn't bring himself to look away from Jask.

"Hi." Jask grinned.

"Hey. We're married."

"Hell yes, we are." Jask went in for another kiss, but Drazan put a hand on his shoulder.

"Hold it, lover boy. You have guests."

"That's how a wedding works, D. The hell are you talking – oh." Vince frowned as Jask looked at something behind him and he closed his eyes, his heart in his throat as he tried to think of what threat or problem might await them. Zaepris and page three, perhaps? Slowly Vince turned and felt only a small amount of relief at the sight of Veris and Riskel, leaning against the door he'd come out of earlier. They sported matching smiles and Vince didn't know if that made him feel better or worse about this new update.

"You guys here for the pie?" Vince laughed nervously. He felt Jask's arm go around him and then their left hands entwined. That relaxed him more than anything else could. They were a team and whatever happened here, they would deal with it together.

"There's pie?" Veris' pleased expression cleared quickly, and he cleared his throat. "No. We're here for something else, but we'll revisit the pie later."

"What he means—" Riskel straightened up from his position against the door and approached them — "is that we're here to give you your wedding gift."

"That really isn't necessary." Vince watched as their namesakes stopped in front of them.

"Are you rejecting our gift, Vincenzo?" Riskel's eyes flashed black and Veris put a hand on his shoulder.

"Calm down, love. They have every right to be cautious. They've dealt with a lot to get here. So tell us, will you accept our gift?" Veris asked quietly. Vince didn't need to look at Jask to know they were having the same thoughts. Rejecting the gift could be disastrous, accepting the gift could be disastrous. After everything they've been through, could they handle more interference from the ancient couple now staring at them?

"Of course." He spoke before anyone else could. "We'd be honored." He only hoped he wasn't making a mistake. He didn't get long to dwell on it because he and Jask were being pulled apart. That wasn't something he'd ever allow to happen again but Veris held him still.

"Don't fret, Vincenzo. This won't take long." Once again, Vince stood in front of Jask. The only difference from the ceremony they'd just completed being the two new additions at the front of the room. Riskel stationed himself behind Jask and Veris behind Vince. One shared nod and Vince searched Jask's face for any hint of discomfort or fear. The next second, all thoughts of negativity vanished as an almost forgotten feeling rushed through him. He didn't need to search Jask's face to understand his emotions because he could *feel* them. The uncertainty that disappeared, the hope that blossomed, and the elation that soared through them both when they realized exactly what the gift being given was. Their broken bond – the one Vince almost died for – restored and whole between them.

"Jask?" Vince couldn't manage more than a whisper.

His mate couldn't manage any words at all — he surged forward and lifted Vince off his feet in a kiss so powerful it rattled the windows of his former home. It was several glorious, long seconds before he finally stopped long enough to say, "I love you."

And with every bone, muscle, and nerve in his body Vince felt the truth in the words. "I love you." A sudden thought made him laugh and he kissed all over Jask's face, repeating the phrase after each kiss.

"Ahhh, stop," Jask said with a chuckle, then blushed as he realized that's exactly what he'd been doing to Vince all that time. "Okay, fine. It's annoying, but I'm still going to do it anyway and you can't stop me."

"I don't want you to. Ever," Vince agreed. He dove back in for another taste of Jask's lips. Slowly he realized they weren't alone and in fact still in front of quite a few people. When he finally forced himself to look away from Jask, the room was filled with soft smiles and an excited-looking Veris.

"You said there would be pie?"

"Angel doesn't fall far from the tree, I guess." Vince pointed to the part of the great hall where the food waited.

Veris grabbed Riskel and dragged him toward the food as Riskel threw an apologetic glance over his shoulder, but Jask held Vince back from following.

"I can't actually believe they were helpful for once. This is... I can't even describe how much better it feels. What if they end up wanting something in return?"

"I believe them when they said it's a gift. And if they do?" Vince placed his hand on the back of Jask's neck and tugged until their foreheads touched. "You're mine again, Jask. Anything is worth that."

JASKIAN

"You did a good job with this place, Vin." Jask looked around the old house and admired the new fixtures and details Vince had added to the woodwork. Considering he'd only had a couple of weeks to fix the place up and a modest budget, Jask really was impressed — though, he thought it was a little silly when they wouldn't be paying attention to anything but each other for the next five days. "Johnny help you at all?"

"Nope. Couldn't trust the job to anyone else." Vince dropped their bags. "I wanted it perfect."

He took another cursory glance around and smiled at the pictures of them on the walls. "You did amazing, Vin. Seriously. We'll have to keep this place for future getaways." Jask turned slowly to face his husband and cocked his head to the side. "But only if we leave the clothes behind next time."

"Trying to get me naked already? We just got here." Vince's face made it clear his words didn't match his thoughts.

"I am. I wasn't allowed to have you last night, and you know how needy I get when you make me wait," he said, like it wasn't his idea in the first place. "There's miles of woods surrounding this place. What do you say you and I revisit that little chase scene we started at home?"

Vince slowly removed his hat and hung it right by the still open door. His face seemed thoughtful but Jask picked up the hint of mischief right before Vince bolted out the front door without speaking a word.

A grin split Jask's face as he skipped out onto the porch and kicked the door shut behind him. The fresh air felt fantastic as he stripped off his shirt and dropped it in a heap on the swing, then tilted his head and extended his grace out to find his mate. The bond acted as a beacon and told Jask exactly where Vince was hiding at the moment, but he wasn't in a rush. He could take his time here.

The leaves crunched under his boots as he headed for the tree line. "Aww, c'mon, Vin. At least make this challenging."

"Why in the hell would I do that? Getting caught is the best part." Yet, Vince didn't show himself. Jask found Vince's shirt hanging from a branch but still no physical sign of the demon himself.

"Tease," he muttered with a fond smile as he tucked the shirt into his waistband. Interested in continuing this pattern, he moved as slowly and silently as he could, eventually coming across Vince's jeans laid over a rock. Jask picked them up and sent them back to the house. "Are you wearing panties for me?" he yelled out.

"Only one way you'll find out, husband mine." Vince replied, the endearment sung out with amusement.

Jask teleported toward the source of the sound and landed ten feet from Vince — Vince, who was just out of reach and hidden from the waist down by foliage. "Gotcha, baby. Better run."

Vince flashed an excited grin and stepped back just

enough for Jask to see the blood red silk panties that adorned his body. Black lace topped them and Jask caught a glimpse of a little black bow before Vince turned and ran.

His pupils blew as he took off on foot after him, pushing past the speed possible for a normal human and tapping into some of his family's power reserve. He became like air, sliding through the trees and barely leaving a trace behind him as he steadily caught up, and with a leap, he tackled Vince to the forest floor and bit the side of his neck. "Say uncle," he growled.

Vince squirmed underneath him, presumably searching for a weakness but Jask kept him trapped. "Uncle. I yield." He didn't sound disappointed.

Part of Jask knew they should go inside first, but he couldn't justify waiting even the few seconds it would take to teleport. He kept Vince pinned with one hand as the other slid down his body to those gorgeous panties, and a second later, they were in his own mouth instead of covering Vince's ass.

He sent a tendril of his grace through his mate to loosen him up, and Jask was impossibly hard just from the chase. *"Hold still, babe,"* he said into Vince's mind as he adjusted his stance and lined up.

"Fuck, Jask, hurry." Vince moaned and dug his fingers into the earth.

The neediness only turned Jask on more, but he eased in slowly, careful that even with the grace, he didn't hurt him. It felt incredible after the long celibacy. "Fuck," he mumbled around the panties as he bottomed out. His eyes closed as he started to move, sticking to long, slow thrusts to drive Vince crazy.

Vince reached back with one hand to grip Jask's hair, turning his head to meet him for a kiss. Jask met it messily and flipped their positions so his back was digging into the ground and Vince was facing the trees, and only then did he start to move faster. He spit Vince's panties out to command, "Ride me, baby."

He leaned back and placed his hands on either side of Jask. He let his head drop as he planted his feet and began to move with determination, and Jask shuddered from how good it felt. Over and over, he drove himself deeper as Vince rocked down until Jask couldn't take it anymore. He held Vince still and planted his feet, fucking up into him hard enough that the trees around them shivered.

Jask's name became a chant on Vince's lips as he met each thrust with a roll of his hips. His mate began to tremble above him and then Vince's entire body tensed. "Fuck, I'm..." his words ended in a shout as his release hit him.

It was more than enough to send Jask over the edge. He growled and buried himself as deep as he could, his cock pulsing inside of Vince as he emptied fully and whispered praises to his mate.

Vince's arms shake as he lowers himself down on top of Jask, his back to Jask's chest. "You should chase me more often."

"I couldn't agree more," he said, breathlessly kissing down the side of his neck and holding him close. "Maybe next time I'll catch you and tie you to a tree first."

"Shit, give me ten minutes and you can do that today." Vince laughed and covered Jask's arms with his own.

Chuckling, Jask tapped him to get him to get up. "Let's worry about getting some food first, okay? I'm starving now. Hunting makes me work up an appetite."

It was reluctant and slow, but they eventually made their way back into the house. Though, instead of actually getting food like Jask said, they made it roughly three steps in and ended up glued to each other again. "Sorry," Jask mumbled, biting Vince's lip and picking him up. "Need you again already."

"Did you get into the bourbon without me?" Vince tilted his head back against the wall as he wrapped his legs around Jask's waist.

He shook his head quickly as he kissed down Vince's neck and lined himself up, sliding in quickly. "Don't need bourbon to want you like this, Vin. I never have."

"Still just as good as the first time." Vince closed his eyes and ran his hands up Jask's back. "Let me see those wings, sweetheart."

They appeared whether he wanted them to or not, and the moment Vince threaded his fingers through them, Jask was lost. Bourbon or no bourbon, the bond itself made it feel so much more intense that Jask dented the door behind Vince with the force of his thrusts. "Vin... pull."

Vince dug deep into the feathers and tugged, sending a pulse of pleasure through his fingertips and into the muscle of Jask's wings. It drove him nuts, lighting his bones on fire in the best way. He tipped his head back and growled as he held Vince up with one shaky hand and stroked him with the other.

"Come for me, Vin."

Vince's grip tightened and he rocked down hard on Jask as he obeyed, emptying over Jask's fist. "Fuck!" Another blast of power shot through his hands as his body clenched down on Jask, and it sent him over for a second time with enough force to make his legs weak.

Slowly, they sank to the ground and Jask sat with Vince still in his lap. "You're amazing, Vin. Seriously. I'm so damn happy no one can interrupt us for the next five days."

Vince curled into Jask's chest, tugging on the feathers until Jask's wings wrapped around them like a makeshift blanket. "If only we'd made it to the bed."

"Eat, then I promise we'll make it to the bed, okay?" Jask held him for a few moments until Vince finally agreed, then forced himself to head to the kitchen to whip something up.

There weren't a lot of options to choose from, so he went with something simple, and even that made him smile at the sense of irony it gave him. Nothing about any of this had been simple, and something told him that even though the bond had been restored, his future with Vince wouldn't necessarily be simple, either. They were different in a lot of ways that would challenge them in the coming years, but that was just life. As long as they held tight to the things that mattered — their families, their hopes, dreams, desires, and above all... their love for each other, they'd be able to weather any storm and push through any fight.

They might not have had the most conventional of beginnings, but their love had changed the world, and Jask could think of worse things than that.

XVIII

EPILOGUE

Forty years of surviving and fighting, Vincenzo Riskel never approached a battle with anything less than his all. He considered every strength and weakness of his newest opponent as they circled each other. Little eyes squinted back at him and Vince noted the cunning and determination he often saw reflected in his husband's gaze. He'd already lost *this* war before it even began.

Vince sighed and sank to the floor, crossing his legs. "Fine. Victory is yours." The celebratory screech almost exploded his eardrums as his daughter flung her little arms around his neck. She immediately grabbed her brush and began to braid and clip his slightly overgrown hair to her satisfaction, and Jask howled with laughter from the couch.

"I don't know why you bother, Vin. She's as stubborn as you are with twice my cunning," Jask pointed out. "You're completely outmatched."

Enolan giggled as she tugged his hair until it complied. "Why don't you ever do this to him, huh? His hair is longer." Vince raised an eyebrow but winced at a particularly vicious tug. "Hey, easy on the goods there, Lanie."

"Sowwy, Poppa," she whispered before gently running the brush through his hair again.

Jask's heart was so full in that moment he feared it would burst right out of his chest, but they were running late as it was. "Hurry up, sweetie. Make sure Poppa is pretty for Uncle Edis', okay? You get to go play with Arro and baby Gradin."

She squealed again and completely abandoned her mission, which Jask should've seen coming. For a four-year-old, she normally had a pretty decent attention span — except for when it came to her cousins. He smiled knowingly at Vince when she raced across the room to grab her pink umbrella despite the fact that the sun was shining in full force. "You're welcome, babe."

"Yes. Now I get to go with only half my hair in pink clips. That won't look nearly as ridiculous," Vince pretended to grumble, but they both knew this wasn't the first or last time it would happen. Vince would do anything for their daughter, even if it meant looking a little ridiculous at the family dinner.

Despite her initial eagerness, actually getting Enolan out the door was an entirely different scenario. She couldn't pick a single stuffed animal to take, and in a last-ditch, desperate attempt to get going, Vince agreed to just let her take all of them.

"You're spoiling her," Jask chastised, but he didn't make a

single attempt to stop it. "Now you get to carry her backpack for her, too."

"It matches my hair." Vince shrugged as he tossed it over his shoulder. He waited for Enolan to get a couple of steps ahead before leaning into Jask's side to whisper, "And the panties I'm wearing too."

He squeezed Vince's ass and smirked playfully. "Then I guess we'll have to make sure she's distracted enough that you can prove it to me in Ed's bathroom."

"I'll bribe Lee with a night of babysitting." Vince watched as Enolan barreled into Edis and Lee's home. "Note to self: teach child about knocking."

Jask snorted as he followed her in and shut the door behind them. "I don't think we've taught her anything at all. Seems like everything we say goes in one ear and out the other, but at least she'll be in school soon."

"Hey, guys," Ed said quietly as he approached. "Gradin's sleeping, so try to be quiet. Lee's been going a little insane with the new baby around and she needs some peace."

"So why'd you invite *us*? When have we ever been peaceful?" Jask teased.

"He has a very valid point, Ed. You'd done better with Draz and Johnny." As if to prove them right, Enolan shot through the hallway after Arro. Vince bent and scooped both kids up, tossing one onto each shoulder and giving Edis a smile. "Just call me keeper of the peace."

He smiled gratefully and led them into the dining room, where Lee already had dinner on the table. "Shut up and eat quickly," she said sharply. She looked exhausted, but the sight of Arro messing with her brother made her smile. "Good boy. Give Uncle Vinnie hell."

"Is that anyway to greet your most favorite brother?"

"You're my only brother." Lee rolled her eyes as Vince got the kids settled in their seats.

Jask almost pointed out that he was technically Lee's brother by marriage, but figured it was better not to poke the bear. Instead, he cut up Enolan's food and ruffled her curly hair until she was swatting his hand away and reaching for an extra roll before she even ate the first one.

They stayed mostly quiet through dinner, but it wasn't awkward. They'd all gotten into a routine over the last several years that meant they didn't always need to fill the silence — sometimes, they could just stuff their faces and enjoy being together.

Jask helped Lee clean up after as Vince rocked Gradin. "If you need a break, we can take the kids tonight. Vin built that really nice bassinet before we realized we were adopting a toddler and not a baby, so we can always put Gradin in there."

"Would you?" She sounded hopeful. "Arro would be ecstatic, and Ed and I could get some *sleep*."

"Of course. Just give me and Vince like twenty minutes to... y'know, then we'll come back and get all three. Sound good?"

She wrinkled her nose at him but nodded and shoved his chest. "Go. And don't lie to me, you need maybe twelve minutes tops."

"You wound me, Lee," Jask joked, but she wasn't wrong. With Enolan around, they'd learned how to speed things up. "We'll be right back."

He found Vince at the mercy of all three kids and carefully extricated him from the dog pile they'd created. "Come on, we gotta hurry."

Vince didn't need to ask what Jask meant, he waved to the kids and pulled on Jask's power to teleport them somewhere private.

"A closet, Vin? Seriously?" Jask laughed, moving the broom to the side and kissing him anyway. It didn't matter to him where they were, but this definitely wasn't what he'd expected. "At least we can clean up after ourselves."

"I got excited. It's been almost a week, Jask. A *week*." Vince pulled his shirt over his head and then quickly got rid of his pants, and Jask simply waved his own away.

A week was absolutely too long, and seeing Vince's body reminded him of that fact so strongly it was nearly painful. Even with his hair a beret-covered mess, the tattoos and panties covering the rest of him were more than enough to steal his attention. "I don't know how I ever survived a week," he whispered, pulling him in and picking him up.

Vince rocked his satin covered length over Jask's equally hard cock. "Me either. Never again."

As Jask kissed him and pulled him impossibly closer, he had his doubts they'd be able to stick to that between work and friends and family — but they had time. Though fate's serrated edge had threatened to rip them apart, it was blunt and harmless now, and they had an entire lifetime ahead of them to enjoy each other.

They'd get there.

Nikola Harvey was born in Atlanta, GA and resides there with her husband and dog.
Kiran Charles lives in her Ohio hometown with her three pups and daughter.

www.ingramcontent.com/pod-product-compliance
Lightning Source LLC
Chambersburg PA
CBHW021303190726
48288CB00003B/659